DARE

THE BLADES OF ACKTAR

BOOK ONE

DARE

TRICIA MINGERINK

Sword & Cross
Publishing

To God, my King and Father
Soli Deo Gloria

Character List

Abel Lachlan (LACK - lan) – Renna and Brandi's uncle

Abigail Alistair – third child of Lord and Lady Alistair. Friend of Brandi's.

Blane Altin – the Nineteenth Blade

Blizzard – Leith's horse

Brandi Faythe (BRAN - dee) – Renna's younger sister. Her full name is Lady Brandiline Faythe.

Esther Alistair – fifth child of Lord and Lady Alistair.

Harrison Vane – the First Blade

Jeremiah Alistair – fourth child of Lord and Lady Alistair.

Jolene Lorraine – Lady Lorraine's daughter.

King Leon Eirdon (ee - EAR - don) – the former king killed by Respen

King Respen Felix (REH - spen) – king of Acktar. He was the lord of Blathe.

Lady Amber Dawson – lady of the town of Hendor

Lady Annita Faythe – Renna and Brandi's mother. She was the sister of King Leon.

Lady Eve Alistair – Lord Alistair's wife

Lady Paula Lorraine – lady of the town of Sierra

Leith Torren (LEETH TOR - ren) – the Third Blade

Lord Doughtry – lord of the town of Calloday

Lord Farthen – lord of the town of Keestone

Lord Hector Emilin (EHM - ih - lihn) – lord of the town of Dently

Lord Henry Alistair – lord of the town of Walden

Lord Laurence Faythe – Renna and Brandi's father

Lord Philip Creston – lord of the town of Arroway

Lord Segon (SEE - gon) – lord of the town of Uster

Lydia Alistair – second child of Lord and Lady Alistair. Friend of Renna's.

Mara Lachlan (MAR - uh LACK - lan) – Renna and Brandi's aunt. She was the sister of Renna's father.

Martyn Hamish (MAR - tin HAY - mish) – the Sixth Blade

Michelle Allen – Sheriff Allen's daughter

Nonden Hess – the Second Blade

Queen Deirdre Eirdon (DEER - dree) – the former queen killed by Harrison Vane.

Quinten Daas – the Twelfth Blade

Ralph Chimb – the Twenty-Second Blade

Renna Faythe (REHN - nuh) – The lady of the town of Stetterly. Her full name is Lady Rennelda Faythe (REHN - nehl - duh).

Shadrach Alistair – Lord Alistair's oldest son

Sheriff Allen – sheriff of Stetterly

Zed Burin – the Seventeenth Blade

Location List

Acktar (AHCK - tar) – a country mostly made up of flat prairie

Nalgar Castle (NAHL - gar) – the capitol of Acktar

Stetterly (STEHT - er - ly) – a town near the Spires Canyon

Walden (WALL - den) – a town near the Sheered Rock Hills

Uster (UH - ster) – a town near the Spires Canyon

Sierra (see - AIR - uh) – a town on the prairie between Walden and Nalgar Castle

Sheered Rock Hills (SHEERD) – the mountain range that forms the northern border of Acktar

Spires Canyon – the canyon that forms the eastern border of Acktar

The Ramparts – the section of steep cliffs that border the Waste

The Waste – the desert on the eastern side of the Sheered Rock Hills

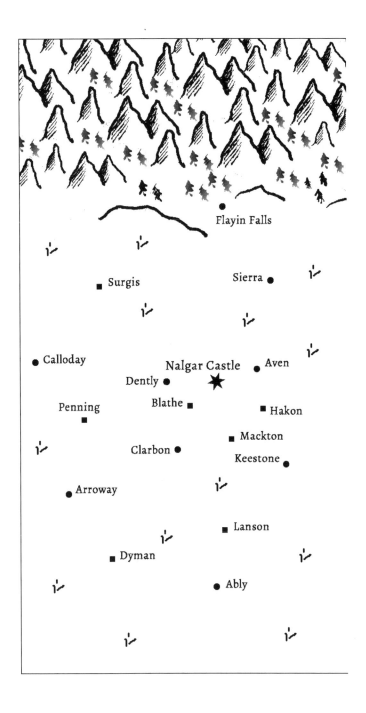

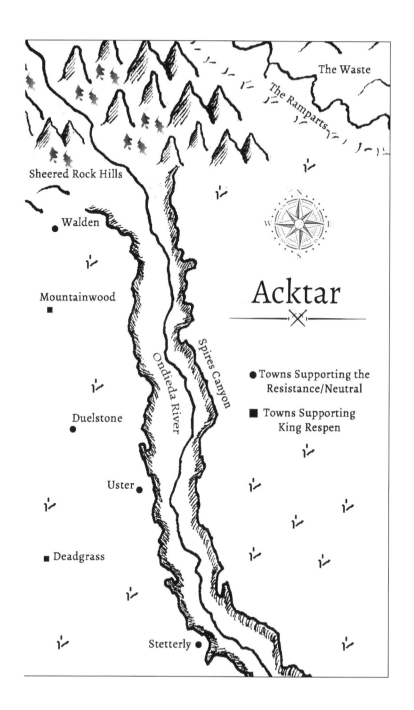

The Waste

The Ramparts

Sheered Rock Hills

Walden

Mountainwood

Acktar

Ondieda River

Spires Canyon

Duelstone

● Towns Supporting the Resistance/Neutral

■ Towns Supporting King Respen

Uster

Deadgrass

Stetterly

Now when Daniel knew that the writing was signed,
he went into his house; and his windows
being open in his chamber toward Jerusalem,
he kneeled upon his knees three times a day,
and prayed, and gave thanks before his God,
as he did aforetime.

Then the king commanded, and they brought Daniel,
and cast him into the den of lions.
Now the king spake and said unto Daniel,
thy God whom thou servest continually,
he will deliver thee.

- Daniel 6:10 & 16

1

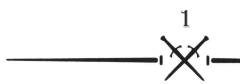

Third Blade Leith Torren knew they were in trouble the moment he saw the girl.

"What is she doing here?" He pointed at the girl Twenty-Second Blade Ralph Chimb had tossed into a corner. The woodshed they were using as shelter rattled with the winter winds that scoured Acktar's prairie. The girl shrank against the grey wall.

Chimb's blond hair spiked with icicles. He shook snow from his cloak and scrubbed at his crooked, snow-reddened nose. The knives strapped to his waist and chest held his black clothes on his angular body. He smirked. "Found her in a tavern. Thought we'd have some fun while we wait."

"We're here to search for Resistance activity, not to have fun." Leith huffed out a misty breath as he tried to calm down. Why did *he* have to be the Blade stuck on Chimb's first mission? Only two years older than Chimb's sixteen years, he felt ages wiser. "Put her back where you found her."

"Why?" Chimb's eyes sparked.

Leith drew his knife and stepped towards Chimb.

1

Chimb raised his sharp chin. The girl in the corner shrieked while the shed shook with another gust of wind. Leith stared at the younger Blade until he squirmed. "Don't question me."

When Chimb backed up a step, Leith sheathed his knife. "You've failed our mission. We won't be able to hide if the townspeople search for her. Better she tell them two Blades are in the area, and they avoid us." Leith snapped his mouth shut. King Respen wouldn't like their failure.

Leith jabbed a finger at the door. "Check outside."

Chimb glanced at the shivering girl, grimaced, and dragged his feet toward the door. Tugging his cloak over his shoulders, he yanked the door open. Snow blasted into the shed. He trudged outside and slammed the door behind him.

Ignoring the girl, Leith rubbed his left shoulder. In his five years as a Blade, he'd never suffered the humiliation of a mark of failure. If not for Chimb's recklessness, he wouldn't be facing the possibility now.

Telling this to Chimb would be a waste of time. Either the boy got discipline or he died.

Chimb stumbled inside and yanked the door closed against the clawing wind. "Didn't see anyone around."

"If you're lucky, you can get her back before anyone notices she's missing." Striding across the shed, Leith reached for his horse's bridle. Even in his gloves, his fingers tingled with cold. With the wind shrieking its way into a blizzard, they wouldn't be scouting around Stetterly Manor as planned.

Chimb scowled and grabbed at the girl. She cowered away from him, whimpering. He rolled his eyes. "I'm taking you back."

2

The door splintered and crashed to the floor. Several men armed with hunting bows burst inside. The burly man in front took one look at Chimb and fired. Chimb fell against the wall and slid to the floor, an arrow in his chest, a vacant look in his eyes.

Leith hesitated a heartbeat. Two long jumps to the girl. Not enough time to use her as a shield. Two of the men swung their bows towards him. No time to negotiate. No chance to fight bows with only his knives. Leith lunged for his saddlehorn.

One man drew his bowstring and fired. Something punched Leith's stomach, slamming him against his horse. Pain ricocheted through his body.

He had to get away. Now. Grabbing his saddlehorn, he slapped his horse's rump. The horse bolted. The men in the doorway dove out of the way as the horse charged through. Leith clung to the saddlehorn, letting his horse drag him from the building.

As they careened into the snowy street, Leith shoved off with his feet and swung into the saddle. The movement tore through his stomach. He cried out and doubled over. He dropped the reins and gave his horse its head.

The wind whipped by him, heavy with flakes. His horse charged down the road and past the snow-covered remains of a church Leith had helped burn down four years ago.

The horse plowed into the ditch bordering the road and stumbled in the snow that reached its chest. The arrow shaft struck the saddle, twisting the broadhead in his gut. Moaning, Leith gripped the shaft and snapped it off, tossing the end away.

The blizzard's breath built into a howl. His horse

galloped into it, heedless of the snow dashing against them. He pressed a hand to his stomach. The red blood—his blood—stained his glove and darkened the snow collecting on his arm and saddle.

His horse staggered through a drift. His arm shifted, snagging on the broken end of the arrow shaft. He gritted his teeth at the fresh rush of pain.

The blizzard screamed around him. The snow stabbed at his cheeks and eyes. He gripped his horse's mane. If he fell off, he would die. He choked on a laugh. He could die right where he was. The blood pooling on his saddle and the lightness in his head warned him death wasn't far away.

He'd failed. He never failed. He'd worked so hard to earn his place, yet he'd been brought down by Chimb's foolishness and a single, peasant's arrow.

He was going to die. Alone. Unwanted.

The dark shape of a building loomed out of the white. A light flickered in a window.

Someone was there. He couldn't count on their help, and he wouldn't beg. A Blade never showed that much weakness. But maybe they'd give him a warm place to rest and stay by him so he didn't have to die alone.

2

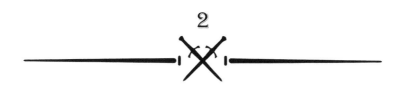

Renna and her sister Brandi huddled beside the fire, wrapped in a mound of blankets against the cold whistling through the manor. She picked up the poker and stirred the fire. The heat struggled to fill the wood-paneled kitchen and warm the red brick floor.

If only Aunt Mara and Uncle Abel were here. They'd gone to Stetterly before the blizzard struck and would be stuck there for as long as this blizzard lasted. Renna prayed for their safety. If Uncle Abel and Aunt Mara decided to try to make it back…if they got lost in the blizzard…Renna added another log to the fire.

Something thumped against the kitchen door. Renna jumped and hugged her thirteen-year-old sister tighter. Brandi's red-blond hair clung to the blanket as she squirmed away from Renna. "What was that?"

Renna peeled herself from the blankets. "Maybe it's Aunt Mara and Uncle Abel." She shivered her way to the door, unbarred it, and turned the latch. It wrenched from her hand and banged against the wall. A body fell into the room. Renna screamed and leapt backwards.

Brandi dashed to Renna's side. "Who's that?"

"I don't know. Here, help me get him inside." Renna grabbed one of the man's arms. Together, she and Brandi dragged him inside. He groaned as Brandi shoved the door closed. His black hair glistened with snow, and melting snowflakes reddened his slim face. Renna knelt next to him. "Ssh, lie still."

"My horse…" The man nodded at the door.

Brandi grabbed her cloak and swung it over her shoulders. "I'll take care of it."

"Be careful." Renna grabbed at her sister's skirt, but Brandi whirled out of her reach.

Brandi rolled her eyes. "I know. It *is* a blizzard."

Renna bit her lip. What if Brandi got disoriented? The swirling white made the buildings nearly invisible from each other. The rope strung between the manor and the stables should guide her, but…Brandi skipped out the door and tugged it shut behind her.

A moan from the floor reminded her that she had another life to worry about. Rolling him to his back, she pulled aside his cloak. A broken shaft stuck from a wet splotch covering his side and stomach.

She clenched her fingers into fists to stop their shaking. She'd never dug out an arrow by herself before. If Aunt Mara were here…but she wasn't. A young man was hurt, and only Renna had the training to help him.

She touched his shoulder, gaining his attention. "I need to move you to the fire. Can you walk if I help?"

He nodded and struggled to sit up. She pulled one of his arms over her shoulder and together they stumbled to the fire. While he propped himself up against a chair, she spread out two blankets and helped him lie down.

As she did, her eyes focused on the two knives hanging in sheaths from his belt. She froze. Her mind whirled as she took in other details. Black clothing. Black leather boots. No sword. More knives strapped across his chest. Stylized initials *LT* etched in the hilts.

She recoiled. He was a Blade. She'd only seen one once, but she'd heard plenty about the black-clothed assassin-spies who served King Respen.

The Blade turned his face towards her. His hand inched toward one of the knives strapped across his chest. Was he going to threaten her?

He didn't beg. But, his eyes, green as the prairie grass in spring, drew her gaze. His hand dropped from his knife.

Renna swallowed. She wanted to run or throw this Blade back into the snow. The Blades had killed her parents, her aunt and uncle, and her cousins. She didn't want to help him. He didn't deserve her help.

All she had to do was sit here, and he'd die within a few hours. His slow death would be small retribution for the blood of her family that stained his hands.

But she was a healer. She grimaced and rubbed her hands together to stop their trembling. She'd helped anyone who'd ever asked it of her. But surely a Blade was exempt. She might even save lives if she let the Blade die.

She buried her face in her hands, trying to shut out the sound of the Blade's ragged breathing. Her heart, her hands, ached to help while her mind railed against the idea.

If only Uncle Abel was here. He'd lay his hand on Renna's arm and quote a Scripture passage so suited to the situation that Renna would know what to do.

What did the Bible say about something like this? *Love your enemies. Bless those who curse you. Do not reward evil with evil but reward evil with good.*

The Blade had his arms wrapped over his wound. Blood soaked his clothes, and sweat beaded on his forehead and upper lip. His body quaked with the effort to continue breathing. If she only focused on his face, he looked young and helpless.

The Blade's life wasn't hers to take. She had to place his life in God's hands. She nearly prayed for the Blade to die but stopped herself. A prayer for her patient's death wasn't the right way to approach healing.

She forced herself to smile and touch the Blade's shoulder. "I'm a healer. Rest easy now. I need to gather a few things before I can tend you."

His eyes widened. Renna turned away, finding calm in the automatic movements of her hands. Fill the kettle with water and hang it over the fire. Gather the bandages. Lay out her silk thread, needle, and small knife. Mix the poultice. Place everything on a tray. The familiar actions soothed her thumping heart and sparking nerves. He was simply another patient.

As she placed the tray on the floor next to the Blade, the door burst open in a flurry of snow. The wind shoved Brandi inside. She slammed the door, barred it, and bounced across the room, flinging her scarf, cloak, and mittens onto a chair.

"His horse is all settled in the stable. I took off its saddle and bridle. I gave it hay, but the water was frozen so I broke the ice and hauled some more water from the well. Is he going to be all right? There was a lot of blood on the saddle."

Brandi plopped onto the ground beside their patient, extending her hands toward the fire and cocking her head to stare at the Blade. "He's not very old, is he?"

Renna paused. Brandi was right. The Blade couldn't be much older than her own seventeen years. He had a smooth face, only a few sparse bristles scattered on his chin. His shoulders lacked the breadth of a full-grown man. Renna heaved a sigh. "He's also awake and can hear you."

"Oh." Brandi scooted closer. "Need my help?"

Renna wanted to keep Brandi as far away from the Blade as possible, but she needed the extra pair of hands since Aunt Mara wasn't there. "Yes. First, we need to get his weapons and cloak off."

The Blade opened his eyes again. "Why would you help me?"

"Why not?" Brandi's tone implied the Blade was stupid to think otherwise. She picked up one of his hands and yanked the glove off. "Renna's a healer. She'll have you fixed up in no time." She tugged off his second glove and tossed them away.

"I'll do my best. Now, I need you to cooperate." Renna squeezed her trembling hands together. She needed to be calm. She could handle tending a Blade.

Maybe.

Leith gathered his strength and pushed himself semi-upright. The arrow shifted, stabbing him in waves of pain. The older girl jumped backwards, fear glimmering in her blue eyes.

The younger girl rushed forward, helping him lean back against the warm stones of the fireplace. He closed his eyes, trying to catch his breath.

He'd killed here. Not this room, but he'd sneaked through here to ambush their guards four years ago. If these girls knew which Blade they helped, they'd toss him back into the snow.

Thankfully he didn't have to threaten them to gain their help. He didn't enjoy that sort of thing, not the way Chimb had or First Blade Harrison Vane did.

But he had considered it. He'd seen death on too many faces. The terror etched in dying eyes that saw into the realm beyond death. Only a few had relaxed into peacefulness, as if the world they saw on the other side welcomed them with cradling arms.

Forcing his eyes open, he fumbled with the buckles of the knife belt around his waist and the straps crossing his chest. The younger sister helped support him while he eased the leather free.

The older girl snatched the weapons away from him and flung them across the room so hard they smacked the opposite wall.

No chance to force their cooperation now. He was at their mercy. Bile joined the metallic tang of blood in his mouth.

"Renna?" The younger girl glanced at her sister. "What'd you do that for?"

"I...just never mind, Brandi." Renna's hands shook as she undid the clasp of his cloak. Leith avoided looking her in the eye and did his best to shrug away the layers of his wool cloak.

"Lie down." Renna set the cloak aside, her light blond braid swinging across her shoulders.

Leith drew in a breath. Even moving a few inches tore at his stomach. Once again, Brandi jumped to help him move. She lifted his head and bunched some of the blanket beneath him for a pillow. Her red-blond hair flowed around her shoulders in untamed abandon, trailing across his face and into his eyes.

Renna—the healer—picked up the small knife she'd set on the tray next to her. "Your shirt is stuck to your wound. I'll need to cut it off."

Leith tensed. She could use that knife to cut more than his shirt. A stab to his stomach, a slice across his throat, that's all it would take. His fingers clenched, but he didn't have his knives to defend himself.

He peeked at her through slitted eyes. Should he remind them what'd happen if they killed a King's Blade?

He felt a tugging on his shirt, a rush of air against his skin, as she sawed through the fabric. Her fingers brushed the base of his throat as she gripped the neckline of his shirt and sliced downward. He gripped the blankets spread beneath him and fought the instinct to knock her hand away.

She wrung out a cloth, the water dripping, and pressed it against his wound. He gritted his teeth, locking the moan inside his mouth.

A cloth dabbed at his forehead. Brandi's voice bubbled above him. "What's your name?"

Renna tugged at the fabric stuck to the wounds. Leith couldn't help moaning this time. Weakness. Vane would laugh if he saw Leith now.

Small fingers touched his forehead. "It's all right. You need to stay still so Renna can help."

Leith tried to focus on the cool cloth dabbing his forehead and cheeks. Brandi started humming. It wasn't a tune he'd heard in the taverns he'd scouted.

He fought for breath, and his voice strained through his teeth. "Leith. My name's Leith Torren." They ought to know. Maybe they'd take the time to carve it into a board for his grave.

Who was he fooling? If he died tonight, he'd end up a

body abandoned to the snow drifts, as unmourned as his father had been.

"There." Renna peeled the last shred of his shirt from the wound.

Leith sensed Brandi leaning over him to get a better look at his wounds. "Oh, that looks bad."

He could hear Renna's sigh. "I'm going to work on getting that arrow out now."

He managed a nod and braced for the rush of pain. She touched the shaft, and the arrowhead shifted. Agony rioted all the way to his toes.

Blackness closed around him.

3

Renna felt his body go limp. His chest rose and fell. He still lived, unfortunately. At least it would be easier tending him while he was unconscious.

She gritted her teeth and examined the arrow. It had a slim shaft like the arrows the local men used to hunt small game on the surrounding prairie. What had the Blade been doing in Stetterly to get himself shot? The possibilities turned her stomach.

She couldn't think about it now. She set to work removing the arrow. She couldn't push it through without hurting him further. Instead, she used her knife to dig the arrow out.

After several minutes, the small broadhead came free. She poured alcohol over the wound to clean it, stitched it closed, and laid a poultice over it. When she was finished, she wrapped the bandage around his waist and placed a blanket over him.

She swiped her hair from her face with the back of her wrist. "Brandi, you should go to bed. It's late."

"I'm not tired." Brandi tossed her long, red-blond hair over her shoulder. "Besides, we never ate supper."

Renna slumped against the hearth. She'd forgotten about food. And she did need to explain to Brandi that their patient was a Blade. They'd have to be careful about what they said and did in front of him. "All right. Help me clean up, then we'll grab something to eat."

Brandi hummed a psalm while they cleaned up the mess. Renna's stomach clenched. Had the Blade recognized it? If he had, he'd know they were Christians. He'd guess they attended one of the secret churches. He'd tell King Respen...and Renna and Brandi would be arrested.

"Brandi." Renna gripped her sister's shoulders, pulled her from the room, and closed the door. Her breath frosted silver in the unheated corridor. "I need you to listen carefully. This is really important."

Brandi's blue eyes darted to Renna's face. "What's wrong?"

Renna waved at the door. "He's a Blade."

Brandi's mouth formed an O as wide as her round eyes. "And we just fixed him up?"

"It was the right thing to do. God tells us to love our enemies." The words grated on her tongue. She was trying to mean them. "But we're going to have to be careful. He could get us in a lot of trouble. He reports directly to King Respen."

"What are we going to do?" Brandi paled and bit her lip. As much as she hated the fear in Brandi's eyes, Renna needed Brandi to be afraid.

"Be careful. Don't mention church. Don't mention Uncle Abel is the minister. Don't mention our Bibles. Don't hum psalms. Don't..." Renna wanted to lay out a few more rules, but Brandi's eyes were already as wide as they would go. "Just don't do anything...Christian."

14

Brandi nodded. Did she understand how serious this was? One mistake and he'd report them to King Respen. With her lecture out of the way, Renna re-heated some stew for supper. If Uncle Abel was there, he'd tend the fires through the night. That responsibility now fell to Renna. She didn't want to run between three rooms, so they'd have to sleep in the kitchen...with the Blade.

They dragged a large mattress from one of the bedrooms and plopped it in one corner of the room. Renna would've preferred to sleep closer to the fire, but their unwanted guest was currently passed out there. Considering all the blood he'd lost, he needed to be near the fire to keep his body warm.

Brandi curled up under the blankets and promptly fell asleep. Renna watched her for a while, soaking in her sister's stillness. Brandi's mouth hung open, a line of drool inch-worming down her cheek, a snuffling snore pouring out. Only her sister could make drooling and snoring look adorable.

Renna leaned over their patient, added a few more logs to the fire, and perched on the edge of the mattress next to Brandi. They had a Blade in their kitchen.

What if the Blade found their Bibles? It wouldn't matter that they didn't participate in the Resistance. King Respen would assume they did. He'd have them tortured and killed. The Blade lying in front of their fire might even carry out that order.

Their Bible. She shot to her feet. They had a Bible hidden in the kitchen. She should move it before the Blade woke up.

Tiptoeing across the room, she eased one of the cabinets open. Several sacks lined up on the shelf. She reached past the first row and pulled out a bag of beans from the back. Digging into it, she drew out the book hidden in the seemingly innocent bag.

Returning the beans to the cupboard, she hesitated, the book heavy in her hands. Where should she hide it? A drawer in a room would be no safer than here if the Blade gained enough strength to search the manor. None of their other Bibles would be safe either.

As the pages fanned in her hand, she caught a glimpse of her favorite verse. *The Lord is my light and my salvation; whom shall I fear? The Lord is the strength of my life; of whom shall I be afraid?*

Renna gripped the book tighter. An ache gnawed at her stomach. Someday King Respen would deem her and Brandi a threat to his throne. They were only cousins to the royal family, daughters and not sons, ineligible to inherit the throne. But if they ever married, if they ever had sons, King Respen couldn't allow them to live.

"What're you reading?"

The voice startled her. Her heart leapt from her throat to her mouth. The Blade blinked at her, his green eyes shadowed. Renna hid the Bible behind her back. She'd hesitated too long. Had he gotten a good look at it?

Setting the Bible on a bench out of the Blade's sight, Renna tried to remain calm as she walked across the room and knelt beside him. "You're awake." Maybe if she distracted him, he'd forget about the Bible. "How are you feeling?"

He stared at the bench, his eyes narrowed, before turning his gaze to her. "Like I got shot with an arrow."

She could hear the strain in his voice. He still could die from the wounds, and he knew it. In a way, that was a relief. She wouldn't have to lie to him like she did some patients.

His eyes pierced her. "Water?"

Renna couldn't deny him water. Besides, she needed to give him laudanum to send him back to sleep so she could sneak the Bible from the room. And it would dull his pain, something that should've been her first concern as a healer.

She dipped a tin cup into the water bucket on the wooden countertop and returned to his side. Lifting his head, she held the cup to his mouth. "Small sips."

He drew in a sip, holding it in his mouth as if savoring it before swallowing. He managed three more sips before Renna laid him down. "I'll give you more in a moment, but first let me get you some laudanum."

Renna fetched the vial from Aunt Mara's cabinet of supplies and measured the drug onto a spoon. Raising his head again, she poured the spoonful into his mouth and helped him wash the taste away with more water.

As she laid his head on the blanket, his eyelids fluttered closed. His breathing slowed, much steadier than it had been several minutes ago.

Renna blew out a breath. This time, he really would sleep for hours. She'd given him enough drug to keep him under until morning. She clasped her hands. There was one thing—a rumor—she had to check. If she dared.

She gripped her hands tighter until her knuckles showed white. She should do it now, while he slept.

Holding her breath, she eased the blanket back from his shoulders. He didn't stir as she tugged the right side of his shirt off his shoulder. The firelight played over parallel lines of scars marching down his arm. Renna started counting but stopped once she reached twenty. She couldn't bring herself to count anymore. He must have over thirty marks.

Her breath scraped in short gasps. Only a high-ranking Blade could have that many marks.

Her hands shaking, she tugged his shirt from his left arm. No marks. He'd never failed. Never.

They were going to die. Renna sat back on her heels, shaking from head to toe. What had she done in healing him? Had she helped kill her own family?

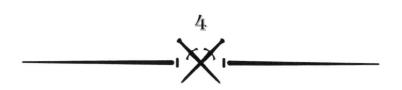

4

The first thing he felt was a clawing pain deep in his stomach. Leith fought to draw in another lungful past the agony. Next to him a fire crackled. A waft of heat brushed across his face.

He heard movement in the room near him, clanging dishes, chattering voices. Forcing his eyes open, he glanced around. The two girls sat at the table, heads bowed over slices of bread.

Leith felt a shiver not caused by the pain. They were praying. Not out loud, but he could guess at what their posture meant. Last night, he'd caught sight of the Bible Renna had been holding. She'd been terrified the moment she'd realized he was awake. No wonder. He was a Blade. He'd report what he'd seen to King Respen.

As Renna raised her head, Leith closed his eyes to slits. She glanced at him, and the tense set of her shoulders relaxed.

When she turned back to her bread, he let his eyes close all the way. They deserved to eat their meal in peace. He dozed. The fire popped. The blizzard wind whined across the chimney.

The chairs scraped on the wooden floor. Water splashed. Pewter dishes clanked together. Leith opened his eyes once again. The girls had their backs to him, laughing and splashing each other with bubbles as they scrubbed their dishes.

He studied their slim figures. Renna's braid swung against the back of her worn, blue dress. She stood a few inches taller than her sister. Brandi's hair gleamed against her faded, green dress as she bounced on her toes. Were the girls servants? Yet he hadn't seen or heard anyone else. Could they be the surviving ladies of Stetterly?

The laughter shriveled the moment Renna turned around. She straightened, her mouth flattening into a hard line. "Brandi, can you take care of the chores?"

"Right now?" Brandi's whole body heaved with a sigh. She set down the dish towel and slumped to the pegs by the door.

She took her time bundling up in her scarf, mittens, boots and cloak before she unbarred the door. The blizzard blasted in, whipping snow around the room. She shoved outside, yanking the door closed behind her.

As soon as she was gone, Renna twisted her hands together in front of her. Leith noted the whiteness around her mouth. Fear was her weakness. All weaknesses could be exploited.

She pulled her shoulders straight. "Which Blade are you?"

Why did his rank matter to her now? He glanced down at himself and caught sight of his bare right shoulder, his first mark peeking over the blanket.

She'd seen his marks and counted the number of scars lining his arm. He met her gaze. "I'm the Third Blade."

"Third Blade." She wrapped her arms around her stomach, hunching over. "We're going to die, aren't we? The King's Third Blade." She squeezed her eyes shut, tears leaking from the corners.

"I might still die." Leith sucked in a breath past the pain in his gut. While the wound felt better without the arrowhead grinding deeper, his pain went too deep for an easy and assured recovery.

He clamped down on his fear. He couldn't give her more weakness. She'd seen enough last night. "That'd solve your problem."

"No, it won't." She swiped at her eyes and shuddered. "We're dead either way. If you don't die, you're bound to see things you'll report to the king. If you do die, the king will send men to investigate. He won't calmly take the death of one of his Blades, much less his Third Blade."

Leith closed his eyes. King Respen would investigate her village regardless of Leith's recovery or death. A Blade had already died.

Leith could stop an investigation. He could protect this girl, neglect to tell the king the things he'd seen. But Leith had never withheld information from King Respen before.

Leith met her blue eyes. She'd taken him in, cared for him, yet his presence rewarded her kindness with danger. He should tell her things would be fine. He owed her that much. But he couldn't lie to her. "I'm sorry."

What had prompted her to tend him? Most of her problems would've been solved had she placed him back on his horse to let him freeze or bleed to death, whichever came first. A frozen corpse found after a blizzard wouldn't point to her family.

21

Leith glanced down at his shoulder once again. "Not all of my marks are killings." The words slipped out before he could reconsider.

Why had he defended himself? He had thirty-four successful marks. No failures. He'd earned his place in King Respen's Blades. He didn't need to defend his actions. Yet, her hunched shoulders begged for something from him.

She backed into the opposite wall. "Most are, aren't they? Were my parents one of those marks?"

"Who were they?" His chest tightened. In this manor, the odds were high he'd recognize the names.

She bowed her head, remaining silent for several moments. With a breath that heaved her shoulders up and down, she lifted her chin and met his gaze. "My parents were Laurence and Annita Faythe, Lord and Lady of Stetterly."

Leith's breath caught in his throat. Those names carried blood-stained knives, frantic screams, heart-wrenching tears. He cleared his throat. "I didn't kill your parents. The Second Blade killed your father, the First Blade your mother."

He turned his face toward the fire. Should he tell her the rest of it? If he did, she'd refuse to help him. But he'd seen the look in her eyes. She'd already guessed too much to be fooled with a lie. "I kept your father's men from saving them."

She made a sound, something in between a cry of pain and a sob. She probably hadn't known all the details of that night. She would've been about thirteen, an innocent girl spirited away by her father's sister while her parents kept the Blades busy.

Leith held his breath, hoping she wouldn't ask the

22

next question. He was the Third Blade, one of the original eight Blades who'd helped Lord Respen take over the kingdom. The night Lord Respen had overthrown King Leon, Leith had the task of killing the king's second son.

He met her gaze. He could see the question building in her eyes. He didn't want her to ask. He didn't feel guilty or anything like that. Of course not. Still, the idea of telling Renna—the girl he owed his life—that he'd killed her cousin made him...uncomfortable.

She turned away and stared into the fire without asking, though the pinched lines around her eyes told him she'd guessed enough.

Leith pressed his hand to the bandages around his waist. She wouldn't continue to help him now. He'd helped kill her parents. He'd killed her cousin.

Perhaps he should climb on his horse and ride into the blizzard. Maybe he could find somewhere else to rest until he recovered or died. It'd save these girls from King Respen's investigation and pay the debt he owed them.

He braced himself and tried to sit up. Pain stabbed through his stomach. Collapsing onto the blanket, he squeezed his eyes shut, sucking short breaths through his teeth.

Footsteps padded across the room. A cold hand touched his forehead. "Lie still. Don't try to move."

Leith fought the black dots bursting behind his eyelids. He didn't understand the kindness in her voice. By any reason on this earth, she should hate him to her core. "I should...leave. It would...spare you."

Her hand stilled. She looked away, tendrils of hair flinging around her face. Thoughts played across her eyes, though Leith couldn't read their meaning. He half-hoped and half-dreaded she'd agree with him.

Her hand pressed against his blanket-clad shoulder. "Don't move. You'll tear the stitches."

"Why try to save me?" By right, she should enjoy his pain, small payment for the years of pain he'd caused her. The lack of understanding itched at him. No one gave anything without expecting something in return. His father taught him that lesson years ago.

"I can't in good conscience refuse to help you or ask you to die in the blizzard." Her voice and face strained. She buried her face in her hands.

At that moment, Leith wished with everything in him that he was something other than a Blade. If he was a better person—a braver person—he'd carry through with his suggestion and leave.

But he'd never sacrificed himself for someone else. It went against everything King Respen had trained him to be. He didn't have the courage to force himself to get up and ride away nor did he have the courage to offer to hide what he learned from King Respen.

In fact, the first option appealed to him more than what would happen to him if the king ever found out that Leith had been less than forthcoming.

The door banged open. A snow bundle tottered in. Forcing the door closed, the snow-clad Brandi shoved the bar in place. She clawed her scarf from her mouth, revealing a wide grin.

"This is an awesome blizzard! There's a drift as tall as the stable next to the house! The animals are all right." She met Leith's gaze. "Your horse is fed and happy. What's his name?"

Leith blinked. "It's a horse. Doesn't have a name."

Brandi shook snow from her hair. "Every horse

needs a name. I named him Blizzard."

"Blizzard? He's dark gray." How did a dark gray horse remind Brandi of a blizzard?

"He came here in a blizzard." Brandi shrugged like it was as obvious as winter. "And he's all speckled with lighter gray fur. Like snow in a blizzard."

She hung her winter things on a peg and scampered across the room towards the fire. Kneeling near his knees, she stretched her hands to the fire, palms out to collect the heat and clasp it close. Her frozen, red-blond hair dripped onto the blanket covering him.

"Brandi, you're dripping on him." Renna laid her hand on Brandi's shoulder, as if to pull her sister away before her melting offended him.

"It's all right. He's too hot anyway. He's sweating." Brandi rolled her eyes.

Leith smiled at her lack of fear. Even though she'd probably been told he was a Blade, Brandi wasn't suppressed for long. He should be plotting how to use her innocence to his advantage. But he could do that later. If he survived.

Renna placed her hand on his forehead. Her hand felt cool and soft. "A little warm." She frowned. "The wound must have an infection."

A draft of air brushed his skin as she pulled the blanket back. He tried to ignore her fingers brushing his skin as she unwrapped the bandages from his stomach.

With firm fingers, she probed his wound. Bolts of pain shot through his body. He clenched his jaws so tightly his teeth ached.

Renna leaned over and asked her sister something in a whisper too quiet for Leith to hear. Brandi's eyes widened, but she nodded and leapt to her feet. She returned a moment later, holding a glass bottle. Amber liquid swirled inside.

Leith gritted his teeth even tighter. Unless he'd guessed wrong, that bottle contained a strong alcohol. She'd probably used it on him before, though he'd been thankfully unconscious at the time.

"Brandi, can you try to hold him still?" Renna's voice was calm and smooth, lacking the pitches and shakes he'd heard earlier.

Brandi placed one hand on his forehead and the other on his chest. Her hands felt like icicles from her time spent outdoors feeding his horse. She leaned her weight on his chest. Although small, he could feel strength in her arms.

Leith braced himself, clenching both his fists and jaws as tight as he could. He heard the splash of liquid as Renna poured the alcohol onto his wound.

A burning pain flared across his stomach. He jerked away from it, but Brandi's hands pinned him down. Tears pricked the corners of his eyes, and a whimper lodged in the back of his throat. Foolish weakness.

"It's all right," Brandi soothed, as if he was a helpless kitten she'd found stranded in the stables. "Renna's almost done."

Leith shivered. He felt cold, deep down cold, as if he still clung to his saddle in the raging blizzard. Breathing was growing more difficult.

"Could he have more laudanum?" The note of concern in Brandi's voice pierced him. When was the last time someone had worried about him? Sixth Blade Martyn Hamish might worry, but he couldn't think of anyone else.

"Yes, I'll fetch it." Renna pushed to her feet. "You

can fetch him a drink of water."

Brandi skipped across the room to the bucket and dipped the pewter cup into the water. Leith focused on breathing.

She breezed back to his side and slid her hand beneath his head. "Here's some water."

Pewter pressed to his mouth. He sipped as best he could. The mouthfuls were pitiful compared to the thirst tightening the back of his throat.

Renna joined her sister, holding a spoon with liquid. She placed it in his mouth. He swallowed, the sour taste curling his tongue. Brandi gave him a few more sips.

Leith closed his eyes as a numbing tiredness spread through his body.

5

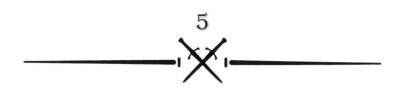

He'd helped kill her parents. Renna rocked back on her heels as the Blade returned to sleep. How was she going to do this? She was supposed to love her enemies, but surely he was exempt.

She clasped her shaking hands. How were she and Brandi going to survive this? Their life had been reduced to a few moments of semi-normality snatched between the minutes of terror whenever their patient was awake.

What would Brandi accidentally say in front of him? Would he use Brandi's innocence to gain more information about them?

Maybe she should've taken him up on his offer to leave. It wouldn't have been that hard to help him out the door and onto his horse. Their problems would be over. He'd be gone, and they'd be safe.

Except that it was wrong. Life belonged to the Lord. She'd placed his life in the Lord's hand when she'd decided to help him the night before. It was God's decision whether the Blade lived or died now, not hers.

The Blade's wound had the redness of a beginning

infection so perhaps his death was God's will. She grimaced. She shouldn't be so happy about that.

Rubbing her scratchy, tired eyes, she pushed herself to her feet. She and Brandi had too much to do to spend her time worrying about things she couldn't change now.

With that in mind, she kept them busy cleaning the kitchen, preparing food for themselves and a broth for their patient should he be able to hold it down, and braving the blizzard, bundled to their eyelashes with scarves, hats, and mittens, to fetch more firewood to last them through the rest of the day and night. The firewood formed a dripping, steaming pile as it warmed after being ice chunks in the cold.

The Blade slept most of the day. He grew restless during the afternoon, flailing and muttering as he slept. Renna spent most of the afternoon and evening dabbing his forehead and face with cloths dipped in cold water.

Were all her efforts really worth it? She wanted him to die. It'd be so much easier if she ignored him and let the fever take him. But, her conscience wouldn't let her turn her back. Aunt Mara had ingrained healing into her heart and fingers from the time she was small.

If only Aunt Mara was here to care for the Blade. But with the blizzard whining around the manor, Uncle Abel and Aunt Mara wouldn't return that night.

Stifling her yawns, she and Brandi sneaked out for a few minutes to hold devotions and read their Bible together in another room where the Blade wouldn't overhear should he wake.

When they returned to the kitchen, Brandi laid a hand on Renna's arm. "You're exhausted. I'll stay up with him for a few hours while you get some sleep."

Renna nearly refused. She didn't want her sister alone with the Blade, even if he was unconscious. He might become delirious with fever. But she was about to fall asleep where she stood. "All right, but wake me in two hours."

When Brandi nodded, Renna collapsed onto their mattress and fell asleep moments later.

She awoke far too soon. Brandi's voice hissed into her ear. "Wake up."

"What?" She pushed herself up and swiped her hair from her face.

"Your turn to watch him." Brandi yawned, yanked off her shoes, and flopped onto the mattress.

Tugging on her shoes, Renna wrapped her cloak around her shoulders and hunched in the chair by the fire. The door rattled under a gust of wind, shards of ice crackling against the window. At her feet, the Blade remained still.

Leaning forward, she spread her fingers toward the warmth of the fire. Her toes bumped the Blade's shoulder. He flinched in his sleep and cringed away from her foot. She watched him for a few minutes, but he didn't move again.

The silence woke her. Renna raised her head and winced at the pain that shot through her neck. Straightening, she groaned as the kinks in her body protested sleeping in the wooden chair.

The persistent howling had gone as silent as her parents' graves in the field behind the manor. She glanced at their patient. His chest rose and fell in a steady rhythm, his sleep restful. Disappointment dragged a bitter taste over her tongue. He hadn't died.

Renna couldn't make herself understand. Her parents had been good people, good Christians, good citizens, but they'd been brutally murdered in their own home just because they were related to the king. This Blade was one of her parents' murderers, yet he survived.

Pushing to her feet, she tiptoed to the window. The undulating snow drifts glittered like handfuls of diamonds had been scattered across their surface, their crests blushing pink with newborn sunlight. Her breath frosted the windowpane.

Renna turned away and padded across the room. The icy brick floor bit at her bare toes. Kneeling, she laid a hand on the Blade's forehead. Her shoulders sagged. His fever had broken.

Shivering, she poked at the coals, blowing on them until their hearts glowed orange. Adding smaller sticks, she waited until they caught fire before stacking bigger logs around them.

When the fire crackled and blasted out heat, she set the pot of broth nearby to heat in case the Blade was hungry. She placed slices of bread on a clean rock next to the flames, letting the heat crisp the edges and warm the inside. The heat on her face and arms soothed like the warm blankets she'd left behind.

"Are either of those for me?"

Renna shrieked and nearly whacked the Blade in the head with the fire poker. But bodily harm wasn't something a healer should inflict. "You scared me."

He turned his face away from her, something flickering in his green eyes. "I do that a lot."

Renna bit her tongue before she said something she'd regret. He was a Blade, a cold-hearted, mark-bearing killer. Of course he scared her. "I'm warming broth for you."

His grimace creased his slim cheeks. Renna grimaced as well. It was a sure sign that he was healing if he was hungry. She did her best to ignore him while she finished toasting the bread.

Brandi didn't wake up until the smell of warm bread and chicken broth filled the room. Her nose lifted first, pulling the rest of her body upright. Her eyes popped open as she pranced to the table, her hair frizzing around her head. "Is breakfast ready?"

Renna nodded and sat on the bench next to the table. She stared at her plate. Yesterday Brandi had convinced her to pray silently while the Blade slept. But this morning Renna could feel his eyes on them.

Across the table, Brandi clasped her hands and glanced at Renna. Her eyes held the question. Would they pray in front of their patient and risk the king's punishment? Or would they hide?

If only she could curl up back in bed. It was too early in the morning to make decisions like this. The right thing would be to boldly declare her faith regardless of the consequences. She shuddered. She didn't want to be arrested, dragged to the king's castle, tortured, and possibly killed.

Hiding would be so much easier. She and Brandi could pray silently, without folding their hands or closing their eyes. She scrubbed her palms against her forehead. Why did she have to choose between what was right and what was safe?

Brandi met her gaze with her blue, trusting eyes. "I'm not afraid."

"You should be." Renna hung her head.

Her sister's voice dropped into a whisper. "If God is

for us, who can be against us?"

Brandi's innocence overwhelmed Renna. But her sister didn't understand. God could be for them, but they still could be arrested, even killed.

Brandi solved the problem for her. She bowed her head, clasped her hands, and prayed out loud as if she didn't care that a Blade was listening. Renna hurriedly bowed her head along with her sister. "God in Heaven, thank-you for stopping the blizzard and keeping Renna and me safe and warm. Thanks for healing Leith and for this food. In Jesus' name, Amen."

Brandi crunched into her toast, tearing it apart as if she hadn't eaten for days. Renna could only blink at her food for several minutes. Brandi hadn't asked for a single thing. She'd only given thanks, including for the Blade's healing.

Renna didn't dare turn around to see the Blade's reaction. Nor did she want him to see the guilt etched in her eyes. Brandi might be thankful that the Blade was healing, but Renna wasn't.

Leith held still as the two sisters finished their breakfast. Brandi had prayed for him. An uncomfortable feeling pinched his stomach. She'd prayed for him, and he'd have to turn her in to King Respen for it.

At least Renna had an accurate picture of who he was. She wasn't blindly trusting like Brandi, and most likely she hadn't prayed for his recovery. In fact, if he wasn't set against gambling, he'd bet on the opposite.

Still, she'd done everything in her power to heal him even though she hated him. He couldn't understand it and wasn't sure he wanted to.

After the girls finished breakfast, they had a

whispered argument over who had to haul the water from the well. Brandi must've lost because she tromped outside a moment later. Renna fetched a bowl and spoon and ladled a scoop of broth. Actually, Leith mused, both sisters lost.

She slid her cold fingers behind his head. He gripped the blankets. She intended to feed him like a baby. He lifted his hand to grab the spoon from her. Pain twisted through his stomach. He gasped and dropped his hand. He was helpless. Thankfully King Respen wasn't here to see his weakness.

Leith opened his mouth and allowed Renna to place a spoonful of broth on his tongue. He swallowed, his stomach rumbling with an awakened hunger. Once he finished the full bowl, his stomach pressed contentedly against the bandages.

He glanced up, catching her blue eyes before she swiveled her gaze away. "I am grateful. I know helping me is the last thing you want to do."

She shook her head, stood, and washed the bowl and spoon. He watched her back, her blond braid swinging between her shoulders.

He was some kind of monster. Who else would allow himself to be healed while intending to betray those who cared for him? He watched the flames lick at the logs in the fireplace. A better person would stand up to King Respen, but Leith wasn't a good person...or brave.

Brandi burst into the room. "Uncle Abel and Aunt Mara are coming! I can see their sleigh!"

Leith studied the relief easing the lines between Renna's eyebrows. Their aunt and uncle? He searched the room, locating his knives tossed against the far wall. He didn't have the strength to reach them, much less defend himself. Whatever strange compassion gripped Renna, he could only hope her aunt and uncle suffered it too.

6

Renna glanced between the Blade and the door. What would her aunt and uncle think when they saw the Blade? How was she going to explain that she'd put them all at risk by taking him in?

She grabbed her cloak, clasped it around her neck, and flung the door open. She stumbled outside, Brandi at her heels, as the sound of the jingling bells rang over the snow drifts.

The black speck in the distance sharpened into a sleigh pulled by a shaggy mule. Aunt Mara and Uncle Abel formed blanket-wrapped lumps on the bench.

They stopped in front of the manor, and Brandi flung herself at Aunt Mara before she had a chance to climb out. Renna followed at a slower pace. No doubt Brandi's over-active mouth would spout the news of their patient before Renna had a chance to say it.

As Renna reached the side of the sleigh, Brandi was indeed gushing with the news of their patient while she gave Stubborn, their easy-going mule, a pat on the nose. But she spent more time talking about the horse now lodged in their stables and befriending their milk goats than she did on the young man lying in front of their fireplace.

Aunt Mara cocked her head at Renna. Renna opened her mouth to speak, but her throat closed. Too many life or death decisions had rested on her shoulders.

Aunt Mara tucked Renna against her in a one-armed hug. "Let's get inside."

"No, wait!" Renna pulled away. Her uncle started towards the stables, but she stopped him. "We need to tell you something first."

Uncle Abel and Aunt Mara glanced between the two of them. Aunt Mara's hands trembled. "Brandi wasn't making stories? There really is a Blade here?"

"I heard a thump the first night of the blizzard. He was slumped against the door with an arrow in his stomach. We dragged him inside and helped him, though we didn't know at first he was a Blade." Renna twisted her hands together, staring at the ground. "I asked him. He's the Third Blade."

Aunt Mara pressed a hand to her mouth and stumbled backwards. Uncle Abel gripped her shoulders. The lines around his mouth deepened into a frown. "We heard there were Blades in the area. Michelle Allen was snatched off the streets two nights ago. Sheriff Allen gathered a few men, and they stumbled upon two men holding his daughter in an abandoned shed."

Renna swallowed. The Blade had kidnapped Michelle Allen. What had he done to her? "What happened?"

"One of the men was shot and killed. The other was wounded but escaped. When they examined the dead man, they learned they'd killed a Blade. Sheriff Allen plans to seek the other one now that the blizzard is over.

He can't have him return to the king and tell who killed the other Blade." Uncle Abel glanced at the manor.

"At least we're here now," Aunt Mara hugged both Renna and Brandi. "He didn't hurt you, did he?"

Renna shook her head. "No." Would he have hurt them if he'd had the chance? What would he do when he recovered?

Brandi cocked her head north towards the town. "Will Sheriff Allen look for him here?"

Uncle Abel nodded. "He might."

"We'll have to hide him. And his horse." Brandi crossed her arms.

Renna clenched her fingers. Hide the Blade? Maybe it would be fine to hide someone good, but was it right to hide an evil person? She glanced at Aunt Mara and Uncle Abel. Both of them wore somber frowns.

Uncle Abel gripped the mule's reins. "Should I go in with you?"

"No, he's safe at the moment. He's too weak to even sit up." Renna dug her fingers into her palms. At least, she thought he was too weak to sit up. Was he stronger than he seemed? Had he been waiting his chance?

Uncle Abel trudged forward. "Brandi, why don't you come to the stables and help me with Stubborn?"

Brandi bounced to his side. "I can show you Blizzard. That's Leith's horse. He let me name him."

Renna resisted the urge to roll her eyes as Brandi skipped through the snowdrifts, Uncle Abel and Stubborn plowing a furrow in the snow behind her. Renna turned to Aunt Mara. "Let's...go in."

Aunt Mara followed her into the kitchen. They hung their cloaks on pegs and stomped the snow from their boots on the front rug. The Blade turned his head to face them, his green eyes expressionless.

Renna tiptoed across the room, swallowed, and waved at her aunt. "This is my Aunt Mara."

The Blade gave a nod by way of greeting. Aunt Mara knelt beside him, lifted the blanket, and undid the bandages. The Blade tensed, the muscles in his arms outlined below his skin. Renna reached a hand towards the fire poker.

Aunt Mara inspected the wound, her face relaxing into the small frown she wore when concentrating. She gave a crisp nod as she rewrapped the bandages. "You did a good job, Renna. He'll live." Those last two words lacked warmth.

The Blade's shoulders relaxed. Renna caught a glimpse of relief in his eyes before he turned his face towards the fire.

Aunt Mara creaked to her feet. She bustled around the kitchen, nudging things here and there to bring the organization back to her standards.

Uncle Abel stomped inside, followed by Brandi. He hung his cloak on a peg, brushed snow from his trousers, and crossed his arms. He faced the Blade, his blue eyes assessing. The Blade met his gaze.

"Did you kidnap that girl in Stetterly?" Uncle Abel's voice rumbled in his chest, a tone that demanded respect and attention when he spoke from the pulpit.

"My fellow Blade kidnapped her. I was ordering him to return her when the men arrived." The Blade continued to hold Uncle Abel's gaze.

"While you're under my roof, there'll be none of that nonsense, understood?"

Renna's heart lodged in her throat. He was giving orders to a Blade?

The Blade nodded, his eyes calm. "Understood, sir."

Uncle Abel turned to Aunt Mara. "Which room would you like him in? I'll build a fire and warm the place up."

Aunt Mara bit her lip. "The one on the end of the hall will do."

Uncle Abel grabbed several logs and pieces of kindling and strode from the room.

Renna stepped aside to let her aunt and uncle take over. Aunt Mara readied the room while Uncle Abel started a fire and fashioned a stretcher.

Together, he, Renna, and Brandi carried the Blade to the last room in the corridor. They laid the stretcher on the edge of the bed and transferred the Blade. Renna flung the blankets over him while Uncle Abel checked the fire.

Aunt Mara gave the Blade a drink and another dose of pain-killer. As the Blade drifted to sleep, Renna hurried from the room. She felt better, knowing she had a door and a long hallway between her and the young man who could learn enough to destroy her family.

7

Leith blinked at the sunlight streaming through the broad window across the room from his bed and studied his new surroundings in the daylight.

The walls were painted a dull blue, chipped in a few places but still serviceable. The bed stood near the center, a small table on one side and a washstand on the other. Along the one wall, a multi-paned window let in the southern sunlight. At one time, this might have been a favorite room among the staff who served the lord and lady of Stetterly.

Leith tried to push himself up but grimaced and fell back onto the pillow. His recovery was going to be slow. Wounds like his didn't heal overnight.

His door breezed open, admitting Brandi. She smiled as soon as she saw he was awake. "Aunt Mara said to check on you. Do you need anything? A drink?"

"A drink would be welcome." Leith couldn't resist the smile that tugged on his mouth as the girl turned to fetch the glass of water. Brandi was so…irrepressible. Nothing scared her for long.

Brandi returned a few minutes later, carrying a cup

of water. "Got it!" She brandished it like fetching water was a hazardous, grueling quest that she'd completed in record time. Judging from the amount of water on her skirt, hazardous wasn't too far off.

She lifted his head and held the cup to his mouth. He managed to drain the full glass.

Brandi plunked it onto the end table and tugged up a chair. "Blizzard's doing good. He and Ginger—that's one of our goats—are best friends. Ginger follows him around."

It took Leith a minute to remember that Blizzard was Brandi's name for his horse. "Thanks for taking care of him."

"It's no problem, really. He's a nice horse. He likes dried apples and carrots."

Leith suppressed a sigh. By the time he recovered, his horse was going to refuse to leave. Not that he blamed it. He clenched his fingers around the spot his knife's hilt normally rested. He should question Brandi while they were alone. She might innocently tell him something worthwhile.

Yet, he hesitated. Using Brandi that way was wrong. Bad enough that he knew they were Christians. If he should learn they were part of the Resistance, King Respen would order them killed immediately.

"Would you like me to tell you a story?" Brandi cocked her head at him.

He nodded. Another minute, and his sense of duty might've banished his hesitation.

"There once was a boy named Daniel. He and his three friends were captured by an evil king and taken far from their home." She leaned forward as she waved her arms to show a long journey. "A bunch of other boys were also captured. When they arrived at the evil king's palace, the king ordered that they all be fed food from his own table. But Daniel and his three friends refused to eat the king's meat."

"Why?" Leith frowned. A captive would be smart to eat all the food he could get.

She rolled her eyes. "He *was* an evil king. They had their reasons. Now do you want me to keep telling this story or what?"

He twitched his hand at her. He had nothing better to do. Might as well let her continue.

"They asked the man in charge of them if they could eat only vegetables instead. The man hesitated. He was scared that if Daniel and his friends looked sickly, he'd be punished." Brandi chopped her hands together.

Leith understood the man's fear. King Respen had executed people for less reason than that.

Brandi leaned her elbows on the edge of the bed. "Daniel proposed a test. He and his friends would eat only vegetables for a certain amount of time. At the end of that time, the man in charge would compare them with the other boys. He agreed, and Daniel and his three friends ate only vegetables for the agreed time. When the test was over, the friends looked much healthier than the other boys, and the friends were allowed to avoid the food from the king's table."

Leith raised an eyebrow at Brandi. "That shouldn't be possible. The other boys would look healthier. They were eating the better food. Daniel and his friends were only eating poor man's food."

Brandi smirked like she knew something he didn't. "Exactly." She waltzed from the room as if she'd accomplished her mission.

Leith stared at her back. What was she doing? She seemed like she didn't have a somber thought in her head and yet there were times she seemed to know more than she let on.

Renna handed another dripping dish to Aunt Mara as Brandi skipped into the room. Brandi dropped a cup into the bucket and splashed scuzzy water onto Renna's bodice.

"Were you with the Blade this whole time? What took you so long?" If that Blade hurt her sister, she'd...there wasn't much she could do.

"I told him a story." Brandi grinned, her eyes scrunching and twinkling.

Fear tore down Renna's spine. "Which story?"

"Daniel and his friends refusing the king's meat."

Renna's heart stuttered to a stop. "Brandi! What if he recognizes that as a Bible story? Do you know how much trouble we could be in?"

Brandi rolled her eyes. "I'm not stupid. I was vague on the details." She grabbed her cloak. "I'm going to the stables." She whisked out the door.

Renna sagged over her tub of dishes. "What are we going to do?"

Aunt Mara brushed at a lock of hair straggling out of her bun. "Don't be too hard on her, Renna. The Bible does say to let your light shine before men."

"Surely Brandi can let her light shine without mentioning the Bible. Or that we're Christians. Or that Uncle Abel is a minister of an underground church that will meet here in *two* days."

Renna gulped in several deep breaths. What would they do? The singing would echo through the whole manor. He'd hear it. Maybe they could drug him so he slept the whole service. That wouldn't make him suspicious, would it?

Aunt Mara shook her head. "The Bible talks about persecution and being hated of men. It never mentions hiding your faith to be safe." The lines of her face deepened. "But hiding is easier."

Renna blinked. "I know. I'm just so scared."

"Me too." Aunt Mara sighed into her hair.

Brandi burst into the house, Uncle Abel on her heels. "Renna! Aunt Mara! Someone's coming!"

Renna glanced from her to Uncle Abel. "Is it Sheriff Allen? Is he looking for the Blade?"

Uncle Abel's jaw set in a hard line while his blue eyes flashed. "I think so. I don't know why he'd be out in this cold otherwise."

Renna eyed her aunt and uncle. What were they going to do? Were they going to hide the Blade? Or let the sheriff find him?

As much as she hated him, she'd made this choice. She'd chosen to save his life once. It made little sense to betray him now. Besides, she could see Brandi's answer. "So, how do we want to do this?"

Uncle Abel gave a short nod. "Brandi will stay here with Aunt Mara and me. We'll answer the door. God willing, he won't do more than ask a few questions. Renna, go to the Blade's room. You'll have to figure out a way to hide him if Sheriff Allen decides to search the house. We'll send Brandi on ahead to give you warning."

Renna waved at the pile of weapons they'd all left untouched along the wall. "Someone will need to hide those. I don't want to hide them in his room."

Aunt Mara picked up the weapons and hurried to the pantry. Renna darted from the kitchen and down the hallway. As she reached the Blade's room, she heard the first knocks echo through the manor. She whirled into his room and stopped herself from slamming the door behind her.

The Blade's eyes flew open. He half-sat up, grabbed at his stomach, and collapsed onto the pillow. "What's going on?"

Renna swallowed to clear her throat. "Sheriff Allen is coming here. Probably looking for you. He wasn't too happy about his daughter's kidnapping, and he doesn't want you to tell King Respen how the other Blade died."

The Blade's green eyes sparked, though Renna couldn't tell if it was fear or something else. He struggled to sit up once again, wincing from his efforts.

Renna hurried across the room and pushed him down. He might tear his healing wound. "No need to move unless he decides to search the manor."

His eyebrows tipped upward. "You aren't turning me over to him?"

"He plans to kill you to keep you quiet." Renna gripped the edge of the blanket. "It'd be murder."

"Even for a Blade?"

The marks on his shoulder drew her gaze. "Even for a Blade." She dragged the chair farther from the bed and perched on it, her head cocked. This room was too far from the kitchen for voices to carry.

The seconds dragged by. She twisted her hands together, picked at her nails, and glanced at the window and around the room, looking anywhere but the Blade.

Footsteps clipped in the hall. Brandi opened the door and pranced through. Renna jumped to her feet. "Is he coming this way? Quick, help me get the Blade under the bed."

Brandi grinned. "Don't panic. Sheriff Allen stepped inside the kitchen for a minute or two to warm up and left. When he asked, Uncle Abel told him the kidnapper wasn't here."

Renna collapsed into the chair. "Hopefully he doesn't come back." Unless he came on Sunday. He hadn't attended church services since King Respen took over, but he might if he wanted a chance to search the manor. What would he do if he found the Blade?

Or, worse, what would the Blade do if he were discovered?

8

Brandi plunked herself on the chair beside Leith's bed. The morning sunlight glinted red in the waves of hair that trailed over her shoulders and down her back. "I'm here to keep you company." Her eyes twinkled with some sort of mischief. "Want another story?"

Leith heard voices—more voices than the family accounted for. "What's happening today?"

She cocked her head. "Do you want to hear my story or not? It's another Daniel story."

Leith tried not to smile. Brandi could dance around a topic as nimbly as a yearling foal. Music and singing echoed somewhere in the distance.

Were they having *church* in this manor? If they were, then they had a lot of guts, having church in the same place as a Blade. No wonder they'd sent Brandi to distract him.

Brandi still stared at him. He adjusted his pillow so he could look at her more comfortably. "Sure. I'm beginning to like this Daniel character."

She grinned, like that had been her plan all along.

"Well, Daniel and his three friends were wise, so they were promoted from captives to positions among the wise men of the kingdom. One night, the king had this dream. So he rounded up the wise men in the country, but he wouldn't tell them what the dream was, claiming that if they really were wise men, they'd be able to tell him his dream and interpret it too. When they couldn't, the king ordered all of them killed. Since Daniel and his friends were wise men, they were going to be killed too."

Leith reached for his knife but patted only air. Daniel and his friends were innocents in danger from an evil king...the story nudged at him. As if this was a parallel with King Respen and...no, don't even think about it. Just enjoy the story.

Brandi straightened her shoulders and puffed out her chest like she was a soldier. "When the king's men came to arrest them, Daniel stopped them and said that he could do as the king asked. So the next day, he went before the king, told the king his dream about a statue made of many different materials that was eventually destroyed by a big stone, and interpreted it. The king was so happy with Daniel that he made Daniel a ruler under him and promoted his friends as well."

"Next time, Daniel will have to control the weather or something. That's the only way to top that story."

Brandi's mouth quirked as one eyebrow arched above her knowing, blue eyes. "Daniel didn't do all those things by himself."

Leith blinked. She was talking in riddles again. Why did he get the feeling he was missing something important?

Brandi chattered away, talking about other things such as his horse and the weather outside. After an hour, music started up once again. He didn't mention it. Brandi seemed intent on distracting him and pretending that both of them couldn't hear anything.

When the music quieted once again, Renna slipped through the door carrying a tray of food. Lines pinched her eyes. What would a smile look like on her face? Had he ever seen her smile? Even without a smile, she looked pretty in a faded, pink dress trimmed with lace.

She placed the tray on the bedside table. "Is everything all right?"

Brandi grinned. "Everything's fine. Except, you might need to check his ears because I think I talked them off."

Leith tugged on one of his ears. "Nope, still attached. I must like your chatter."

Renna pursed her lips. Leith should promise that he wouldn't harm Brandi. But, he couldn't. A Blade couldn't make those kinds of promises.

"I told him the story of Daniel and the king's dream of the big statue." Brandi crossed her arms and raised her eyebrows. Renna's eyes narrowed, a frown tugging on her mouth. Brandi replied with a roll of her eyes, as if saying, *Give me some credit. I'm not dumb.*

Leith studied their expressions. Renna didn't want Brandi to tell him the Daniel stories. Why? They were nothing more than tales, right? Unless they could get Brandi in trouble somehow.

Renna headed for the door. Leith waved at the tray. "Why don't you stay?" His heart thumped for her to stay.

She clasped her hands, her eyes darting between him and the door. Her shoulders sagging, she turned back to him and Brandi. "I can probably stay a few minutes."

She glanced around. Leith searched as well. The

chair Brandi sat on was the only seat in the whole room. A strange feeling lurched in his chest. Renna might have to sit at the end of the bed.

Brandi popped up. "Take my seat." With a bounce that rattled the whole mattress and sent a spasm of pain through Leith, she plopped onto the bed near the middle. Leith gritted his teeth and sucked in a breath. He didn't want his pain to curb Brandi's exuberance.

To disguise the source of his discomfort, he pushed himself into a sitting position. His wound twisted and shot fresh pain through his body. He pressed a hand to the bandage as if he could hold the pain there. A hand under his elbow steadied him while someone tugged his pillow into a better position behind him.

He glanced up. Renna hovered next to him, adjusting his pillow and steadying him. She retreated back to the chair and swiped her hands on her skirt. Her eyes flicked to his arm before swerving to the tray.

Leith glanced down at his right arm. His marks stood out starkly, thirty-four reasons to fear him. Should he tug the blanket to his chin to cover them? No, that'd admit he felt ashamed. He couldn't show a weakness like that. Not to her. Not to anyone.

Renna handed out the food. Leith smiled when he received his plate of beef roast and mashed potatoes. Finally some decent food.

Brandi glanced at Renna and bowed her head. Renna's gaze flicked in his direction before she also bowed her head. "Our Father God in Heaven…"

Father. Leith's breath caught in his throat. The word rolled from Renna's mouth so easily, as if the title meant something warm and comforting.

Not someone to be feared.

"Amen." Renna raised her head and glared at him. He focused his gaze on his plate. She wouldn't understand this. He'd seen her father sacrifice himself to save her. Leith's father...Leith clenched his fingers. His father had sacrificed Leith to save himself.

Renna nibbled at her lunch. Her worry ate at her appetite. Brandi didn't seem to care that the Blade posed a danger to them. If Renna were to guess, she'd say that Brandi thought of the Blade as a friend. Was the Blade using her little sister to gain information?

The Blade wiggled into a better sitting position. The muscles in his arms and chest rippled. She swallowed at the knot in her throat. Every day he could move a bit more by himself. Soon, he'd be up and walking.

What dangers would he pose then? He claimed he'd had nothing to do with Michelle Allen's kidnapping, but he was a Blade. He couldn't be trusted.

She glanced at the door. She'd only stayed because she'd wanted to keep an eye on how he was treating Brandi. She shouldn't have worried. Brandi had him as wrapped around her finger as she had everyone else, the goats and horses in the stables included.

He set the tray on the bedside table, the food half-eaten. A frown lined his face and scrunched his forehead, a look he'd worn since she'd prayed before the meal. Was he angry they kept praying in front of him?

"You shouldn't waste good food like that." The heat in her chest straightened her spine. "But I guess you're used to having so much food you can waste it."

Brandi glanced at her, cheeks bulging, eyebrows tilted.

His green eyes speared her. "We're given our portion

at the castle but no more than that. I'm grateful to have that much. You were rich once. You grew up with plentiful food, servants, new clothes. I didn't."

Renna picked at a clump of lint on her skirt. At one time, she hadn't worried about the food for their next meal. She'd had several new dresses every year instead of one whenever her last dress fell apart. Her parents had sheltered her from work, all except learning healing with Aunt Mara, an amusement to indulge a child.

Time to change the subject. "How did you grow up?" Where had the Blades come from? They seemed like they'd always been men, always killers, always Blades.

Brandi stopped chewing and stared at the Blade.

He turned his face away. "You're poor, but you have good food on the table every day, a nice house providing a roof over your head, and a family who cares for you."

"I should have more family." Fire rushed across her face and curled in her chest.

"At least they cared about you." He wrapped his arms over his stomach. "My father was a drunk. My mother and I wore clothes she could patch together from the charity bin and ate burnt and leftover food we could beg from shopkeepers at the end of the day. Our house, if you could call it that, was smaller than this room."

Renna tried to imagine a house smaller than the tiny bedroom. Pity stabbed her chest. No, not pity. She couldn't pity him. He was a Blade.

"I ended up a servant to King Respen when he was lord of Blathe. He trained me to be a Blade. He's been decent, at least. We get a roof over our heads and food. He rewards us with marks."

Renna blinked at him. She'd always thought Blades were voluntary, paid killers. That they'd joined the ranks of the Blades willingly, reaping vast rewards for their evil deeds. But the picture this Blade painted...

"You're a slave to him."

His head shot up, his green eyes widening. "No, it's not like that."

"You're provided with food, shelter, and clothes, but nothing more. You have to obey every order he gives you. Are you punished for failing?"

"Yes, but only after three failures."

"Are you allowed to quit or leave?" Renna leaned on the bedpost.

"No." His voice dropped, as if he didn't want to admit the truth. "King Respen hunts us down if we don't return."

"And then what? You mentioned punishment. What kind of punishment?"

The eyes he turned her way had been stripped of their hardness. "Death. Death for three failures. Death for trying to avoid punishment. Death if we try to run." He squeezed his eyes shut, hanging his head.

She needed time to think, and she could hear the strains of the second service starting. She rushed from the room, releasing out a long breath when she was safe in the hallway.

Renna's words rattled in his head. King Respen owned him. He hadn't told Renna and Brandi the full truth. King Respen owned him more than they thought.

But being a Blade was a privilege only to be won by those tough enough to survive the training and skilled enough to never fail afterwards.

He'd never seen himself as a slave. After the first time he'd been asked to kill, he hadn't felt forced. His will had been King Respen's will. He'd never questioned it, never resisted it.

Until now. Renna and Brandi had cared for him. They'd given him his life and didn't demand anything in return. When he reported to King Respen, he'd reward that kindness with danger, if not death.

Unless he listened to the desire to *resist.*

Resistance was a bad idea. Bad things happened to those that resisted King Respen. To spare them, he'd have to risk death himself. And he wasn't brave enough for that.

Brandi bounced off the end of the bed and set her plate on the table. She waved at his unfinished meal. "Are you going to eat any more?"

Leith shook his head. He cleared his throat. "Do you have any more Daniel stories?" Somehow, the Daniel stories tasted like a sweet form of resistance.

That devious, almost scary grin returned to Brandi's face. Her eyes sparkled with the gleam of a hunter who has her prey right where she wants it. "Well, this story isn't really a Daniel story since he isn't in it. But his three friends are."

Brandi settled into her story-telling voice. Leith relaxed along with her. "The evil king liked the huge statue from his dream so much that he decided to make one himself, though his would be all gold. After he built this statue, he decreed that everybody had to bow down and worship it when he gave the signal. If they didn't, they'd be thrown into a furnace and burned up."

Leith got a sour taste in his mouth. He could see where this story was going. Daniel's three friends had refused the king's food. They weren't going to bow down to this statue. The king was going to punish them, and they'd die in that furnace.

"When the time came, the king ordered all these musical instruments to play. Everyone bowed down, except for Daniel's three friends. Some of the men, who were not happy that these three captives had been promoted over them, told the king. The king was very angry, so he had the three friends arrested and dragged to his throne room." She gripped fistfuls of air and dragged it towards her.

Could Brandi see his hands shaking? He saw another king's darkened room, King Respen meeting with his Blades, one of them chained against the wall awaiting punishment.

Even now, First Blade Vane hunted Zed Burin. After his third failure, Zed had run into the Waste, the desert on the eastern side of the Sheered Rock Hills. A foolish chance. Vane would catch him. Vane always did.

"The king asked the three men if it was true. He even gave them a way out to say that they hadn't been ready the first time and would bow the second time. But, they refused. They could not worship the statue. The king was so angry that he ordered his men to make the furnace seven times hotter than it already was."

Brandi's voice built as she made tying motions with her hands. "The three friends were tied up, dragged to the furnace, and thrown in!"

Leith couldn't help the small noise in the back of his throat. He needed the friends to get out of it somehow, to succeed in their resistance.

"The fire was so hot that it killed the men who'd thrown the friends into the furnace." Brandi leaned closer, her voice deepening as if imparting a secret. "But, the king looked into that furnace, and he turned to his men and asked, 'Didn't we throw three men, bound, into that fire?' His men agreed. The king pointed at the furnace. 'I see four men, unhurt, untied, and walking in there, and the fourth man looks like the Son of God.'"

Leith gaped at Brandi. This story had turned really strange. "How can someone look like the son of God?"

She smirked and raised her eyebrows. "Do you want to hear the rest of the story or not?"

He slammed his mouth shut. Of course he did, no matter how strange it got from here.

"So the king told the three friends to get out of that furnace. They did and the whole court looked at them. The men weren't hurt. Their clothes and hair weren't even singed, and they didn't even smell like smoke. The king was so astonished that he made a new decree that anyone who spoke against the God of the three friends would be punished."

Leith stared at Brandi for several minutes, not sure which of his thoughts to say first, if any. "You really believe these stories?"

She gave him a look, like he was the strange one. "You don't?"

Grabbing the lunch tray, she waltzed from the room, a satisfied smile on her face.

Leith fell back on the pillow. Great. Now both sisters gave him too much to think about. His life had been so simple before. Now everything jumbled in a knot he didn't want to unravel because he didn't know what else would unravel with it.

9

By the time Thursday crawled in, Leith couldn't stand lying in bed any longer. Sitting up, he swung his legs over the edge of the bed.

Yesterday, Brandi had fetched his saddlebags for him. He dug out his second black shirt and tugged it over his head. The fabric fell over his shoulders, covering his marks. For a moment, he could almost pretend he wasn't a Blade.

He tottered over to the door of his room and swung it open. The corridor to the kitchen stretched into the distance. Each step shot pain down his legs.

Glancing back, he groaned. He'd only gone about five feet from his door. Closing his eyes, he leaned against the wall.

When he'd caught his breath, Leith managed to hobble down the rest of the corridor. As he entered, the lively conversation died a quick death.

He slumped into a seat by the table and rested his arms on the wooden surface. He glanced around at the blank faces and let his head sag.

With a laden silence pressing on the room, Brandi

placed pewter plates onto the table. Mara set a pot on the table while Renna added cups and a jug of goat's milk.

Lachlan slid into the seat at the head of the table. Mara and Renna clustered at the end of the table as far away from Leith as possible. Brandi hopped into the seat across from him. At least someone didn't fear him.

After a brief hesitation, Lachlan bowed his head. To be polite, Leith bowed his head too as Lachlan's voice drifted around the table. "Our God in Heaven, bless this meal we are about to eat. Strengthen us to walk on the right path. In Jesus' name, Amen."

As Leith raised his head, he stifled the questions that burned his tongue. Who was this Jesus they kept mentioning? Brandi had ended her prayer in Jesus's name also. What power could a mere name hold?

Mara pushed to her feet and picked up the pot with a cloth-wrapped hand. Brandi scrabbled for her bowl and held it out. Mara's mouth tipped into a frown as her blue eyes flicked towards him. "Guests first."

"Oh, right." Brandi plunked her bowl back on the table and stared at Leith.

Wait, he was the guest? He was a nuisance. Perhaps a burden. He held up his bowl, and Mara ladled a portion of vegetable soup into it. The air filled with salt and basil.

He should say something. What was the polite thing to say? He forced a smile. "Thank-you. It looks delicious."

She halted, her eyes darting back and forth as she studied him. "You're welcome." A smile creased her face into layers of wrinkles. A strand of gray-blond hair drifted out of her bun.

An ache stabbed Leith's chest. The last time he'd seen his mother, she'd smiled at him just like that, her black hair falling around her shoulders as she gave him a bowl of watery soup made from a bone he'd scavenged. He'd never had a chance to say goodbye. Not that it mattered. His mother must not have wanted him any more than his father did.

The ladle clanked and soup splashed as the family received their meal. Leith blew on a spoonful and eyed them.

The silence curled around him. Did they expect him to start a conversation? What did people normally talk about over family meals? He and Martyn Hamish usually talked about their last mission or knives or something like that when they ate their meals in the Tower common room.

He met Brandi's gaze. He could count on her to break the silence. "How's my horse?"

"Well, Ginger—that's our goat—has decided Blizzard's back is the best place to nap. I don't think Blizzard minds. He doesn't stand up unless she starts moving around too much."

Leith popped another spoonful of soup into his mouth to stop his grin. Just like that, the tense silence melted under Brandi's chatter.

As everyone swiped the last of the food from their plates, Leith caught the surreptitious looks shared around the table. He glanced between them. "I already know you're Christians, you pray before meals, you hold Sunday services in your home, and you own a Bible."

Renna gasped and hunched her shoulders.

Brandi smirked as if she didn't care he knew enough to get her killed. "And you know the first few chapters of Daniel. We're up to Daniel 5. Would you read it tonight, Uncle Abel?"

With a last glance at Leith, Lachlan stood and strode to the pantry. After a few minutes of rummaging, he returned with a worn book in his hand.

So the Daniel stories were in the Bible. Leith scrubbed his damp palms across his thighs. He shouldn't listen to them. They were banned by King Respen, and he'd be participating by listening. Worse, he'd enjoyed the stories. Had asked for more. Remained silent even now as Lachlan read.

The words flowed differently than Brandi's re-worded versions, but the story had a familiar feel. The evil king's grandson was now king. This grandson liked to host wild parties. While he was at one of these parties, God's hand wrote words on the wall. Everyone stopped what they were doing. Daniel was summoned, and he interpreted those words as a warning that the kingdom would be overtaken by a different kingdom, and that night it happened just as Daniel said.

Leith shifted. Perhaps this explained why King Respen didn't like the Bible. In the last story Brandi told him, the king lived like an animal for seven years to humble his pride. In this story, the king was overthrown as God's judgment. King Respen wouldn't want to be told that he was under anyone's control, even God's.

But it shouldn't matter. King Respen didn't believe in this stuff. Nor did Leith. So why did it scratch at him? They were just stories. Nothing more.

When Lachlan finished, Renna and Brandi stood and gathered the plates. Leith placed his hands on the table. He should offer to help. That was the polite thing, wasn't it?

As he gathered his strength to stand, the kitchen door resounded under a firm knock. Renna peeked out the window. Her face paled. "It's Sheriff Allen."

Mara glanced between the door and Leith. "He must want to search the manor this time."

Leith's stomach clenched. Surely after all the time they'd spent healing him, they wouldn't hand him over to be killed now? He hung his head. Why should he trust the goodness of these people? They had no reason to spare his life.

As the door rattled again, Lachlan pushed away from the table. "Mara, see if you can delay him. Brandi, offer to take care of his horse. Don't let him go into the stable. Renna, you and I will take care of the Blade."

That's all he was to them. The Blade.

Leith sucked in a breath as Lachlan yanked him to his feet. Renna wrapped his other arm over her shoulders.

Together, they hauled him from the room. As the door closed behind them, Leith could hear Mara welcoming the sheriff into the manor.

"Where are we going to put him?" Renna leaned her face away from him.

Leith stumbled. His wound throbbed with the exertion. The meal he'd eaten threatened to come back up, coating his tongue with vinegar.

"In here will work." Lachlan dragged him into a bedchamber.

The room contained nothing more than a bed, the quilt thrown back at the end, a washstand, a wardrobe, and a bedside table. Grey paint covered the walls while worn boards creaked under his feet. A haphazard pile of books tumbled across the bedside table while a basket sat on the floor, the linens from the bed piled in it.

"Mara was planning to wash the sheets. We'll hide him here."

Leith stared at the basket. "I'm supposed to curl up in that?"

Renna slid away from him and tossed the linens out. Lachlan gave him a sharp gaze. Leith grimaced. He didn't have much of a choice.

He climbed into the basket and curled up as tightly as he could, pain twinging through his gut. Before he could catch a decent breath, Renna and Lachlan piled the fabric on top of him. He heard Lachlan leave the room, though Renna's footsteps continued to scurry around.

He huddled in the basket, breathing as quietly as possible. His legs ached as they fell asleep. His spine cramped. His breath hovered in the space around his nose while the fabric smothered him.

Still, he didn't move. He closed his eyes. Another cramped space dragged from a corner of his memory. It had been winter then also, the space a woodbox by the kitchen door of Blathe Manor. Lord Respen's voice boomed in his ears. *Stay. Don't move.* He'd stayed, freezing, for five hours. When Lord Respen finally came for him, he'd asked Leith to repeat all the servant gossip he'd overheard while curled in the woodbox.

The door creaked open. Several sets of feet clumped on the floorboards. Mara's voice floated somewhere above him. "Renna, dear, thanks for trying, but I fear it's too late to clean my mess before our visitor sees it."

A man laughed. "I'm here to find a Blade, not inspect your house."

Leith held his breath. His palms dampened, but he couldn't move to swipe them dry.

Lachlan's footsteps stopped near the door. "I doubt the Blade would hide in here. Perhaps in an unused room, but we'd notice if he were in our bedchamber."

"Can't be too careful with those Blades." The sheriff's footsteps pounded further into the room. Leith heard him open the doors to the wardrobe and rifle through the clothes.

The footsteps scuffed closer. A boot kicked the basket. Leith winced as pain shot up his spine. Was the man going to search the bed sheets?

Something clumped to the floor. The sheriff spoke on the other side of the woven reeds, "Nothing under the bed." A grunt, and his boots vibrated the floor.

Mara's and Renna's footsteps left the room. The sheriff's boots pounded toward the door, but he halted, the door clicking closed.

"You don't have to hunt this Blade." Lachlan's voice pitched low.

"Don't preach to me." The sheriff growled the words with more menace than Leith would've expected. Had Lachlan tried to talk the sheriff out of this before?

The sheriff's boots knocked against the floor, as if he'd yanked his arm out of Lachlan's grasp. "You know what he did to Michelle."

"More killing isn't the answer."

"With a Blade it is. It's the only way to stop them. Or have you forgotten four years ago?"

Lachlan's footsteps paced closer to the basket. "You know I haven't." His voice wavered. Not with anger. Regret? Sadness? Leith squeezed his eyes shut. He was responsible for the events of four years ago.

"Good." The sheriff's tone announced the matter was settled. When he spoke again, he'd lowered his voice. "Have you decoded the last message from Walden yet?"

Leith jerked in surprise, then froze as the basket gave a tiny creak. Lord Henry Alistair, suspected to be a leader in the Resistance, was the lord of Walden. If Lachlan received coded messages from Lord Alistair, it could mean only one thing.

Lachlan was not just a Christian. He was part of the Resistance.

Lachlan's voice cut sharply. "Not here. Renna might come back." Their footsteps pounded out the door. The latch clicked shut.

Leith released a slow breath, but he couldn't relax. He should search the room. If Lachlan had a message from Walden, he'd keep it close. It was Leith's duty to find it.

Almost he wanted to remain where he was. If he didn't search, he could pretend Lachlan had nothing to do with the Resistance. But he'd fail King Respen. And Leith never failed.

Tossing the sheet aside, Leith levered himself upright. His head swam as he tottered to his feet. Painful tingles surged into his toes. He sat on the edge of the bed, fighting to keep his breathing steady as pain engulfed his awakening legs.

Where would Lachlan hide it? Leith scanned the room. The pile of books on the bedside table was too open, yet Leith searched through them anyways. He didn't find anything.

The back of his neck prickled. Someone was bound to return soon. He lowered himself to the floor and felt under the bed. Nothing.

As he drew his arm back, his elbow bumped something wooden on the underside of the bed. He felt along it and discovered a narrow shelf attached to the bedframe. A heavy book lay on it. He drew the book out and perched on the edge of the bed again. A Bible.

He flipped the pages until they fell open to reveal a slip of paper. Rows of numbers lined the page. A few of the numbers had words written under them. *If you are concerned for the girls' safety, the Resistance is strong enough to protect them. The Leader is...*

The rest wasn't decoded. Leith studied the numbers. Why had Lachlan tucked the paper in this particular spot? Random? Or not? Leith found the next set of numbers and counted verses and words on the page. The corresponding letters spelled the next words. *...almost ready.*

The Bible was the key to the code. He stared at the pages in front of him. Lachlan was neck deep in the Resistance. King Respen wouldn't ignore this.

Renna and Brandi weren't involved, but the king would order them killed anyway along with their aunt and uncle. He held their death sentence in his hands.

Maybe he could put it back. Pretend he never saw it.

But he'd fail King Respen. He'd worked for nine years to earn King Respen's respect. He couldn't throw that away now, could he?

Lachlan's footsteps plodded into the room. The door clunked shut. Leith didn't look up from the Bible on his lap. He felt like a little boy again, waiting for his father's blow after yet another failure.

"You found it, I see. I suspected you would once Sheriff Allen mentioned it."

The disappointment in Lachlan's voice hurt worse than a blow to the face. Leith tried to gather a measure of defiance. He was a Blade. He shouldn't feel guilty about doing his duty.

"At least promise me one thing. When you tell the king, you'll tell him the girls know nothing of this."

It wouldn't do any good. King Respen would order them killed anyway. The king couldn't let the Resistance rally behind them.

But surely Leith could make this one promise, this one tiny resistance. "I promise."

He glanced up at Lachlan. Lachlan leaned a shoulder against the door, his head hanging. "Why did you hide me? Again?"

Leith needed to hear the answer. No one was as good or selfless as these people seemed to be. While they claimed they saved his life out of kindness, there had to be another motive. There always was.

Lachlan clasped his hands behind his back. "I asked in Stetterly. The witnesses saw one man snatch Michelle Allen. The man's description matched the body of the other Blade."

"I told him to return her. He failed our mission." Leith gripped the straw mattress. He couldn't dredge up the anger he'd once felt towards Chimb.

Lachlan's face tightened. "I believe you're telling the truth. Sheriff Allen has his reasons for pursuing vengeance, not just for this latest incident."

The sheriff had said something about four years ago. Leith gripped the edge of the mattress. The sheriff had lost someone in the attack on Stetterly Manor.

"So far you've given me no cause to fear for my nieces' safety, at least not while you're under this roof."

Leith caught the implication. "So why did you hide me? If the sheriff killed me, I would no longer be a danger to you."

Lachlan should've done it. He should've betrayed Leith the moment the sheriff mentioned the Resistance message. Leith had been helpless. It would've been easy and would've saved Lachlan's family.

"You're a danger to us dead or alive." Lachlan shifted his clasped hands. "If you were actively threatening us, I wouldn't hesitate to allow Sheriff Allen to deal with you. But you came here asking for nothing but healing. It'd be unjust to allow him to kill you for something you haven't done."

Leith couldn't wrap his mind around Lachlan's way of thinking. "You talk of justice. Then you know I deserve death. Maybe not for this, but I have killed. You've seen my marks."

Lachlan had to know whose blood tainted Leith's hands. Surely Renna had told him Leith's role in the deaths of his brother- and sister-in-law. If she hadn't, then he'd probably guessed as much. He had to know Leith killed one of Acktar's princes. Yet he still protected Leith from death. It didn't make sense.

Lachlan paced across the room. "Justice belongs to God. It's not up to me to wrest it from His hands." He sighed and shook his head. "But my main reason is Renna. She made the decision to save your life. If I were to have you killed, I'd disrespect her decision. It would appear as if I believed her actions in healing you were wrong. In hiding you, I'm showing her I'm proud of her. I believe she made the right decision, even if the consequences aren't easy to deal with."

Leith turned Lachlan's words over in his mind. That explanation made sense. Leith didn't buy Lachlan's calling on principles, but Lachlan would do it for his niece. Renna had a way of making a person want to protect her. Leith paused. Did he want to protect her?

No, he couldn't. He was a Blade, and Blades protected no one but the king.

71

10

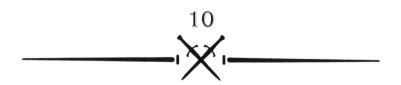

Leith lay on his back in the upper gallery surrounding what had once been the ballroom. His wound tightened. He tried to keep his gasps for breath as quiet as possible, though he doubted the worshippers could hear him past the thick drapes separating him from the railing and the room below.

Renna leaned against the wall a few feet away, hugging her knees and looking anywhere but him.

For some reason, they'd agreed to let him listen to their church service. Though, Lachlan had probably allowed it because whatever Leith learned couldn't put them in any more danger than they were already in.

What would a church service be like? Did they preach some kind of sedition against King Respen? It had to be something like that, otherwise why would the king ban them?

He closed his eyes, listening to the deep hum of people gathering in the room below. Eventually, everyone quieted. Lachlan's voice boomed across the room.

Leith pressed his palms against the floor. Not only did they host this underground church but Lachlan was the minister. Yet another thing that would get the entire family killed if Leith told this to King Respen.

If...when had Leith started thinking in terms of if instead of when? Bile licked at the back of his throat. Did he dare defy King Respen? What would he have to gain through a foolish move like that except death?

He locked those thoughts away. Right now, he should concentrate on this church service. He might never have another chance to satisfy his curiosity.

So far he hadn't heard anything that would explain King Respen's laws against church services, but perhaps Lachlan changed things around since he knew Leith was listening.

The worshippers in the ballroom below sang two songs Leith had never heard before. Then Lachlan announced the Bible passage: Daniel 6. Leith looked at Renna for the first time since the service started. "Daniel?"

She nodded, her blue eyes focused on the drapes. "Brandi's suggestion."

Leith could only shake his head. That girl and her fascination with Daniel. If it wasn't for her, he never would've gotten curious enough to be here in the first place. Had that been Brandi's plan all along? Was that what her smug smiles were about?

In this story, Daniel held a high position under the conquering power. Daniel's enemies talked the new king into making it illegal to pray to anyone besides the king for the next thirty days. Disobedience to the law would be punished by being thrown to a den filled with lions. All Daniel had to do was change his routine for a few days, and he'd be safe.

Instead, Daniel prayed as he always did. His

enemies, of course, told the king. With reluctance because he liked Daniel, the king ordered Daniel thrown to the lions. But, like the fire in the story about Daniel's three friends, the lions didn't hurt him. In the morning, the king went out early to see if Daniel was still alive. The king took him out of the lions' den, and his enemies were thrown in instead. This time, the lions attacked. Daniel told the king that he was spared because God sent his angels to stop the lions' mouths.

A weight crushed Leith's chest. If the names and situation were changed, that story was the one he lived right now, with Brandi and Renna as Daniel, King Respen as a not-at-all-reluctant king, and Leith's fellow Blades as the lions.

All Renna and Brandi had to do was pretend they weren't Christians for a few weeks. Instead, they'd risked King Respen's lions rather than hide their faith even for a few days.

What did that make him? Leith's hands shook. When he'd listened to Brandi tell these stories, he'd been on Daniel's side. Now he saw the truth. He was the people he'd hated in those stories.

He was Daniel's enemy.

Renna studied the expressions crossing the Blade's face as he listened to Uncle Abel's sermon. His face had gone pale as the snow outside, his eyes squeezed shut. He looked like he might be sick.

When Uncle Abel's sermon ended and the congregation in the ballroom below sang the final song, Renna crept closer. "Are you all right?"

For a moment, she wasn't sure he'd heard her. When he did speak, he didn't answer her question. "If King

Respen threw you to a den of lions, would you survive the way Daniel did?"

Renna caught her breath. She could imagine herself and Brandi in a dark pit, hungry lions circling them, springing on Brandi, her screams…Renna shook herself, drew in a deep breath, and pieced her thoughts together. "God doesn't always work that way anymore. Miracles like that are no longer needed. God works through other ways."

"What other ways?"

She blew out a breath. Why couldn't the Blade ask Uncle Abel these questions? "God says that all things work together for good for His people. Maybe we don't see outright miracles, but we can see how every event that has ever happened and will happen is for our good."

"Even your parents' murder?"

Renna swallowed hard. She believed the truth of the Bible, but for four years she'd struggled to apply it to herself. She could say the right answers out loud, but it was hard to mean them deep in her soul. She cleared her throat again. "Yes."

"And King Respen's rise to power?"

Renna clenched her fists. "Yes."

The Blade opened his eyes. "Even me being here?"

Renna couldn't meet his gaze. Why did he have to be the one to remind her of that?

She stared at the curtain above his head. "God must have some purpose in bringing you here. I don't know what it is yet, and I'm not good at trusting it will work out for good eventually. But God brought you here. This manor is the only building for miles in this direction. In that blizzard, you couldn't have been able to see twenty feet. If this was all chance, then chances were you would've missed this manor and kept riding until you either froze or plunged into the Spires Canyon."

His face paled further, and he shook his head as if he could deny her words. "So, your God wouldn't protect you if you were thrown in a den of lions?"

From below, Renna could hear the sounds of the church goers talking as they sat around the tables set up in the ballroom, plates and utensils clinking, ladles clanking on tureens. The noise blended into a nondescript roar.

She hugged her knees tighter. "God works all things for the good of His people. That good isn't necessarily what we would call our physical good. God looks at our spiritual good—our trust, faith, and love in and for Him—and works the things in our life toward that good. So maybe God would spare me but maybe not. Either way, He'd give me the strength and grace I'd need."

The Blade looked at her strangely again. She shrugged. She'd explained the best she could.

Brandi waltzed up the stairs to the upper walk, carrying a tray heaped with food. She set it down on the floor between them. "I brought lunch." Her voice was subdued but well above a whisper.

The Blade pushed himself up to a sitting position. He winced but managed by himself. That scared Renna. He grew stronger each day. How long would it be before he was able to ride away, back to King Respen? She could feel her family's time ticking away.

Brandi and the Blade wolfed down their meals as if they'd been starving all morning. Renna choked down a few bites. Had Daniel in the Bible ever felt this scared? The Bible never mentioned him nor his friends feeling fear, but Renna had to imagine that they'd felt afraid.

Or perhaps they were so exceptionally strong in their faith that they didn't feel fear.

When lunch ended, the Blade remained quiet during the second service. Renna tried to concentrate, but her fears bubbled in her brain in a relentless swirl. She'd said all the correct answers to the Blade earlier, but meaning them was a totally different thing.

Four years later, she didn't want to believe that her parents' death had been good. Surely this constant fear, this constant doubt, wasn't what was best for her.

She rested her head on her knees. She tried to form a prayer but failed.

11

Leith faced the family around the breakfast table. He'd delayed long enough. If he didn't leave today, he'd never make it to Nalgar Castle in time for the Meeting of the Blades. "I'm leaving today."

Brandi's head jerked up, crumbs stuck to the corners of her mouth. "Today?"

Nodding, he hunched over his toast. Why did she have to look at him like that?

While Renna and Brandi cleared the dishes, Lachlan laid Leith's weapons on the table. Lachlan's jaw tightened, his eyebrows arching.

Leith avoided his gaze. He buckled his belt around his waist and looped two more leather straps across his chest. He should've felt comfortable. These knives were as bonded to him as his horse and as shaped to him as his saddle. Yet, they now clunked against his body.

When he glanced up, the level of fear had risen in everyone's eyes. "I'll go saddle my horse."

He grabbed his cloak and limped into the snow-covered yard, following the trench Lachlan had shoveled through the snow from the manor to the stable. Inside, his horse greeted him with a low nicker, accompanied by the bleat of a brown goat.

Leith saddled his horse and led it from the stable. It tugged on the reins, as if unhappy about being led away from its warm stall. The goat called uproariously from the stable behind them, as if it sensed that Leith was taking away its friend without allowing a proper goodbye.

Outside, he found the whole family gathered to see him off. As if he was a guest. As if they cared about him.

He stopped in front of them. How did he go about saying a decent goodbye?

Mara handed him a cloth-wrapped bundle. "Some provisions for your way."

"Thanks." Still they helped him. Even though his leaving brought danger that much closer. When was the last time someone had cared if he'd had enough to eat?

He placed the bundle in a saddlebag. When he turned, he found Brandi petting his horse's nose and choking on a goodbye. His horse bent its head and nudged her shoulder.

Brandi patted the horse's neck one last time. Then she faced him, tears glittering in her blue eyes. "Why do you have to go?"

"Brandi, I…" He crouched in the snow. He could feel Renna's gaze on him, daring him to tell Brandi the truth he'd ignored for the past few weeks. Tell her he planned to report to King Respen. Tell her his report would get her killed. If not by his hand, then by another Blade's.

He might as well kill her now. He inched one hand toward his knives. They'd lured him into forgetting his duty. And forgetfulness was the next step to failure.

His hand closed over one of the knives strapped

across his chest where the others couldn't see. He was the Third Blade. He didn't fail.

He should yank it out and stab her now. As a Blade, he had to kill anyone on King Respen's order. Even Brandi. If he couldn't, then he'd already failed.

Draw his knife. Draw it. He could do this. His hand trembled on the knife's hilt. He could plunge his knife into Brandi's chest and watch her blood pool on the snow.

He dropped his hand. He couldn't do it. He'd failed King Respen. His perfect record. All his successful marks. All gone.

But it didn't matter. He couldn't kill Brandi.

A heady freedom buzzed his head. He didn't have to be Daniel's enemy. If he stayed silent, Renna and Brandi could continue their lives as if he'd never been here.

Why did he have to return? He could ride away. With this much of a head start, he might be able to outrun Vane. What would it be like to be free?

Leith gripped Brandi's shoulders, ignoring Renna's intake of breath and Lachlan's step forward. "I have to return. If I were to disappear, King Respen would have me hunted. He'd send Blades here, and I can't let that happen. You understand?"

He needed her to understand. He'd give anything to stay here, to never kill again, never follow another order. But he was a Blade, and Blades couldn't quit any way except death.

She nodded and sniffled. Then she did the most unexpected thing of all.

She hugged him.

As her arms wrapped around his neck, Leith held his breath. When was the last time he'd been hugged? Perhaps by his mother? He gave in and wrapped his arms around Brandi's slim back.

Brandi pulled away and placed her hands on her hips. "You take good care of Blizzard."

He stood and squeezed her shoulders. "Of course."

Brandi gave him a glare like she was going to hold him to that promise. As she whirled and trudged back to her family, Leith's eyes met Renna's. She twisted her hands in her skirt. Had he really planned to betray her?

He glanced at Abel and Mara Lachlan before turning his gaze back to Renna. "As far as King Respen will know, I was never here."

Her scrunched eyebrows told him she didn't believe him. No matter. He'd given her no reason to trust him.

With a final nod in their direction, he turned to his horse. Placing his foot in the stirrup, he pulled himself into the saddle. His wound burned. When he settled into the saddle, the pain eased to a dull ache.

He pointed the horse away from the manor and nudged with his heels. "Come on, horse. Let's go."

The horse didn't budge. He nudged it again. What was Brandi's name for it? "All right, Blizzard. Time to go." The horse walked forward, turning its head and tugging on the reins like it wanted to turn back. Leith forced himself not to turn around, not to wave. A Blade shouldn't—wouldn't—feel any regret at leaving.

As his horse trotted deeper into the rolling hills of Acktar's snow-drifted prairie, he spotted a horse cresting one of the hills, headed towards him. The distance prevented him from recognizing the rider.

He drew his horse to a stop and glanced over his shoulder. The hills they'd crossed hid both the town and manor from sight.

He studied the rider and weighed his options. He

could urge his horse into a gallop. He didn't doubt his horse's ability even in the deep snow, but he didn't know the speed of the other horse. Nor was his wound healed enough to take the strain.

He had to stay and see what the man wanted. Leith swept his cloak out of the way and touched the hilt of his knife. If only he'd mastered the art of throwing knives. He didn't have the hand-eye coordination necessary. Only a few Blades did.

Leith tensed and gripped the knife. Stetterly's sheriff rode towards him, his hunting bow held loosely in his hands. It wasn't drawn back. Leith would have a few minutes warning before the sheriff fired at him.

The sheriff halted his horse. "I knew you had to be hiding in the manor. But I didn't expect the Lachlans would purposefully hide you."

"They tried to prevent you from doing something you'd regret." Leith kept his face expressionless, hiding his churning stomach. He couldn't die here. Not now. He needed to protect Renna and Brandi. "You already killed one Blade. If you kill me, you'll have the deaths of two Blades on your head."

"You touched my daughter." The sheriff raised the bow and pointed the arrow at Leith's chest.

"I never laid a hand on her." Of all things to die for, he'd rather not die for the one thing he hadn't done. "If you want to punish someone, punish your daughter for unwisely being in that tavern in the first place."

The sheriff's nose flared. Leith raised his eyebrows. What story had that girl told her father? It certainly wasn't the truth. "I see she didn't tell you that part. You should be grateful nothing worse than a scare happened to her."

The sheriff ground his teeth and prepared to draw the string. "Doesn't matter. You'll still tell the king I killed a Blade."

Leith drew one of his knives. "The Lachlans have more reason to fear what I'll tell the king than you do, yet they let me go. I would suggest you do the same." Leith twisted his knife so it caught the morning light. "You might be able to shoot me. But I'll live long enough to kill you."

The sheriff's hand tugged on the string, the arrow rubbing back and forth against the bow. A bitter taste flooded Leith's mouth. The bow started to lower.

Leith stared at the sheriff until the bow pointed at the ground. The sheriff's shoulders slumped. Leith nudged Blizzard forward. The sheriff didn't move.

His shoulders prickled, but Leith didn't look back as he rode away. The sheriff didn't shoot. He'd frightened him into submission. A sick feeling settled into Leith's stomach, a feeling he thought he'd left behind years ago.

12

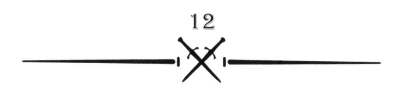

Leith halted Blizzard on the hilltop overlooking Nalgar Castle. Their breaths puffed into the evening. Leith flexed his fingers. His gloves and cloak failed to ward off the late winter chill slithering across his skin.

In the valley below, the grey stones glowed orange in the setting sun, gleaming against the snow that drifted over the prairie. Icicles glittered from the overhanging battlements and drooled from the flag poles jutting over the arched gates. The blue flags emblazoned with black, crossed daggers hung stiff with frost.

As Blizzard's hooves clattered over the cobbled ramp leading to the iron-bound gates, each beat pressed against his heart. Could he lie to King Respen? His fellow Blades? If he failed to be convincing, he'd be punished and the girls would die.

Inside the gates, the bustle of the castle surrounded him. A stableboy appeared at Leith's elbow as soon as he dismounted. Leith handed him the reins, grabbed his saddlebags, and tossed them over his shoulder.

As the stableboy led Blizzard away, Leith stopped himself from patting Blizzard's rump. A Blade didn't care about his horse.

First Blade Harrison Vane strolled from the tall, stone archway next to the stables. His blue eyes, cold as the layer of ice covering the courtyard, froze Leith's skin. If Vane had returned, then he'd captured Zed.

Leith limped forward. Could Vane read Leith's intentions? Drawing in a deep breath, Leith clenched his right fist and thumped it over his heart. "Third Blade reporting in."

Vane's gaze raked over him. "Alive, I see. We heard rumors to the contrary."

"Chimb didn't make it." Leith rubbed his wound as he and Vane passed the guards guarding the entrance to the arched passageway that connected the cobbled main courtyard to the southern, grass-covered courtyard that belonged to the king and privileged guests. "I took an arrow."

In the middle of the passageway, Vane halted. To their right, a set of stairs led into King Respen's chambers. An arched doorway to their left opened onto the wooden bridge spanning the moat surrounding the Blades' Tower.

Vane arched one, light brown eyebrow. "Did you learn anything?"

Leith couldn't swallow. He couldn't lick his lips. He couldn't do anything to betray the nerves twisting his chest. "Nothing that can't wait until the Meeting."

Vane drew his knife and twisted it in his hands. A smile shivered across his face. "Did you see the ladies Brandiline and Rennelda?" His voice lingered on the girls' full names.

Ice slicked along Leith's skin. Renna and Brandi marked the single failure on Vane's left arm. Leith met

Vane's blue eyes. "No, I never saw them."

Vane tapped the tip of his knife against his teeth. His blue eyes scoured Leith. Leith held his gaze. If he squirmed, Vane would know he lied.

"Pity." Vane sheathed his knife. He waved towards the bridge. "Supper was served a few minutes ago." With a tip of his head in Leith's direction, Vane strode up the stairs to report Leith's arrival to King Respen.

When he disappeared, Leith shuddered. How was he going to fool both King Respen and Vane? He swiped his damp palms on his shirt.

He headed for the Blades' Tower, a five-story monolith looming above him. The moat had frozen into a sheet of grey ice glazed with snow. The bridge thumped with Leith's footsteps, echoing his heartbeat and Renna's words. *You're a slave.*

Before, he'd believed the separation of the Blades from the rest of the castle was due to their status. They were above everyone else, separated to maintain their mystery and secrecy. Perhaps that was true, but it also cut them off from contact with everyone else.

At the end of the bridge, he rapped on the wooden gate set in the wall of the Tower. Two crossed knives, the symbol of the Blades, was carved into the stone above the door.

A hatch swished. A boy peered through, glanced at Leith, and closed the hatch. The door creaked open. The boy stepped aside, clasped his fist, and pressed his arm across his chest. "Third Blade."

Leith returned the boy's salute, one of the young Blade trainees. Only Blades, their trainees, a handful of servants, and the king were allowed in this tower.

As he tottered into the darkened common room that

formed the main floor of the tower, warmth smacked his chapped face. The massive, central fireplace roared, casting dancing tongues of light across the black shapes of his fellow Blades hunched around the long tables.

Nodding at a few of them, Leith crossed the room to the kitchen tucked along one wall. Fetching a plate and receiving his portion of food, he sat by himself at a table.

A strange feeling swept through him. As if he should pray before his meal. Not that he believed in all that stuff, but three weeks of doing it made it something of a habit.

His eyes swept the room, the clusters of dark-clad men, the shadows spreading across the room as if intending to smother the half-hearted light from the four candelabras. Why had he never noticed how oppressively dark this room, this tower, this entire castle were all the time?

Martyn slid onto the bench beside him. "Heard rumors of trouble up in Stetterly. Glad to see you made it back in one piece. Where's Chimb?"

"Didn't make it." Leith didn't want to talk about it, not even to Martyn. The less he said about the past month, the better for Renna and Brandi.

Martyn's mouth pressed into a thin line. "The king won't be happy with that."

"No." Leith took a bite of his meal. A Blade had died. Even if Leith said nothing about Renna, Brandi, their family's Bible, the underground church, and the Resistance, the king's attention would still focus on Stetterly. Leith struggled to swallow his meat.

He was going to fail no matter what he did.

"Vane caught Zed." Martyn stirred his meat.

"Did he take him back alive?"

Martyn's blond curls glinting in the candlelight.

"Been here about a week." He stabbed at his plate. "It hasn't been pleasant."

Leith's food rotted on his tongue. He didn't have to ask. The look in Martyn's brown eyes told him enough. Martyn had helped carry out Zed's torture, the price Zed paid for running.

Choking down the rest of his meal, Leith pushed away from the table. His wound twinged.

Martyn leapt to his feet. "Are you all right?"

Leith pressed his palm on the tabletop. "Took an arrow in Stetterly when they killed Chimb."

Martyn's gaze searched him. "How bad?"

"Bad enough I thought I might die." Leith touched his shirt above the wound. How was he going to manage the four flights of stairs to his room? Martyn fell into step with him as he limped across the common room and forced himself up the first few stairs.

Once they'd turned the first corner of the winding staircase, Martyn grabbed Leith's saddlebags and tossed them over his shoulder. He drew Leith's arm over his other shoulder. "Can't have you passing out and falling down the stairs."

"Thanks." Leith leaned his weight on his friend's sturdy shoulder. Martyn's height wrenched Leith's arm above his head, but the pressure eased on his wound.

Together, they hobbled up the staircase that spiraled along the outer wall of the Tower. At each floor, the stairs leveled into a corridor between the outer wall and the inner rooms barred with heavy, oak doors. The crossed knives symbol marked each door with a number carved in the center. *22. 21. 20.* Arrow slits in the outer wall, the only windows in the entire Tower, filtered light onto the stairs and corridors.

At the third floor, Leith glanced at the rooms, the stairs behind them, and the corridor ahead of them. No one in sight. "Do you wonder what it would be like if we weren't Blades? If we didn't have to obey King Respen?"

Martyn halted. "What put a thought like that in your head?"

Leith shrugged as best he could with his arm over Martyn's shoulder. "Too much time to think the last couple of weeks."

"Well, stop thinking it. We're Blades. That's our duty." Martyn started walking again, tugging Leith with him. "You're the one who taught me that."

Leith turned his face away from Martyn as they climbed the stairs to the fourth floor. *Do your duty and you'll survive.* He'd believed that. Once. He'd done everything King Respen had asked of him and earned his place in the Blades.

But all he'd done was work himself into the same slavery he'd had when cringing from his father's fist.

He didn't want that slavery anymore, and he didn't want to leave Martyn in it either. "But what if things were different? And we were free. What then?"

Martyn shook his head as they reached the corridor. "It's nonsense, and you know it. Stick to what we know and put thoughts like that out of your head before Vane hears them."

A weight snagged in Leith's chest. His friend refused to listen. They halted in front of his door. Leith tugged his arm free. "I can manage on my own from here."

Martyn held out his saddlebags but didn't let go. "Stop thinking crazy. I don't want to see you end up tortured and killed like Zed."

Leith met Martyn's gaze. "I won't. I'll be fine."

"Good." Martyn slapped him on the shoulder. "Glad you're back." He strolled down the corridor towards his room, the last one on this floor. Leith watched until he disappeared around the curve of corridor.

The truth ached inside him, but Leith couldn't voice the words, not even to his best friend. No one could know what Leith had seen and learned in Stetterly.

Stepping inside his room at last, he lit the single candle and locked the door behind him. He hung his saddlebags on the pegs along one wall, set the candle on the table at the head of the iron-framed cot, and pressed his hands flat against the back wall. The central chimney radiated enough heat to warm the stones.

When his fingers lost their stiff chill, he sank onto the cot. The darkness surged through the room and over his head, choking him, choking his soul. He shivered at the stale air that pressed around him. If he could, he'd run from this place.

But, he couldn't. Vane would hunt him. King Respen would torture him. He didn't dare brave either of those threats. Besides, running would only draw attention to Renna and Brandi. For their sakes, he had to stay.

Leith's stomach clenched. Who was he to dare even this much resistance to King Respen? King Respen was the absolute ruler of Acktar. With a word, he could send his Blades anywhere he chose, kill anyone he desired.

If—most likely when—he learned of Leith's omission of detail, he'd punish Leith like he'd punished Zed. Leith hugged his arms to his body. He didn't have the courage. He wasn't like Daniel in Brandi's stories. He couldn't stand alone against a king's wrath.

But Daniel didn't stand alone. Leith turned the thought over in his mind as if to learn its taste before he swallowed. That was his secret. That was the secret that put the smirk on Brandi's face and stiffened Renna's spine.

They were not alone.

He couldn't pray to their God for himself. He was the enemy. But their God might help him for their sakes.

Leith checked the lock on the door and inspected the stones in the walls that separated his room from the Second and Fourth Blades'.

When he was satisfied his room was secure, he knelt on the floor. How did Renna and Brandi go about praying? He had to get this right. God had enough reasons to ignore him already.

Leith clasped his hands and closed his eyes. "I know I'm not worthy to be heard. I have blood on my hands. But please hear me for the sake of Renna and Brandi. I know they are loved. Give me the words tomorrow to shield them from King Respen."

He paused. What word did they use to end their prayers? He mumbled something that sounded similar and opened his eyes. The room was still dark, the one candle striving to clear a small section of light around his bed.

But he felt a little braver.

13

When Leith woke, he felt like someone stirred his stomach with a soup spoon. He skipped the dry toast the Blades were given for breakfast.

A few minutes before eight in the morning, he climbed the staircase to the fifth floor of the Tower and filed into the meeting room with the rest of the Blades.

Two candles, set at intervals along the dark table, provided meager light in the circular room. At the foot of the table, a form, barely recognizable as Zed, writhed and moaned, tugging at the chains that held him against the wall. His shirtless torso dribbled blood across swollen bruises and burns.

Leith turned his face away and hung his weapons from his peg along the wall. He slipped into his seat, second from the head of the table on the right side.

Across from him, the Fourth Blade claimed his seat while the First and Fifth Blades sat on either side of him. Two seats, one at the end of the table and one near the middle, remained empty.

At precisely eight, King Respen swept into the room. Leith's stomach dropped into his toes as he rose to his feet with the other Blades in a concerted movement. Could he fool King Respen?

The king stood in front of his throne at the head of the table with his back to the chimney. He fisted his right hand and clasped it over his chest. "My Blades." King Respen's voice rumbled in deep tone of thunder over the mountains.

The sound of fists thumping against chests reverberated around the room, but Leith's fist clumped off-rhythm. "My king."

The king reclined on his throne. His sword and daggers clunked against the armrests. As Leith sat with the rest of the Blades, invisible shackles dragged on his wrists.

King Respen was the only one allowed to wear weapons at this meeting. Supposedly, it was to show that the Blades were a brotherhood so united and dedicated to each other that this was the only place they could leave their weapons behind.

But what if the truth was more sinister? Having weapons while the Blades were unarmed gave King Respen control over his Blades. Renna had been right all along. The Blades weren't honored servants. They were all slaves.

Leith fought to keep his face blank. He'd be chained along the wall like Zed if King Respen noticed even a flicker of his current thoughts on his face.

"The Blades have been dishonored." The king's voice flowed through the darkness like midnight clouds scudding across the sky.

Leith's skin prickled. Did King Respen know? Had he heard rumors? Had someone seen him leave Stetterly Manor?

King Respen tipped his hand towards the foot of the table. "The dishonored one awaits his punishment."

The figure along the wall gave a piteous moan. Leith hid his shaking hand by gripping the seat of his chair. The king would order one of his Blades to carry out his judgment on Zed.

Please not me. Without meaning to, the thought came out as a prayer.

"Fourth Blade Craven, restore the honor of the Blades."

Leith sagged against the back of his chair. King Respen hadn't picked him. Almost as if his prayer had been answered…but that was impossible. God wouldn't hear someone like him.

The Fourth Blade stood and bowed before the king. King Respen handed him a knife. Gripping the knife, the Blade strode to the foot of the table. Leith couldn't look away. He was a Blade. He was supposed to have the stomach for killing.

The Fourth Blade halted in front of the prisoner chained to the wall and rested his knife against his neck. Zed whimpered. His face hard, the Fourth Blade dragged the knife across Zed's throat.

Leith flinched at the choking sound Zed made as he died. With long, unaffected strides, the Fourth Blade returned the knife to the king and regained his seat.

Leith remained motionless and struggled to remain expressionless. Out. He had to get out. But the only way out was to die the way Zed had a few moments ago.

"Twentieth Blade Beeson."

The Twentieth Blade slid to his feet, strode towards the head of the table, and knelt before King Respen. He clasped his fist across his chest as he bowed. "My king."

"Your report?" King Respen's voice rolled across the table.

The Twentieth Blade raised his head and met the king's eyes. "I accompanied the First and Second Blades to the foot of the Ramparts. The Second Blade and I waited outside the Waste in case Burin doubled back while the First Blade went into the Waste after him. When the First Blade returned from the Waste with Burin, we helped escort the prisoner."

Leith drew in a deep breath to remain calm. He could do this. He had to do this.

King Respen remained still and silent for a long minute, the fingers of his left hand tapping a slow rhythm on the armrest. The tapping stopped as he leaned forward and drew his knife. "You have done well, my Twentieth Blade."

The Twentieth Blade pulled up the black fabric of his right sleeve. He jumped only a fraction as King Respen slashed the knife across his arm below the other three marks already clustered there.

The Twentieth Blade thumped his fist on his chest one last time, rose to his feet, and strode back to his seat. Once he was seated, King Respen's dark brown eyes swiveled to the next Blade. "Nineteenth Blade Altin."

The fifteen-year-old Blade slid to his feet. Leith noted the tremble to his hands and the shake to his stride. Altin knelt in front of King Respen. "My king."

"Your report?"

"I rode into the Sheered Rock Hills above Walden looking for signs of recent travel. The blizzard snowed me into a ravine for a week before I could get my horse out. I searched for the next three weeks, but I couldn't find any signs of travel."

"None? In three weeks?" The king's tone deepened to a chilled rumble.

Chills scurried across Leith's skin. If King Respen was angry over this failure, one that Altin had no control over, what would he think when Leith had little information to offer? It wouldn't matter that he'd been wounded. He was the Third Blade. He was expected to return with information regardless. Worse, Leith had information. He planned to hide it.

Altin hunched before the king. "None."

King Respen leaned forward until his face was only inches from the Blade's. "You have failed, my Nineteenth Blade. Do not let it happen again."

Altin swallowed and pushed his left sleeve up to his shoulder. A single white scar marked the top of his shoulder. The king slashed his knife across the Blade's arm below the scar. Blood dribbled down his bicep. One more mark, and he'd die.

Leith gripped his chair tighter as Altin hurried back to his chair. He'd been there the day Altin became a Blade and had seen the look in the boy's eyes as he stared down at his first kill, the blood dripping from his knife. Altin shouldn't be a Blade. He shouldn't have to kill to stay alive.

"Twelfth Blade Daas."

Leith shifted. He'd missed several reports because of his preoccupation. He scrabbled at whatever courage he possessed. His tongue cracked as every bit of moisture fled his mouth. If only he had even a measure of Daniel's courage.

"Sixth Blade Hamish."

Martyn slid to his feet, crossed the space in three

strides, and knelt in front of the king. "My king."

"What do you have to report?"

"I watched the town of Sierra. A number of riders came to Sierra from the direction of Walden. I managed to search one rider's saddlebags but didn't find anything. If they carried any messages, they kept the messages on their person. Because of the snow, I wasn't able to get close enough to the manor to search it."

Leith had seen one of those messages. He even knew how to translate it. Yet he couldn't breathe a word about it without putting Renna and her family in danger.

"You found possible evidence of Resistance activity as ordered." King Respen picked up his knife. "You have done well, my Sixth Blade."

After the king sliced Martyn's successful mark, Martyn returned to his seat. Leith slowly scrubbed his palms against his trousers.

Two more reports.

One more report.

"Third Blade Torren." King Respen's voice shuddered through the shadows.

Leith stood. He needed to be cold to bluff his way through this report. He knelt at the king's side and bowed his head. "My king."

"What do you have to report?" King Respen's deep voice shivered across the beads of sweat gathering between his shoulder blades.

Leith resisted the urge to take a deep breath. He lifted his head and met King Respen's gaze. "Twenty-Second Blade Chimb and I arrived in Stetterly the night the blizzard started. We took temporary shelter in a woodshed, and I sent Chimb into the town to gather information and scout a better place to wait out the storm. When he returned, he brought a girl with him."

"A girl?" King Respen leaned back in his throne, stroking his beard into a stiffer point.

"Yes. The daughter of Stetterly's sheriff, as I learned later." Leith didn't break eye contact. He couldn't deviate from his normal rhythm or the king would sense his hesitation. "I ordered Chimb to return her before she was missed, but before he could, the sheriff and his men discovered us. Chimb was shot and killed. I took an arrow to the stomach, but got to my horse in time to escape."

King Respen's eyes narrowed, but his fingers continued stroking his beard.

"I rode into the blizzard. My horse took me far out of town until I thought the blizzard or my wound would claim me before I found shelter. At last, I spotted the dark shape of a building. I nudged my horse towards it and fell off on the doorstep."

The king leaned forward.

Leith paused a heartbeat. Time to do something he'd never dared before. Hide information from King Respen. "I passed out. I spent a week delirious with fever and hovering near death. When I finally awoke, I discovered I'd been rescued by an old man named Daniel."

Leith resisted the smile that tugged his mouth. "He had enough healing skills to remove the arrow and close my wound. I was very weak and couldn't get out of bed for several more days. I spent another week and a half with him before I returned here."

"Show me your wound." King Respen motioned with his hand.

Leith raised his shirt, revealing the pink scar on the left side of his stomach. King Respen's gaze raked across his skin like a finger with a long, sharpened fingernail. With a nod, the king signaled he'd satisfactorily assessed that Leith's wound matched his story. Leith released his shirt, nearly letting out a sigh of relief along with it.

"Your mission was to study the rumored unrest in Stetterly. Did you accomplish this?"

Leith met King Respen's eyes once again. "I failed to gather much information due to my injury. The fact that the Twenty-Second Blade and I were attacked points to a growing boldness among those living in the countryside. The sheriff actively hunted me, even though he knew I was a Blade."

He suppressed the guilt heating his chest. The sheriff had hunted him too openly. Leith couldn't hide that from the king. Better to betray the sheriff and save Renna and Brandi.

"They are emboldened." King Respen drummed his fingers on the armrest. "They do not fear my Blades as they once did. Do you think the attack you suffered could have been a trap?"

Leith turned the memory over in his mind. The girl's kidnapping had been a reckless impulse, and the sheriff never would've purposely placed his daughter in a tavern. But, it'd be easy to plant suspicion of something more in the king's mind, something that would take his attention away from Stetterly.

"The Twenty-Second Blade was impulsive. If the town knew ahead of time that we were going to be there, it's possible they could've put the girl in the tavern as a means to trap us."

The king's dark eyes sharpened. He didn't say the words out loud, but Leith could see the suspicion growing in his mind. The only way for Stetterly to know the Blades' movements ahead of time would be if they had a spy among the Blades. As the one caught in the ambush in Stetterly and reporting the possible existence of a spy, King Respen wouldn't suspect Leith.

King Respen picked up his knife, the tip stained red with the marks he'd already given that Meeting. "In spite of your injury, you have done well, my Third Blade."

A thrill zimmed through Leith's stomach, but he kept his expression blank. He pulled up his right sleeve. The king sliced the knife across Leith's arm, drawing a line of blood. He should be proud. Thirty-five marks and no failures.

Leith slid into his seat before anyone noticed his shaking. The warmth of success soured. Had he done enough to protect Renna, Brandi, and their family? If King Respen scrutinized the sheriff, would he notice his connection with Lachlan?

The Second Blade returned to his seat across the table. Leith clenched his fists. He'd missed yet another report.

"First Blade Vane."

Vane rose to his feet, glided the single stride that separated his chair from the king's, and knelt. "My king."

King Respen waved for him to make his report. Chills danced across Leith's skin. Vane didn't have to prove his success to King Respen. His proof hung from the chains at the far end of the room, dripping blood onto the floor.

Vane cocked his head and met the king's eyes. "I tracked Burin into the Waste. I caught him a day's journey in."

A day's journey into the Waste. Thirst tightened Leith's throat. The Waste stretched into a dead zone of sand and rock. From the jagged cliffs known as the Ramparts to the far eastern side, no known water source provided relief from the heat. A few Blades had run into their depths to avoid the First Blade. None ever succeeded.

"You have done well, my First Blade."

Vane's mouth curled into a smile as King Respen slashed his thirty-ninth successful mark across his arm above his elbow. Vane slipped into his chair.

Leith tensed. Where would he be sent now?

King Respen leaned back in his chair. "First Blade Vane, you will go to Stetterly to investigate the trouble there."

Leith flinched before he caught himself. Every eye around the table swiveled in his direction. Stomach churning, Leith met King Respen's eyes. "I'd like to return to Stetterly."

Vane's blue eyes sparked as he crossed his arms. King Respen studied him. "Why?"

Leith rubbed his dry tongue against the inside of his teeth. If he messed up now... "I would like to complete the mission in Stetterly. I failed to bring as much information as I could have if I hadn't been wounded."

King Respen shook his head. "You do not have the strength. You will remain here to work with the trainees. Nineteenth Blade Altin will also remain here."

Altin hunched in his chair. Leith bowed his head as if in obedience of the king's decision, but instead he hid the burning in his chest.

The First Blade had been sent to Stetterly.

14

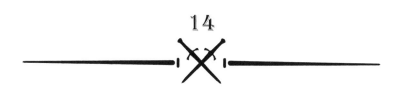

Renna stood on the kitchen step, the sun beaming on her face. In the yard, piles of snow slowly lost their fluff. The blizzard had been the last gust of winter. In a few more weeks, spring would reclaim the earth from ice, but for now winter lingered in a mild hush.

She stared at the hills surrounding the manor. Would she and Brandi live to see the spring?

Her skin crawled with the feeling of being watched. A few days ago, she'd seen a flash of black. Uncle Abel found footprints in the slushy snow. Was a Blade watching her even now, planning how to kill her?

Shivering, she stepped back into the house. The walls wrapped around her, giving an illusion of protection.

Aunt Mara glanced up from kneading a ball of dough. Renna swiveled her gaze away, but not fast enough. She heard Aunt Mara wipe her hands on a cloth and hustle towards her. A moment later, soft arms enveloped her.

Renna couldn't lean her head against Aunt Mara's shoulder the way she used to now that they stood the same height, but she still hugged her aunt, breathing in the scent of herbs and bread.

Aunt Mara stroked her hair. "God has protected us this far. He will protect us going forward."

"I know, but…" Renna pulled away. Cold filled her chest and trembled into her hands. "What if the Blade told the king about us? A Blade could be out there now."

Aunt Mara's gaze shifted to the window, the wrinkles on her face deepening. "I've wondered the same thing since that Blade left, but living in fear is a terrible place to be."

She shook her head and waved at the ball of dough. "Can you finish kneading that for me?"

Renna nodded and pounded the dough. Too bad she didn't have the courage to pound any Blade that came to kill her sister.

Brandi blasted into the room and flung her mittens onto the table. "Stubborn is starting to shed. It's going to be spring soon."

Renna forced a smile. Their mule didn't have a stubborn thought in his thick head, though Brandi seemed to think he needed the name to remind him he was *supposed* to be stubborn. "Don't get too close. I don't want fur in our bread."

Brandi plopped into a seat at the table. "Do you think Blizzard is doing all right? He should be shedding too. Leith will have to brush him a lot."

Renna forced herself to continue kneading. Brandi brought up the Blade's name every chance she got. Her sister had no doubt the Blade had kept his word.

But Renna had seen the fear in the Blade's eyes. She understood that kind of fear. It made a person do strange things. Yet she couldn't destroy the hope bouncing Brandi's step. "I'm sure Blizzard's fine."

Aunt Mara flapped her hands at Brandi. "Now go wash up for supper. You can't sit at the table shedding mule fur over everything."

As Brandi skipped to the washbasin, Renna placed the dough in a pan and placed the pan in the coals. Her knees rested on the bricks where the Blade had lain during that blizzard. What had he told the king?

But, she couldn't trust him. He was a Blade, and Blades didn't protect anyone. They killed. They didn't change.

Uncle Abel stomped in the door, flakes of packed snow tumbling from the soles of his boots. He hung his cloak on a peg and knelt in front of the fire next to Renna. "Looks warmer than it is outside."

She managed a small smile. "According to Brandi, Stubborn's fur told her spring is coming."

Uncle Abel searched her eyes, then rubbed her back. Clasping her shoulder, he rose to his feet, both knees popping. "I talked to Sheriff Allen. He's going to step up his patrols around the manor. That should scare away any prowlers."

Unless the prowler was a Blade. But Renna didn't mention that.

She slipped onto the bench as Aunt Mara placed the vegetable soup on the table. Renna could only sip at her soup, the salty taste souring on her tongue.

Would this fear never end? Uncle Abel and Aunt Mara seemed intent on pretending everything was fine. Brandi didn't think anything was wrong. Was Renna the only one who saw the danger they were in?

As soon as she could, Renna retreated to her room. Perhaps re-reading her favorite psalm would ease the painful knot in her chest. She knelt on the floor and reached under her bed for her Bible on its hidden shelf attached to the frame.

It was empty. She felt back and forth, then peered under the bed. She patted the floor and bedside table.

Nothing.

Her heart pounded. She hurried to the window and checked the latch. It was open. Faint marks showed on the wood of the frame. Something sharp had nicked the paint below the latch.

Someone had been in her room. Not only that, but the stranger had been watching her long enough to know where she kept her Bible.

Her stomach lurched. She dashed from her room and skidded down the hall. She pounded on her aunt and uncle's door.

When Uncle Abel yanked the door open, she took one look at his face and knew.

Someone had been in their room too.

"This is what comes of harboring Blades. I told you he was trouble." Sheriff Allen paced across their kitchen.

Renna clenched her fists and hunched in her seat beside the table. She'd brought this danger onto her family. It wasn't Uncle Abel's fault. It was hers.

"We don't know if Leith Torren stole our Bibles." Uncle Abel crossed his arms and leaned against the chimney. "We don't even know if it was a Blade. Could have been anybody."

The sheriff huffed and waved at the door. "Who else would steal a Bible? No one wants to be caught with one. Did the Blade know about those hidden shelves?"

Uncle Abel's shoulders slumped. "Yes, he did."

When had the Blade learned about them? Renna had never shown him one. His room didn't have one. She rubbed her upper arms. Had he prowled the manor when she wasn't looking? What else had he learned?

Brandi crossed her arms and glowered at the sheriff. "Leith didn't do it. He wouldn't steal from us."

"Why would he come back to steal them? He could've taken several while he was here." Uncle Abel pointed at the pantry. "He knew where the one in this room is hidden, yet that one is still here."

Renna hunched further. He'd learned that location because of her hesitation. Her mistake.

Sheriff Allen glared at him. "I don't know. Maybe he doesn't want you to know it's him."

Aunt Mara bustled between them and laid a hand on each of their arms. "I think it is safest to assume it was a Blade, and it doesn't really matter which Blade it was. The girls are in danger."

Renna glanced at her sister perched on the bench across the table. Brandi still had her arms crossed, her eyes and mouth scrunched. No trace of fear.

Renna tore her gaze back to Uncle Abel. "Can we hide in the cabin again?" The shack hidden in a crevice deep in the Spires Canyon had saved her and Brandi's lives four years ago.

If only they were already there. Safe. Hidden.

Sheriff Allen shook his head. "Better not. There's still too much snow and mud. Your tracks would be plain as a mule's face leading the Blade right to you."

No place to hide. Renna twined her cold fingers in her skirt. They were trapped in their own home.

"I'll ask around town for a few volunteers. We can set up a guard here." Sheriff Allen frowned as he surveyed the kitchen. "This room isn't the most secure, but it's the best this manor has. I suggest all of you sleep in here at night where you can bar the doors. That window's too small for anyone to climb through."

Little good it'd do. Renna scrubbed her fingers together. A few untrained men from town and a locked door weren't going to stop a Blade.

Uncle Abel nodded and motioned to Renna and Brandi. "Go fetch a few of your things. I'll be there in a minute."

Brandi jumped to her feet and darted from the room, but Renna eased to the door. As she left, Uncle Abel lowered his voice. "I'm going to need a message sent to Uster, and from there to Walden."

The door closed behind her, cutting off the sheriff's answer. Renna hesitated in the corridor. Walden? Shadrach Alistair's town? Why would Uncle Abel want to send a message there?

She rubbed her arms. Would Uncle Abel send them away to be safe? Or was he asking for help to be sent here? Would Shadrach come to Stetterly when he heard she was in danger?

A pair of dark brown eyes under a mop of tousled hair flashed through her memory. She'd once fancied herself in love with Shadrach, Lord Henry Alistair's oldest son.

But that was nonsense. He'd been sixteen years old, too old to notice his sister's scrawny, freckled, thirteen-year-old friend.

She shook the thoughts from her head. It didn't matter even if Shadrach did come. She didn't dare court anyone, much less think about marriage. It'd only get her killed faster.

As she tiptoed down the hall, the corridor leading to the rest of the manor yawned to her right, opposite her door. A flicker in the darkness caught her eye.

A man dressed all in black leaned against the corner. He twisted a knife in his hands, as if inspecting the blade for flaws and finding none. When he lifted his gaze to hers, his pale blue eyes gleamed. A smile broke through the stubble shadowing his chin.

Her throat clogged. She opened her mouth, but she couldn't scream. She couldn't move.

A door burst open. Brandi skipped through.

Brandi. She couldn't let the Blade harm Brandi. Renna grabbed her sister's arm and dashed down the corridor. Brandi stumbled and started running to stay on her feet. "Renna, what—"

Renna reached for the latch, but the door swung open, knocking into her hand. She plowed into Uncle Abel while Brandi tripped into Sheriff Allen.

Uncle Abel gripped her shoulders. "Renna, what happened?"

She glanced over her shoulder. The corridor was empty. When she turned, Uncle Abel's soft, blue eyes searched her face, their depths warm. So different than the blue eyes she'd seen a moment ago.

She pointed down the corridor. "I saw a Blade. Just standing there. He...he isn't there now."

Brandi gaped at the corridor. She leaned forward and whispered, "Was it Leith?"

Renna shook her head. "No."

An image of those light blue eyes slammed into her, but this time they stared at her over her mother's body, blood dripping from the Blade's knife in time with the stream from her mother's throat. "It was the Blade that killed Mother."

The Second Blade killed your father, the First Blade your mother. That's what the Blade Leith Torren had told her the night she'd asked.

The First Blade. He was here. Waiting to kill her and Brandi like he'd killed their mother. This time, they had nowhere to run and no one to protect them.

Uncle Abel hurried the two of them into the kitchen while Sherriff Allen shut and barred the door. Aunt Mara hugged Brandi and glanced between them, her forehead furrowing.

Uncle Abel jabbed a finger at Sheriff Allen. "I want that message sent. Now."

Sheriff Allen nodded and reached for his cloak. "I'll send it right away."

"And tell everyone that church services will be canceled Sunday." Uncle Abel leaned a hand against the fireplace, lines dragging around his mouth and eyes.

"Why?" Renna grasped the whiff of heat tightening her spine. "Why now? What's different this time?"

"The Third Blade never gave us cause to treat him as anything but a guest. He seemed genuinely interested in the truth. It would've been wrong to hide it from him." Uncle Abel pinched the bridge of his nose. "But there's a time to take a stand, and a time to exercise caution."

"How do you know this is a time for caution and last time wasn't?" She couldn't understand Uncle Abel's logic. They'd had a Blade living in the manor, and he hadn't canceled services. But now she merely glimpsed a Blade and he panicked?

Uncle Abel crossed the room and rested his hands on her shoulders. "When Leith Torren was here, I never saw terror on your face like I did just now. And that's how I know this time is different."

His words settled in her chest. With the Third Blade, she hadn't been terrified he'd hurt her. Yes, she'd worried about the danger he'd pose after he left, but nothing more.

But this Blade...he wanted to hurt her.

15

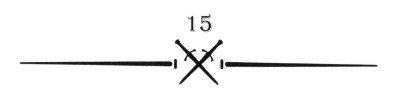

Leith glanced at the orange stain of sunrise in the southeast. Was Renna all right? Had the First Blade bothered her?

Of course the First Blade had bothered her. He thrived on the thrill of the hunt. Since he couldn't kill her yet, he'd terrify her.

And Leith could do nothing to stop him.

"Third Blade?" A tiny voice tugged at him.

Leith shook himself and glanced down at the six boys, ages seven through thirteen, standing in front of him. He and the trainees gathered on the strip of muddy grass between the base of the Blades' Tower and the outer wall where the servants and trainees lived.

Nineteenth Blade Altin stood a few feet away, as if to pretend he wasn't there to train like one of the boys.

"Are we going to learn to throw knives today?" One of the boys leaned closer, his small hands closing around the knife he had stuffed in his belt.

Leith shook his head. "Only a few of the Blades can throw knives accurately. There are more important skills that need to be learned first."

He studied their faces. They looked too eager about fighting and killing. Only the thirteen-year-old shifted uncomfortably. Once it hadn't bothered Leith to teach the trainees. He'd told himself he was teaching them to survive. Instead, he'd taught them to kill.

Straightening his spine, Leith wiped his weakness from his face. He couldn't let these boys see any of his regrets. They were too apt to blurt out things they'd been told or observed.

Leith pulled out a canvas bag and dumped the contents onto the grass. Several beat up and bent knives clanked onto the ground. The boys shoved each other as they crowded closer.

He picked up two of the knives. "Today I'm going to show you how to climb a wall using a pair of knives to act as handholds. A few of you have done this before, but the review and practice never hurts. Nineteenth Blade, please demonstrate."

Altin picked up two of the knives and approached the Tower wall. After examining the wall, he jabbed a knife into the crack between two stones where the mortar was already crumbling.

Holding himself against the wall, Altin wedged his toes into gaps between the stones, boosted himself higher, and jammed the other knife into a crack above his head.

Leith scratched his chin. Altin had decent technique. His form could be improved by keeping his body straighter and closer to the wall, but overall an adequate demonstration.

Leith waved at the trainees. "Any questions?" When the boys shook their head, he pointed to the pile of knives. "Go ahead and try it. Climb to the base of that arrow slit and back down." He pointed at an arrow slit one story from the ground.

The boys scrambled to pick out their knives and find places along the wall. The thirteen-year-old scrabbled up first, the younger boys trailing behind him. But this wasn't a race. Leith wasn't going to use the same methods King Respen used on him.

Altin dropped to the ground, panting from his climb to the window and back. "May I ask you something, Third Blade?"

The fear in his voice hurt. "Sure."

"Who taught you?"

Leith rubbed his knuckles. The rain-lashed stones had scraped his fingers that night as his hunger twisted his stomach. "I had to learn fast."

Altin still eyed him. Leith craned his neck to keep an eye on the younger boys. "It was just Harrison Vane and I back then. The king was still lord of Blathe. He took us outside one night in the middle of a rainstorm and told us to climb to the top of the south tower and back. Last one down lost his supper."

"Who won?"

Leith glanced away from the boys on the wall long enough to see the curiosity sparking in Altin's light brown eyes. "I did."

The victory had been short lived, though. Vane gave him a beating and stole his food anyways.

Footsteps scuttled across the wooden bridge behind him. A tenor voice coughed. "Third Blade Torren?"

Leith raised his eyebrows at the king's clerk rocking on his toes in the middle of the bridge. "Yes?"

"I..." The man cleared his throat again. "His Majesty would like to speak with you in his chambers." Another cough as the man cringed. "Immediately."

Why did the king wish to speak with him? A dozen reasons flooded through his head, none of them good. Had the king learned of his deception? Had the First Blade returned from Stetterly already?

Leith touched the knives strapped across his chest. "Tell him I'm on my way."

The clerk bobbed and scurried back the way he'd come as fast as his thin legs could carry him. Leith waited for a few more heartbeats before he turned to Altin. "Can you take over?"

Altin nodded. He'd been a trainee with a few of them. He wouldn't stand there and let them fall if they made a mistake.

Leith strolled across the bridge and crossed the passageway, his heart pounding even before he started up the stairs to King Respen's chambers. No Blade besides Vane reported directly to the king.

At the top of the stairs, Leith halted and knocked on the thick oak door. King Respen's voice called, "Enter."

Leith lifted the latch and stepped into the room, closing the door behind him. Burgundy rugs sprawled across the floor while dark wood paneling covered the walls.

King Respen stood in front of a window overlooking the cobblestone courtyard, his desk beside him.

Crossing the room, Leith knelt on the rug in front of King Respen and thumped his fist across his chest. "My king."

"You have always been loyal to me, haven't you, my Third Blade?" King Respen clasped his hands behind his back and faced the window.

Leith struggled to keep his breathing even. Why was

he questioning Leith's loyalty? "Yes, my king."

"And what is your opinion of the First Blade's loyalty?" King Respen didn't turn around.

Dangerous ground. Leith swallowed. What answer did King Respen want to hear? "The First Blade likes power, and he likes having it over others."

King Respen turned around then and tapped his fingers on the windowsill. "Has he ever wanted the power I have?"

"Not that I know of." When had King Respen become suspicious of Vane? "Vane has no desire to be king."

"No, but he might want a longer chain." King Respen's fingers stopped tapping the windowsill. "But you have no ambitions, do you?"

Leith didn't want a longer chain; he wanted no chain at all. But he couldn't let King Respen see that thought in his eyes. "I want no rank beyond what I've been given."

"Very good. Return to the Tower."

"Yes, my king." Leith pressed his fist to his chest one last time and hurried from the room.

If King Respen suspected Harrison Vane, his right-hand Blade, of disloyalty, then how long would it be before he also suspected Leith?

16

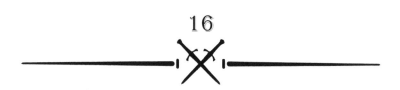

The kitchen door thumped with a knock. Renna jumped and dropped her spoon in her oatmeal. Drops splashed the back of her hand. On the mattress across the room, Brandi still snored and drooled on her pillow.

Uncle Abel leapt to his feet so fast his knees bashed the table. He reached for the dagger he'd taken to carrying around.

Renna couldn't help but stare at it. Her father's dagger. The same one her father had carried the night he'd died. It had remained in a trunk with the rest of her father's weapons for the past four years, and she wasn't sure what Uncle Abel planned to do with it now. If her father, trained warrior that he was, couldn't fight off the Blades, then Uncle Abel didn't stand a chance.

After peeking out the window, he opened the door. Sheriff Allen brushed past Uncle Abel and shoved the door closed. "The messenger didn't get through. His body was left on my doorstep this morning."

Renna clapped her hands over her mouth. The Blade had killed the messenger her uncle sent to Uster. Was it a warning? Was she next?

Uncle Abel sagged against the wall. "And the message?"

"Gone." Sheriff Allen scrubbed a hand over his face. "It was in code. He might not guess how to translate it."

"Maybe." Uncle Abel rested a hand on the fireplace mantle. "So no help is coming from Uster or Walden."

Renna's heart pounded. "What are we going to do?"

Aunt Mara rubbed her hand along Uncle Abel's arm. "We'll have to head for the cabin now. Perhaps if we're careful, we won't leave too many tracks."

Sheriff Allen scratched at the brown stubble across his chin and cheeks. "At this point, I think that's your best option. I'll patrol the manor tonight as if I'm still guarding you. Hopefully the Blade will be too busy watching me to follow you."

Renna glanced at her sister's sleeping form curled into a ball under her blankets. And if the Blade did follow them? What would happen to them then?

Renna clasped her cloak around her shoulders and slipped her bag across her shoulders. The leather satchel hung next to her hip, filled with a few pieces of clothing, medical supplies, and her hairbrush.

Aunt Mara handed her a leather sack. Renna heaved it across her shoulders, the weight settling onto her back. Uncle Abel handed Brandi a smaller bag. Brandi grinned and slung it over her shoulder. "Think we have enough food?"

Uncle Abel picked up a third, larger sack. "We should. Unless you eat too much."

Brandi pressed both hands over her mouth, but a tiny giggle slipped out. Renna glanced towards the window. Was the Blade out there now? Had he heard?

In the distance, a glow marked the single lamp kept burning in the center of town. Would the town be all right without their healer and their minister?

Aunt Mara caught Renna's gaze, stepped towards her, and wrapped an arm around her shoulders. "You're our first duty."

As they'd been that night four years ago. Could Aunt Mara have saved any of the men that died that night had she been there? What had Renna and Brandi's safety cost back then? What would it cost now?

Aunt Mara nodded to Uncle Abel. Waving them forward, Uncle Abel led them into the night. The ground crinkled beneath Renna's boots, her breath misting in the starlight. She followed Uncle Abel's footsteps as closely as she could to avoid the slushy piles of snow.

Brandi's footsteps crunched behind her, Aunt Mara trailing her. The hills rolled into the blue night. The cold stung Renna's nose. Tears leaked from the corners of her eyes when the breeze whipped across her face.

The darkness prowled around them, its breath cold and dank with snow. Renna's skin prickled. Was the Blade hunting them? Did he lurk out there?

Her toes numbed by the time they reached the edge of the Spires Canyon. Uncle Abel led the way down a thin path. Pines brushed against her cloak and face.

She shoved a branch out of her way and ducked. Brandi spluttered, and Renna winced. She'd snapped the branch into her sister's face.

As they hiked deeper into the canyon, the waning moon crested the treetops above them, brushing the pine needles with silver. Mist drifted across the Ondieda River at the bottom of the canyon.

Too much like another night when they'd dashed

down the path, Aunt Mara shushing Renna's tears, Uncle Abel carrying Brandi, the sounds of bloodshed ringing behind them.

Uncle Abel reached the bottom and turned towards them. Renna halted beside him, wiggling her toes inside her boots. Brandi skidded down the last few feet of trail while Aunt Mara eased down the incline, gasping for breath.

Renna steadied Aunt Mara's elbow. Would she be all right? Aunt Mara was four years older than the last time she'd done this hike.

After Aunt Mara caught her breath, Uncle Abel helped her over the rocks as they hiked north up the canyon. Renna stumbled over the rocks, but Brandi scrambled up them like Ginger their goat.

The path led into the darkness below the pine trees and the grotesque spires of rock pointing at the sky. Renna tightened her grip on her cloak, but the wool couldn't stop her shivers.

Uncle Abel shoved through a screen of pines and held the branches for Aunt Mara. Brandi bounced forward to hold the branches while Uncle Abel and Aunt Mara eased through a crack in the rocks.

Renna tiptoed after them. After a few yards, the rocks opened into a small clearing set against the canyon wall. The cabin tucked under a shelf in the cliff, hiding it from above. Spruce and white pines clustered around the edge of the clearing, the needles glowing in the moonlight.

Renna misted a breath into the air. This place felt like safety. Like warmth and solid walls and healing.

Brandi skipped toward the cabin. Aunt Mara and Uncle Abel strolled through the tall grass, so close together than Renna only caught a glimpse of their clasped hands. She stepped forward to join them.

Something cold and sharp pressed against her neck. She stiffened. A body radiated heat behind her. Chills spiked into her toes. The Blade had returned to kill her.

"I will enjoy killing you." The tenor crawled down her spine like a hairy spider creeping along her skin.

A hand on her shoulder turned her around. She faced a pair of light blue eyes, flat, almost dead in their depths, set in a slim face. The Blade's light brown hair waved down to his collar, highlighted with moonlight.

His mouth twisted in a thin smile. "You thought I wouldn't know this place? That I wouldn't track it down after you disappeared here last time?"

Her breath caught. She was going to die. They'd tried to run, but they'd failed. Now the Blade would kill her. She shook so violently only the Blade's hand on her arm and knife under her chin kept her standing.

After she was dead, would he go after Brandi? Uncle Abel and Aunt Mara? Unlike last time, there were no guards to jump between them. No one to intervene.

She opened her mouth but couldn't gather enough air to scream a warning.

She didn't want to die. Didn't want to drop to the ground in a pool of her own blood. Like her father. Like her mother. Like the rest of her family killed by the Blades. Perhaps she should beg God for rescue, but He'd remained silent four years ago. And He was silent now.

The Blade's smile slicked across his face. The steel of his knife brushed down one side of her neck and up the other as if searching for the place it wanted to bite.

If only she could find the words to pray, the breath to scream.

He let her go. She collapsed to the ground, her palms sinking into the snow. By the time she glanced up, the Blade had disappeared into the darkness.

"Renna?" Uncle Abel's voice hissed across the clearing. His running footsteps crunched the snow. He knelt next to her, one hand on her shoulder, the other gripping his knife. "What is it? What happened?"

"He was here." She forced the words through her chattering teeth. Why wasn't she dead? Surely it wasn't mercy that stayed the Blade's hand. Then what? Why did he want to prolong her death like this?

But one thing was certain. When the Blade wanted to kill her, she would die.

17

Her eyes gritty, Renna trudged into Stetterly Manor's kitchen. She slumped onto a bench next to the table.

Brandi plopped onto the bench next to her and leaned her forehead on her arms. Aunt Mara bustled to light the fire while Uncle Abel leaned his arm against the mantle.

"What are we going to do now?" Renna glanced at Aunt Mara and Uncle Abel. The sag to their shoulders told her their answer. They'd run out of options.

Aunt Mara met Uncle Abel's gaze. "Do you think we could get to Uster?"

He shook his head and scrubbed a hand over his short, grey hair. "It's a three day ride with no shelter. If the Blade could track us to the cabin, he could track us there."

Boots stomped on the front step, and Sheriff Allen burst into the kitchen. "What are you doing back here? I thought you'd be safe in the cabin by now."

Uncle Abel rubbed his palm along the mantle. "The First Blade tracked us there. He threatened Renna."

Sheriff Allen's eyebrows rose. "And he didn't kill her?"

Renna shivered. If she closed her eyes, she could still feel the Blade's knife caressing her throat, his breath hot on the back of her neck.

"No, and we don't know why." Uncle Abel turned to Sheriff Allen. "We need to try to send a message to Walden again."

Sheriff Allen massaged the back of his neck. "I'll go myself. I don't think I'll get another volunteer. I'll leave tonight."

Renna wrapped her arms over her stomach. Bowing her head, she blinked at the tears heating her eyes. Her mother had fought back against the First Blade. She'd sacrificed herself to buy Renna and Brandi enough time to escape.

If Renna were braver—if she were like her mother—she'd ride to Uster herself. She wouldn't ask anyone else to take the danger meant for her.

But she wasn't brave. She wasn't her mother.

The door to the common room creaked open. As Leith glanced up from oiling his knife, Vane strolled in, his lips curled.

Leith fought the urge to jump to his feet and interrogate Vane. What had the First Blade done to Renna and Brandi? Had he hurt them? Leith's chest tightened.

Vane strode towards the stairs. As he passed the bench where Leith sat, Leith leaned forward as casually as he could manage. "Learn anything?"

Halting, Vane's smile widened while his pale, blue eyes sparked with the candlelight. "A few things. It's a pity you never met the lady Rennelda while you were in Stetterly. She's quite the charming girl."

Leith's fingers clenched around his knife's hilt. If Vane had hurt Renna, he would...

What would he do? What *could* he do? He couldn't prevent Vane from hurting Renna anymore than he could prevent King Respen from ordering Renna killed.

He cleared his throat. "Yes, a pity." Even to him the words sounded strained.

Vane eyed him for a moment longer before he turned away and headed up the stairs.

"You all right?" Martyn's elbow nudged him.

Leith turned to Martyn. Martyn's curls, damp from washing off the trail dust when he'd returned a few hours ago, flopped against his forehead. Leith gave him what he hoped was a nonchalant shrug. "I'm fine. Why?"

"You're just acting...strange." Martyn's brown eyes twitched back and forth as he searched Leith's face. Could he read the secrets Leith hid? Leith tried to hold Martyn's gaze, but he couldn't.

He stood and gathered his knives. "It's late, and I don't want to be too tired at the Meeting tomorrow." Did that sound as off to Martyn as it did to him?

Martyn nodded and turned back to his work, but his eyebrows remained scrunched.

Leith pressed his hands against his knees to stop his legs from bouncing.

The First Blade knelt in front of the king and saluted. "My king, I completed my mission of spying on Stetterly Manor. I discovered that they have been very disobedient to your laws, my lord."

King Respen stroked his pointed beard. A frown tugged at the corner of his mouth.

Vane pulled two books from a leather bag and set

them on the table in front of King Respen. The black cover of one flaked onto the table. Leith had held that book. Lachlan's Bible.

Leith jumped and gripped the edge of his chair. Martyn raised his eyebrows at Leith. Leith forced himself to relax against the back of his chair.

Vane traced the brown cover of the second book with his index finger. "These Bibles were hidden in the rooms of Abel and Mara Lachlan and Lady Rennelda Faythe."

Renna's Bible. Leith clenched his fists under the table. Vane had been in Renna's bedchamber.

"Besides these Bibles, they host an illegal church each Sunday. Abel Lachlan is the minister." Vane placed a slip of paper on top of Lachlan's Bible.

Leith peered at the note. He could make out numbers, but no words. An untranslated message?

Vane's smile grew. "I intercepted a messenger. After some...persuasion, he told me he'd been sent to Walden by Stetterly's sheriff. The message is in a code the messenger didn't know how to translate."

King Respen tapped his fingers on the note. "Perhaps."

Leith fought to keep his shoulders from curling in defeat. He'd tried to protect them. He could've told King Respen all this information a month ago. He could translate the note that now lay under the king's fingertips. He'd hidden all of that.

But it wasn't enough.

"You have done well, my First Blade." King Respen held up his knife as Vane bared his right arm. The king swiped the knife across Vane's skin, drawing a line of blood at Vane's elbow below the long rows of scars that marched down his arm. "Your fortieth successful mark.

You are truly my First Blade."

The First Blade saluted and returned to his seat. His mouth thinned into a slippery smile. A suspicion niggled the back of Leith's mind. Vane hadn't told everything. He'd left something out, something he'd enjoyed.

A variety of possibilities whirled through Leith's mind, none of them good. Was Renna all right? Brandi? Their aunt and uncle?

He had to do more. Silence was not enough. He had to take some kind of action. Something to protect Renna and Brandi once and for all.

And perhaps, while he saved them, he'd taste a portion of the freedom he craved. He couldn't be free—only death released him from the Blades—but a taste might satisfy.

"The Eleventh and Eighteenth Blades will remain here." King Respen's dark eyes glittered in his hard features, his beard cutting across his face and coming to a point as sharp as Leith's knife.

The Eleventh and Eighteenth Blades saluted, though the Eleventh Blade's eyes tipped down as if disappointed to be staying behind.

King Respen leaned forward. "But I have a special mission for the rest of you, my Blades. For the next month, you will each spy on a nobleman and his manor. I want to know the guard routine, number of guards, layout of the manor, and where each member of the family sleeps. I want you to know their life and routine better than you know your own."

The dread in Leith's chest curled tight, as if to choke the life from his heart. He focused on breathing evenly. Martyn's mouth tightened into a line. The Second Blade leaned forward, hands twitching as if he longed to grab the knives that hung from his belt on the wall. A gleam flickered in Vane's pale eyes.

King Respen tipped his head towards Vane. "First Blade Vane, you will watch Stetterly for only two weeks. I do not believe it will take longer than that to gather the necessary information. Then I would like you to return to Nalgar. I will need you here."

Leith hunched in his chair and tried to breathe. Vane had been sent to Stetterly. Again. Even two weeks was too long. Yet what could Leith do? He was helplessly bound to follow his own orders.

"Second Blade Hess, you will go to Sierra. Lady Paula Lorraine has proven to be as troublesome as her husband. Watch her carefully."

The Second Blade's teeth flashed in the candlelight. "It will be my pleasure to deal with her as I dealt with Lord Lorraine."

"Third Blade Torren."

Leith tensed. Where would he be sent? If not Stetterly, then where?

King Respen tapped the coded message. "Your target is Walden. Lord Alistair grows bold in organizing rebellion against me."

Leith bowed his head and pressed his fist over his heart. "Yes, my king."

Something stirred in his chest. Hope? A chance? Henry Alistair, lord of Walden, was rumored to be a leader of the Resistance, if not the leader. Leith might be helpless to stop Vane and King Respen from killing Renna and Brandi, but Lord Alistair wasn't.

18

Leith crouched on a window seat in a small alcove. Curtains separated him from the main room. The brick wall next to the window pressed against his back.

A shaft of light cut through the gap in the curtains. From inside the room, he could hear a pen scratching at a piece of paper.

Peeking through the gap, Leith spotted Lord Alistair bent over a ledger. His gray-streaked, brown hair was falling out of his queue while his hands moved the pen efficiently over the page. A thick, neatly trimmed beard covered the lower half of his face.

His broad shoulders and wide chest pressed against his dark blue shirt, but even from his hiding place Leith could see muscle, not fat, rippling beneath the fabric.

With a soft snick, a lady entered the room. Her long, brown hair flowed down her back to her waist, a sharp contrast with her red gown, flounces trailing down her sleeves and skirt.

Leith studied the lines of gold embroidery shimmering in the candlelight. Lord Alistair might be rebelling against King Respen, but he wasn't living in poverty if his wife could dress like that.

Lady Alistair glided across the room and rested her hands on Lord Alistair's shoulders. "The girls are waiting to be tucked in."

Lord Alistair drew her hand over his shoulder and kissed her fingers. Leith shifted and stared at the floor for a moment.

"Is it that late already?" Lord Alistair squeezed his wife's hand. "Tell them I'll be there in a minute. Is Jeremiah still up studying?"

Lady Alistair's hair slipped over her shoulders as she kissed Lord Alistair's cheek. "Of course. You might have to remind him to get some sleep when you say goodnight to the girls."

Releasing her hand, Lord Alistair turned back to his paperwork. Lady Alistair slipped from the room while the lord scratched a few more lines in the ledger.

Leith didn't move as Lord Alistair sighed, stuffed his quill into the inkwell, and snapped the book shut. Placing the ledger in a drawer, he lit a candle, blew out the lamp on his desk, and strode from the room.

Leith waited for half an hour before he crept from his hiding place. The deep green rugs muffled his footsteps. Light oak shelves bordered the room while a large map of Acktar took up most of one wall.

Underneath the map, the oak desk was placed a few feet into the room. Leith inched the curtains open another few inches to let the light from the rising moon stream into the room. He didn't dare light a candle.

But he needed to find proof of Lord Alistair's involvement in the Resistance. Not to give to King Respen, but to prove to himself that Lord Alistair could save Renna and Brandi.

He padded across the room and methodically searched the desk. The ledger was an account of the fields to be planted that spring. Nothing out of the ordinary.

The top desk drawer on the right side contained a knife while the bottom drawer held nothing but more ledgers. Neither told Leith anything besides that Lord Alistair was mildly paranoid and kept up on his paperwork.

After the desk turned up nothing, Leith searched the shelves for anything unusual. Partway through the second set of shelves, Leith paused, his hand hovering over a hard-bound book with a gilt title: *A Farmer's Manual for Crop Control*. He glanced over the shelves he'd searched. He'd seen this book before.

He tugged it off the shelf. The pages slipped from the hard cover. He managed to catch the pages before they fell. Flipping through them, he smiled. He'd stumbled onto one of Lord Alistair's hidden Bibles.

A longing rose into Leith's throat. What would it be like to read for himself the stories that Brandi told him? What did this book hold that would prompt equally vehement love from Renna and hate from King Respen?

Leith arranged the cover on the shelf so it looked like it still contained the Bible. He searched the rest of the shelves but discovered nothing else. If Lord Alistair was in the Resistance, he was too canny to hide anything in his study. Still, Leith would need more proof. He didn't dare trust Renna's and Brandi's lives— not to mention his own—on finding one Bible.

With a final glance around, Leith slipped through the curtains and out of the manor. With the moon beaming down from overhead, sneaking back to his horse was more challenging than getting in, but he managed without being seen.

Taking Blizzard's reins, Leith led him at a walk below the crests of the rolling hills. He eyed the night around him warily. Acktar's rolling prairie offered little in the way of shelter except for the occasional creek bottom or ravine. Only the thick forests of the Sheered Rock Hills provided decent cover.

Half a mile from the manor, Leith mounted and nudged the horse into a steady lope, avoiding a herd of cattle lowing in a valley, circled by men on horseback.

Several miles to the north of Walden, Leith reached the foothills. Winding his way up a ridge and partially down the other side, he slipped into the protected hollow he'd found the day before. The small campsite remained as he'd left it earlier that evening.

After Blizzard had enough to drink, Leith tied a length of rawhide between the horse's front legs. This hobble would keep the horse from going too far from camp while Leith slept but also allow the horse some freedom to wander in pursuit of grass. With Blizzard taken care of, Leith slipped into his bedroll for a few hours of rest.

Leith woke in the grey haze of early dawn. The silence wrapped around him as the night crickets slept and the first birds of morning ruffled their feathers to begin the day song. He rolled from his blanket, shook out his boots to make sure nothing had crawled into them while he'd slept, and tugged them on.

Blizzard nibbled on a patch of grass a few yards away. His ears swiveled towards Leith, but his stance remained relaxed, assuring Leith that they were alone in their hollow.

After eating a dry biscuit, Leith dressed in the light brown-colored clothing all Blades carried for stealth missions like this. He packed the Bible and a few more biscuits in a leather pack, and patted Blizzard's neck. The prairie provided no place to hide the horse, and a lone horse drew too much attention. "I'll be back tonight, boy."

Blizzard huffed a breath and returned to his grazing. Leith rolled his eyes and set out on foot over the ridge and across the prairie.

He reached the hill overlooking Walden as the sun's first fingers wiggled over the horizon. Dropping to his hands and knees, Leith crawled the last few feet to the top of the hill, slinking on his belly at the top. The tall grass waved over him, covering him so well a person would have to step on him to spot him. He parted the stalks in front of him to peer at the town and manor house below.

Walden Manor lay below him, two stories built of a light brown stone with ledge running between the first and second floors. The garden he'd slipped through the night before was to his right, the front door to his left.

The tiny figures of the guards walked their circuit around the manor's grounds. To the north, the town arranged along two dirt tracks, one heading east to Flayin Falls and west to Duelstone and the other coming from Uster to the south, past Walden Manor, and ending at the edge of town.

Leith settled in for a long day of watching the manor house. He ignored the spider crawling over the grass a few inches from his face and the mound of ants bustling near his feet. Easing the Bible from his pack, he placed it on the ground in front of him and slowly turned the pages until he reached the book of Daniel.

Between reading a few verses, Leith watched Walden Manor. A few peasants and merchants streamed back and forth from the town to the manor and back again. Farmers could be seen on the far hills, walking behind their mules as they plowed into the winter-hardened earth. Behind Leith, cattle and sheep grazed the grassland.

As he read farther in Daniel, he had to remind himself to glance up every once and a while. The words were familiar from Brandi's stories, but she'd left out much of the story to draw him in before he discovered they were Bible stories.

Chewing dry rations for lunch, Leith set the Bible aside. After the story about the lions' den, the rest of the book seemed to be a confusing muddle of some sort. Leith needed a break, and activity around the manor demanded his attention.

A group of guards practiced with swords and pikes on the lawn behind the manor. Leith frowned as the numbers grew until there were far too many people for this to be simply a training session for the manor guards. Even the farmers in the fields abandoned their plowing to pick up wooden swords.

A rider crested the south hill at a full gallop. As he reined his horse to a skidding halt before the manor, Lord Alistair, recognizable in his blue tunic, strode to meet him. They conversed for a moment, and Leith caught sight of a flash of white. A note?

Was this the proof he was looking for? A courier and a small army in training?

Was he ready to take that first step? A shiver trickled along his spine. He could still leave now. Once he stepped forward, he could never go back to the way things were. That was assuming, of course, that Lord Alistair even listened to him, much less let him live.

Did he dare? The consequences would be as harsh as the punishments that evil king had dished out to Daniel and his three friends. Leith might not face a fiery furnace or a den of lions, but King Respen would see that he'd suffer torture and death just the same.

Daniel and his three friends were exceptions, perhaps bolstered by their mysterious God. If that was the case, then Leith would never have a hope of having their courage. Their God would never pay attention to someone like Leith.

Leith fought to control the shakes that threatened to give away his position in the grass. He wasn't brave enough to make that kind of stand. Could he face King Respen and refuse to follow an order?

But if he didn't, Renna and Brandi would die. And he'd be bound to King Respen forever.

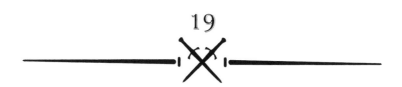

19

Dressed in his black clothing, Leith slipped onto the same, darkened windowseat in Lord Alistair's study. His heart pounded in his throat and drummed in his ears. He froze in the darkness.

Step forward or step back. Each beat of his heart swayed him between decisions. A beat of courage. A beat of fear. Once the decision was made, nothing could alter it.

With a deep breath, Leith stepped into the lighted room. Lord Alistair hunched over his desk, scratching numbers into the leather-bound ledger. He stroked his close-cropped beard.

Leith got within fifteen feet of the desk before Lord Alistair froze, his pen hovering in midair on its way back to the inkwell. With deliberate slowness, he placed his pen on the desk and looked up.

"What do you want, Blade?" His tone was even, but Leith could hear the undercurrent of defiance. Lord Alistair inched his hand toward his desk drawer.

"You won't need the knife you have hidden in your desk." Leith spread his hands out in front of him so the lord could see that all his knives remained sheathed.

"I'm here to talk, not kill you. If I'd wanted to kill you, you'd already be dead."

Lord Alistair eyed him, but he placed his hand on the desk where Leith could see it. "Give me Respen's message and leave."

"I'm not here on behalf of the king." The words tasted strange, but it was a good strange, like the first hint of spring scurrying across the melting snow.

Lord Alistair raised both eyebrows. "You're a Blade. Your only business is Respen's business."

"Not this time." Leith took a deep breath. "I'd like to return the Bible I stole from your bookshelf." Reaching out slowly, Leith placed the book on the desk. He hadn't read as much as he'd like, but he should return it.

Lord Alistair stared at the book, his eyes flicking towards the bookshelf where the false cover hid nothing but air. "You were in here last night." Only a flash in his eyes and the tips of white on his clenched knuckles betrayed his fear at learning his private sanctuary had been invaded before. "What else did you take?"

"Nothing." Leith met his gaze. "I know you're a leader in the Resistance. I'd like to be your spy in the Blades."

Lord Alistair shot to his feet. "Get out. Whatever Respen's plan is, it won't work."

Leith blew out a breath. Convincing him would take time. "Please, I'm not going to hurt you. Just listen to what I have to say."

Lord Alistair crossed his arms and glared. Leith resisted the urge to cross his arms and glare back. King Respen had taught him to be tougher, stronger, quicker than anyone else. That strength was the last thing Leith needed now. He had to do the unthinkable in King

Respen's world and become meek.

Slowly, so slowly that Lord Alistair couldn't mistake his actions as threatening, Leith undid the buckle of his belt. He held it away from him and dropped it, the knives in their sheaths clanking. He unstrapped the rest of his weapons, adding them to the growing pile. Pulling off his boots, he tossed them aside.

A glance at Lord Alistair showed he was still unconvinced. With shaking hands, Leith pulled his shirt over his head and dropped that to the side as well.

With bowed head, Leith stepped away from his weapons and knelt on the ground. The hair along his arms prickled with the cool air brushing his chest.

The muscles along his spine cramped. What would Lord Alistair do now that Leith was defenseless?

A desk drawer scraped open and closed. Hushed footsteps strode around the desk. Leith didn't move. The boots stopped in front of him.

He could feel Lord Alistair's eyes counting the marks on his arm. A knife rested against the vulnerable skin of his neck and forced his chin up.

Leith met Lord Alistair's hard, brown-eyed gaze. Lord Alistair was testing him, testing his meekness. He wanted Leith to break. But Leith didn't look away.

"What's your game, Blade?" Lord Alistair growled and pressed the knife harder against Leith's throat. "Did Respen order you to lure me into killing you? It'd give him reason to kill me and my family."

"He already knows you're a part of the Resistance." Leith's words scraped past the knife, but he didn't fight it. "I want to prevent more killing."

Lord Alistair's eyes cut towards the scars on his arm. "Your marks say otherwise."

"Not all of them." Leith eased his hand to his stomach and touched the scar. "On my last mission, I was wounded. I was rescued by Lady Rennelda and Lady Brandiline of Stetterly."

Lord Alistair jerked at the words. Leith winced as the knife pricked his skin. Lord Alistair grabbed a fistful of Leith's hair and yanked his head back. Pain tore across Leith's scalp. He struggled to breathe with his neck craned backwards.

But he held himself as still as possible, fighting the years of training that screamed at him to fight back.

Lord Alistair bent closer, his breath slicing against Leith's cheek. "What did you do to them?"

"Nothing. They helped me." Leith fought the urge to claw away from that fist pulling out his hair. "I didn't tell the king anything. I didn't even tell him who had healed me. But another Blade reported them."

"Why should I believe you?" Lord Alistair tugged Leith's head back farther. "It's just your word."

"Listen." The word came out as a gasp. The unnatural angle of his neck, the pain from his hair being dragged from his head, and the knife pressing down on his throat strangled him. "You have to believe me. They're in danger."

Lord Alistair released him and stepped back. Leith gasped his first decent breath in several minutes. His fingers shook. Had Lord Alistair noticed?

"What proof do I have that this isn't one of Respen's plots?" Lord Alistair pointed his knife at Leith. "You could be the Blade that told him everything, and decided to use this incident to make it look like you've had a change of heart. It would give you a convenient means to work your way into my trust."

Leith bowed his head. He had no way to prove he was anything other than the king's pawn. Every action he did could be taken two ways. Lord Alistair couldn't read his heart. Only One could.

Leith's heart pounded. Would he be struck with fire from Heaven for daring to invoke the name of Renna's God? "God in Heaven as my witness, I mean you no harm."

Lord Alistair's knife was back at Leith's throat in an instant. He forced Leith to meet his burning eyes. "If you take the Almighty Lord's name in vain, it will be His eternal wrath you face, not mine."

Leith didn't look away. The words should've filled him with fear, but they didn't. He deserved the wrath of God for plenty of things, but he didn't invoke Him in vain now.

Lord Alistair stepped back once again. This time, he placed the knife on top of the desk and faced Leith. "You pose quite a problem. If you're lying and I trust you, I'll be opening myself to my greatest threat. If you're telling the truth and I turn you away, I'll be sending away my greatest asset."

Leith stayed silent. He sensed words now would harm his cause more than help.

Lord Alistair gave him a glare to stay put. With several glances back over his shoulder, he walked to the door of his study, cracked it open, and spoke to the guard outside the door. Shutting the door, he returned to his spot near the desk.

Leith didn't move. He needed to appear as non-threatening as possible.

A knock sounded on the door. Lord Alistair kept his eyes fixed on Leith. "Come in."

A young man strode into the room. His eyes took in the scene even as his hand shut the door behind him. He focused on the line of marks on Leith's shoulder and arm. To his credit, he didn't speak as he strolled across the room.

Leith studied him, taking in the leather, guard's uniform, the easy swing of the sword at his side, and the comfortable way a quiver of arrows and unstrung bow rested across his back. This young man was a trained fighter, skilled with the bow and sword. His brown eyes flicked toward Leith before he faced Lord Alistair.

Lord Alistair waved at Leith. "Shadrach, this Blade claims he wants to switch sides."

The guard, Shadrach, crossed his arms, his brown hair falling into his eyes. "You believe him?"

"No. But we can't afford to dismiss him entirely either. He could be the answer to our prayers."

"Or our worst enemy." Shadrach's hand strayed to his sword's hilt. Leith's stomach clenched. This young man might decide it'd be easier to slit Leith's throat and ask questions later.

"I don't trust him, but I feel we must investigate this." Lord Alistair studied Leith, as if really seeing him for the first time. "How old are you, boy?"

"Eighteen."

His eyebrows rose. "Which Blade are you? The Fifteenth? Maybe the Tenth?"

Leith pressed his palms against his knees. What would they do when they realized which Blade they had in their manor? "I'm the Third Blade."

While Lord Alistair didn't recoil the way Renna had, Leith could see disgust flash into his eyes. Leith's rank in the Blades announced he was one of the original eight that had taken Acktar, participated in the bloodshed of that battle, and had killed King Leon, Queen Deirdre and their four sons. No amount of meekness could undo all that.

Shadrach's hand tightened on his sword hilt. "How many marks do you have?"

Leith fisted his hands tighter. His marks ranged down his arm, visible in the lamplight. He couldn't lie. "Thirty-five."

Lord Alistair and Shadrach shared a glance. Lord Alistair gave a small nod. Shadrach circled Leith, picked up his shirt from the pile he'd left on the floor, and pushed the weapons farther away. "Stand up."

Leith did as he was told, standing still as Shadrach frisked him for any additional weapons hiding under his trousers. Shadrach stood several inches taller than Leith, with broader shoulders and thicker arms.

When he was satisfied, he tossed Leith his shirt. Leith pulled it on. The fabric covered the rows of scars on his arm, hiding his shame. Shadrach inspected Leith's boots and flung them to him. Leith tugged those on as well.

"Sit." Lord Alistair waved at the two leather armchairs facing his desk.

Leith perched on one where he could keep an eye on both Shadrach and Lord Alistair. Shadrach planted his feet beside Leith's weapons.

"What's your name?" Leather creaked as Lord Alistair settled into his high-backed chair.

"Leith Torren." Leith itched at the time this was taking. Even now, Vane was on his way to Stetterly.

"What Bible stories did Lady Brandiline tell you while you were in Stetterly?"

145

A chill tingled down Leith's arms. He'd told no one about that, not even Martyn. "How do you—"

"Answer the question." Lord Alistair's gaze didn't waver.

He had no choice but to trust them. "Brandi told me stories about Daniel." The pieces clicked together. "Abel Lachlan wrote you. He told you."

"Yes. He sent me a message shortly after you left Stetterly. We decided to wait and see what would happen before we took any action regarding the girls' safety."

A sinking feeling dropped into Leith's toes. "The First Blade intercepted a message. He didn't know how to translate it, but King Respen might guess." What was in that message? If Lachlan mentioned Leith, and King Respen did translate it...

Lord Alistair leaned back in his chair. "If he does, he'll only learn how his First Blade tormented Lady Rennelda."

Leith bolted upright. "Is she all right? Did he hurt her?" He gripped the edge of his seat. What had Vane done to her?

Lord Alistair's sharp, brown eyes studied him across the desk. "She's fine but scared." He picked up a piece of paper. "The First Blade threatened to kill her. Abel Lachlan has asked me to bring Renna and Brandi to Walden to protect them."

"Here?" Shadrach's voice rose. Leith wasn't sure why having Renna and Brandi come to Walden would cause such a strong response.

"Yes. Here." Lord Alistair tapped the paper on his desk. "It took me longer than expected to translate the code or I would've informed you sooner."

Probably because Leith had stolen the Bible he

needed to translate it. Leith glanced at the Bible still sitting on the corner of the desk, guilt squirming in his chest. It most likely wasn't Lord Alistair's only Bible, but searching for it and checking for other things missing would've taken time.

But Leith wasn't going to apologize. He wasn't sorry he'd stolen it. If only he could've read more before he'd had to return it.

"He won't kill her. Not yet." Leith could at least be sure of that much. Still, the knot in his stomach refused to relax. "He might bend his orders, but he won't break them."

"I see." Lord Alistair steepled his fingers. "What do you get out of this? I understand you are...concerned about Rennelda and Brandiline's safety. Perhaps you feel you owe them for saving your life. But that can't be your only reason. You're risking death if Respen finds out. So what do you want from us?"

What did he want? Leith let the question settle into his bones. The swirl of things he wanted bubbled inside him. A life. Dreams. The ability to look Renna in the eye without shame. The freedom to return Brandi's smile. "I want to leave the Blades."

A thrill buzzed into his toes. Did he dare dream of something after the Blades? He couldn't even picture what that would be like.

"Leave the Blades?" Shadrach's eyebrows lowered as he clenched his hand around the hilt of his sword. "Why would you need our help to leave the Blades?"

"Because I can't leave on my own. The First Blade would track me down like he does all the other Blades that leave. But you must have somewhere safe, somewhere the First Blade couldn't find me."

Perhaps it was a ridiculous thought. Vane could track a Blade across the Waste. Where could the Resistance take him that Vane couldn't track down? Leith slumped against the back of the chair.

Lord Alistair studied him over his fingers, his eyes so shadowed Leith couldn't read their expression. "That's the deal, then. You'll spy for us if we agree to help you leave the Blades?"

"Yes."

"I believe that should be manageable, provided you keep your part of the bargain."

"You're going to trust me?" The tension drained from Leith's shoulders. He'd done it. He'd joined the Resistance.

He could end up dead long before Lord Alistair ever got around to helping him leave the Blades. But having the possibility there, dangling in the air like crystals from a cave wall, was more than Leith had ever dared before.

Lord Alistair placed his elbows on his desk. "Trust is a strong word. Let's just say I'm prepared to give you a chance, but I trust you as much as I trust a rattlesnake. Only time will tell which side you decide to bite."

Not the most glowing of statements, but Leith would take it. He straightened his spine. Time to prove his worth. "Renna and Brandi aren't the only ones in danger."

"Explain." Lord Alistair tapped his beard. Shadrach crossed his arms and leaned against the wall.

"All but three of the Blades are on two-month spy missions. We were instructed to get detailed layouts of each of the towns and manors we were sent to watch, including daily routines."

"What does Respen plan to do with that

information?" Shadrach rubbed his square jaw.

Leith glanced at Lord Alistair. He could tell by the pale cast to his face that he'd already guessed the king's plan. "I believe the king plans to kill off a number of the lords and their families."

Lord Alistair nodded. "For four years, Respen hasn't touched us because of the threat of instability. But now the country is stable, and he can afford to kill off those who oppose him."

"Including Renna and Brandi." Leith swallowed hard. With so much death all at once, King Respen would break the spirit of resistance instead of inflaming it. "When do you plan to bring them here? The First Blade is on his way there as we speak."

How much would he terrify Renna this time before Lord Alistair could get to her?

"I had planned to leave in the morning." Lord Alistair raised his eyebrows at Leith. "But you complicate matters."

"I'd have to follow you. It'd give everything away if a Blade spotted you and I wasn't trailing behind. And the First Blade will be at Stetterly expecting me to report to him when you arrive."

Lord Alistair frowned. "How will I know you haven't stayed at Walden?"

Leith scrubbed his boot against the green rug. A rattlesnake. That's how Lord Alistair saw him. "Your family will be safe while you're gone."

Raising his eyebrows, Lord Alistair stared at him, as if he could read Leith's heart if he looked long enough.

Shadrach stepped forward. "I'll tag along with him. If he wants to prove he's on our side, he'll have to let me come."

"No. Out of the question." Lord Alistair slapped a hand on his desk. "If he's lying, he'd kill you."

"He won't." Shadrach scowled at Lord Alistair. Lord Alistair glared back. Shadrach's eyes narrowed.

Leith watched the war crinkling the air. He wasn't the only cause of this tension. Something else was going on here.

Lord Alistair raked a hand through his beard. "Fine. We leave in the morning."

Not the outcome Leith wanted. "He can't tag along. Another Blade might see."

Shadrach turned towards him, square jaw set, arms crossed over his chest. "Tough. You claim to be good enough to spy for us. You'd better be good enough to avoid the other Blades."

Leith shrugged. He couldn't argue. The risk should be small. Few of the others lords would be traveling this time of year, and the Blades were tied to their missions. "Meet me in the foothills north of here at dawn."

Shadrach nodded. He tapped a toe against the pile of Leith's weapons. "I'm keeping these for now."

"All right. Don't leave them behind." Leith slid to his feet, but he couldn't bring himself to leave yet. "When you arrive in Stetterly, could you tell Brandi that I'm taking care of Blizzard? Blizzard's my horse. Brandi named him. And tell Renna that I told the king I was saved by a man called Daniel."

Lord Alistair's gaze sharpened at Leith's words, but he remained silent.

Leith glanced at the Bible that still lay on the corner of the desk. His fingers itched to snatch the book and flee into the darkness with it. A desire to read more, if just to quench the curiosity burning his brain, urged him to steal the book again.

"Would you like to keep the Bible for a while longer?" Lord Alistair's tone softened a fraction from the iron it'd been all evening.

"No, I…" Leith wasn't going to admit he felt drawn to that book. He backed away.

"You might not get another chance. I doubt you'd want to risk smuggling a Bible into Nalgar Castle."

Leith swayed, torn between the desire to read that book and the fear of what he might discover if he did. He didn't trust gifts. Lord Alistair must have some plot in mind if he was offering his Bible to Leith. As Lord Alistair had said, no one did anything without wanting something in return.

"Go ahead. Take it. You've stolen it once already." A smile tugged at the corners of Lord Alistair's mouth.

Leith swiped the Bible from the desk, whirled, and slipped out the window as quickly as he could. He didn't look back, and he definitely didn't question why he cradled the Bible like it was the most precious thing he'd ever held.

20

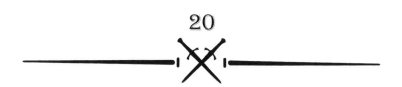

When the sky lightened to misty grey, Leith woke, dressed in his light brown clothing, and packed his gear since he wouldn't be returning to this campsite. When he'd strapped everything to Blizzard's saddle, he scattered leaves and sticks to return the hollow to its natural state once again.

He walked Blizzard to a hidden vantage point in the foothills, hobbling his horse behind an outcropping of rock while he worked his way into the gnarled branches of a small fir tree.

After half an hour of waiting, he spotted the black dot of a rider on the horizon. As the rider drew closer, he noted the quiver of arrows poking up over his shoulder. Even from this distance, Leith could see he had his bow strung. After several more minutes, the rider drew up below the crest of a hill, waiting.

Leith slipped from the fir and crept through the trees. Shadrach faced the ridge ahead of him, eyes scanning for movement. Leith circled through the firs and exited the tree line behind Shadrach.

After sneaking a few yards closer, Leith purposely

stepped on a stick. The snap echoed around the hillside.

Shadrach drew an arrow from the quiver, nocked it to his bow, and whirled in one motion. He was well-trained, but not jumpy. Leith wasn't going to be stuck with someone who lacked discretion in dangerous situations.

"Now that you have me out here alone, what do you intend to do, Blade?" Shadrach's voice cut like the steel of Leith's knives.

Leith spread his hands. Not that he had any weapons to draw if he wanted to. "I know you don't trust me, but this will work a lot better if you aren't pointing an arrow at my chest."

Shadrach glared at him, the arrow never wavering. "What's your interest in Lady Rennelda?"

"What?" Leith lowered his hands. That wasn't the first question he'd thought Shadrach would ask. "Nothing."

"You mentioned her just about every other sentence last night. That isn't nothing."

"I just want to make sure she's safe. That's all." Shadrach didn't understand. Renna hated Leith. She'd never see him as anything other than a Blade. Leith crossed his arms. "So what's your interest in her?"

Shadrach scowled, relaxed the bow, and slipped the arrow into his quiver. "We were friends a long time ago."

Leith sensed it wasn't that simple. But he wasn't going to press for answers. Not yet.

Shadrach unstrung the bow, his movements slow and deliberate. With his bow tucked across his shoulders, he crossed his arms as if to mimic Leith's stance. "What now, Blade?"

So that's how it was going to be. Undisguised hostility. "We're going to sneak back to Walden to watch

Lord Alistair leave. And, it's Leith."

Shadrach eyed him, as if debating what to tell him. "I'm Shad. Shadrach Alistair."

Leith straightened. "You're the lord's eldest son." He should've noticed Shad had the same brown hair and eyes as his father, though his face and build was leaner and taller.

Lord Alistair risked his son's life by placing him as Leith's watchdog. Yet, why had Shad been so eager to volunteer?

Shad rested a hand on his sword's hilt. "That knowledge won't do you any good."

Leith shrugged. No, it probably wouldn't. "Better hobble your horse. We have to walk."

Shad loosened the girth on his horse's saddle and hobbled its front legs. Leith's weapons hung from the saddlehorn.

Leith led the way out of the foothills and onto the prairie. It was later and lighter than Leith would've liked, but they stayed below the horizon line and slipped up the hill that overlooked the town.

As he wiggled on his belly and parted the grass, Leith spotted the bustle of activity below. A horse pawed at the dirt in front of the manor. A few guards darted around, tightening the girths of their horses' saddles.

Leith counted a five-man guard party going with Lord Alistair. Small, but perhaps small enough to be unnoticeable.

Mid-morning, the group headed to the east. Leith waited another half an hour, but Shad didn't fidget. Another mark in his favor. He could be patient.

With a small nod of his head, Leith directed Shad to crawl down the hill. Shad wiggled through the grass, and Leith followed, rising to his feet when they reached the bottom. Hiking back the way they'd come two hours ago, they retrieved their horses.

Leith swung onto Blizzard and led the way through the scrub brush, junipers, and conifers covering the hills. To their left, gray rock crags poked above the spikes of firs and pines. Below and to their right, the prairie rolled away in waves of grass to the horizon.

Blizzard flicked his tail, his ears swiveling to track Shad's horse. He snorted, weaving his head to get a glance behind him. Leith scratched his horse's sleek neck. "It's all right, boy."

Leith glanced over his shoulder. Shad's eyes were locked on Leith's back. The sun glinted on his sword's hilt and shimmered over his horse's chestnut fur. The chestnut would stand out more than Blizzard's dark gray, but Leith didn't dare argue with Shadrach's choice of horses. They had bigger issues to deal with.

They followed the ridgeline until they were well east of the town. Then they exited the foothills and skirted farmers' fields before picking up the line of beaten grass left by Lord Alistair and his guards.

Occassionally, Leith dismounted and studied the shape and particular nicks and cracks that made each hoof print distinct.

The third time Leith dismounted, Shad did as well. "What're you looking for?" His tone was too casual.

Leith hunched and pointed at a hoof print in a patch of soil. "Studying for later. This horse's hooves need a trim. See how the front is long and deep?"

Shad bent and studied the hoof print. "You can tell all that just by looking at the ground?"

Leith nodded. Out of the corner of his eye, he spotted

Shad eying Blizzard's tracks left in the soft ground. He got the feeling Shad wasn't as untrained in tracking as he pretended.

They followed the trail until nightfall. Leith found a curve in the hillside that provided some shelter and called a halt. They ate dry rations and curled in their blankets several yards away from each other.

Shad lay with his and Leith's weapons close to hand. As he tried to sleep, Leith's back prickled with the feeling of being watched.

"I'm not going to kill you in your sleep." Leith didn't bother to open his eyes. If Shad wanted to keep himself awake all night to keep an eye on Leith, then let him. He'd pay for it in a few hours.

When Leith woke, the moon inched below its zenith, showing they had several hours until dawn. He rolled from his blankets. Across from him, Shad still slept, huffing in and out.

How to wake him without getting killed? Leith slipped around Shad's sleeping form, stretched out, and nudged his shoulder.

Shad jerked awake, swiping his knife from the ground. Leith jumped back, hands in the air. "Sssh, it's just me. Time to get moving."

With a glare, Shad sheathed his knife and gathered his weapons. Leith rolled his bedroll and strapped the bundle onto Blizzard's back.

With the moon painting the prairie silver, Leith took his horse's reins and walked along the trail left by Lord Alistair and his guards. Shad fell into step beside him.

After a quarter hour of walking, Leith spotted the glow of a dying fire ahead of them. He halted, scanning the area. Lord Alistair and his guards had chosen to camp in a valley next to a creek. Trees scattered in clumps across the hillside, breaking up the monotony of the prairie.

Leith waved Shad to a clump of trees, below the rim of a hill out of sight of the camp up ahead. Together, they slipped through the grass and brush to overlook the campsite.

Lord Alistair slept in the center of a ring of guards. One guard walked around the campsite, eyeing the darkness behind the glow of the embers. The horses bobbed their heads in restless sleep a few yards away on their tether lines.

Leith settled down to watch and wait. Shad sprawled beside him. A frown tugged at the corners of his mouth and puckered his forehead.

By the time the sun splashed pink across the landscape, the camp below them stirred. Lord Alistair glanced towards the different hills surrounding the campsite, as if searching for Leith and Shad, but his eyes never focused in their direction.

After an hour, Lord Alistair and his guards turned their horses east and disappeared over the horizon. Shad glanced at Leith, his eyes wide. "The guards never knew we were here."

"They had no reason to scout farther away than their immediate campsite." Leith watched the faint dust cloud rising from the horizon.

"That's going to change." Shad muttered under his breath, but Leith heard it anyway. "Do we start following them now?"

Leith shook his head. "We'll give them a two-hour head start. We don't want to get too close while they're climbing the trail into the canyon."

If he'd been by himself, he would've kept Lord Alistair in sight. But as good as Shad was proving to be at sneaking, Leith couldn't trust him not to make a mistake. Lord Alistair knew he was being followed, but his guards didn't.

Shad nodded and crawled out of the brush. After hiking back to their campsite, Leith waved at Shad's bedroll. "Catch a nap. I'll wake you in an hour."

Climbing to the hill above their campsite, Leith settled in as comfortably as he could. The time passed in a buzz of insects and rustle of animals in the grass. When an hour was up, Leith woke Shad. This time, he came awake without pulling a knife.

Leith stretched out on the grass. "Keep a watch on the hill. Make sure no other travelers decide to pass through this area."

Shad grabbed all of his and Leith's weapons and headed off. When he was gone, Leith fished the Bible out of his pack. He should take the opportunity for a few minutes of sleep. But he could handle the lack of rest. Satisfying his curiosity was more important.

Wiggling into a comfortable position, Leith opened the book to the first page and started reading. The stories wrapped around him. What if the world had been created with just a few commands? That kind of power was overwhelming. It made the power that King Respen wielded over Acktar seem...small. Like an ant declaring absolute rule over his tiny anthill without realizing that he could be crushed in a single footstep.

Something nudged Leith's foot. Leith dropped the book and reached for his knife. His hand closed over air. Shad stood over him, arms crossed. He had the audacity to smirk. Leith scowled, picked up the book, and brushed it off. "Has it been an hour?"

Shad's smirk still hovered on his face. "Interesting reading?"

Leith shrugged. "Time to get moving." He swung onto Blizzard. He and Shad trotted their horses east until the Spires Canyon sliced across the land in front of them.

Leith located the same game trail Lord Alistair had used. The first section of trail hugged the side of the canyon in a thin, winding ledge. Dismounting, they led their horses and eased forward one foot at a time.

Near the bottom, the ledges disappeared into a steep incline of shale and gravel. Leith started downward, trusting Blizzard to pick his way down the slope.

Shad's horse followed without hesitation, as if he was used to sliding down slopes and scrabbling along cliff faces. Did Shad do a lot of travelling through the Spires Canyon and the Sheered Rock Hills? Why? He'd have no reason to venture into the Hills unless...

Unless he was as much a part of the Resistance as his father.

Leith's feet slid on the shale. He would've fallen except for his grip on Blizzard's reins. Blizzard planted his feet until Leith regained his footing.

Of course Lord Alistair wouldn't keep his Resistance activities from his son the way Lachlan protected Renna. But how much was Shad involved? Was Shad the Leader mentioned in Lord Alistair's message?

Leith slid the last few feet to the level ground at the floor of the canyon. Pebbles lined the banks of the river while tufts of grass poked through the muddy breaks in the stone. Shad and his horse trotted down the last few feet and halted next to him.

As they swung on their horses and started off again, Leith glanced at Shadrach. "So, you're Lord Alistair's son? I wouldn't have guessed that two nights ago."

Shad settled into his saddle. He stared at the canyon ahead of them. "I'm the captain of the guard, and I'm his son. It's best to keep those two things separate." His jaw tightened.

Leith sensed an edge to Shad's words, but he didn't dare probe too deeply. He understood father issues all too well. He scanned the cliffs above them. "You aren't going to be missed at Walden? Won't the guards notice their captain disappeared?"

Shad's shrug rattled the arrows in his quiver. "No. This isn't the first time I've had to leave."

There it was again. The hint that Shad travelled a lot. What was the Resistance doing that would cause Shad to travel so much? How organized was the Resistance? Was there more to it than even King Respen had guessed?

21

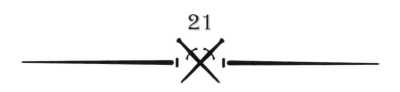

The eyes were back. Renna shivered as she tossed the wash water into the yard. Two guards from Uster patrolled the yard in front of her while a third strolled around the stable. None of them seemed to sense anything wrong.

She dashed into the kitchen and slammed the door behind her. She leaned against it, panting even though she'd only run a few steps.

For over a week, the nagging sense of being watched had vanished, especially after Sheriff Allen managed to get the message to Uster and returned with a ten-man squad of guards with Lord Segon's compliments. But now the icy feeling of staring eyes prickled across her skin.

Aunt Mara paused in wiping down the wooden countertops. Uncle Abel looked up from his sermon notes spread across the table. "What's wrong?"

Renna glanced over her shoulder. "I felt watched again." Was the First Blade back? She hadn't seen him since that night outside the hidden cabin.

Uncle Abel eyed the window. "Did the guards see anything?"

"No." She pressed her palms against the wood behind her. Was she imagining things? Perhaps she was simply becoming paranoid.

Uncle Abel gathered his notes. "Our message got through. Henry Alistair should be getting it any day now. He'll have a solution. The guards from Uster will be here until then."

Aunt Mara frowned. The delicate lines on her face deepened. "Where's Brandi?"

"Out in the stable." Renna's pulse hammered at her temples. What if the First Blade held a knife to Brandi's throat like he had Renna's? "I'll fetch her."

"Let's go together. I don't want either of you girls going out alone." Aunt Mara set down her towel. "Best not to take any chances."

Uncle Abel tapped his sermon notes into a neat pile, tucked them into the Bible, and returned them all to the pantry. Picking up her father's knife, Uncle Abel cracked the door open and peered out. Nodding to them, he stepped outside.

Renna slipped out the door, Aunt Mara following on her heels. The guards nodded at them in greeting. Uncle Abel spoke to one of them briefly before they squished across the yard and entered the stables. The musty smell of hay drifted on the breeze. "Brandi?"

"Over here." Brandi's voice came from the back of the stables.

Renna hurried between the long lines of empty stalls. The place had once been filled with stomping stallions and sleek mares.

Brandi sat on a short beam in the goat pen. She scratched a brown goat between its curving horns. The goat tilted its head and rolled its eyes. "Ginger makes funny faces when you scratch her head like this."

Renna forced a smile to her face. "Yes, she does. Now come back to the manor."

Brandi's eyes flashed up. "Are we being watched again?"

Aunt Mara knelt and wrapped an arm around Brandi's shoulders. "We think so. But don't panic. We'll be all right."

Renna squeezed her hands together to hide their trembling. Her skin crawled with the feeling of a knife dragging across her skin. Had the First Blade come back to kill her? Or taunt her some more?

As Aunt Mara stood, Uncle Abel pressed the knife into her hand. "Get the girls inside and bar the doors. I need to warn Sheriff Allen and let everyone know church services will be canceled again."

Aunt Mara nodded, her lips pressed flat. Her fingers curled around the knife like she was prepared to use it. Renna hadn't seen her look that dangerous since the night Renna's parents died. "Come on, girls. Let's go inside."

Brandi popped to her feet and bounced ahead of them. Uncle Abel reached for their worn saddle for Stubborn.

As they exited the stables, Renna scanned the surrounding hills. She couldn't spot anyone, but then again, if there was a watcher and he was a Blade, she'd only spot him if he wanted to be spotted.

22

Leith studied the hoof prints in the dust of the game trail descending the canyon's side from the direction of Uster. The early afternoon sun flayed the back of his neck, but at least the canyon wall would provide shade in another hour.

He searched for footprints, but he didn't see any. Martyn must still be out on the prairie.

Standing, Leith dusted off his knees and returned to where he'd left Shad around a bend in the canyon wall. "Looks like your father took an hour or so to meet with Lord Segon in Uster. Sixth Blade Martyn Hamish is stationed there. As soon as he can sneak away safely, he's going to be headed this way expecting to meet me."

"Do you have to talk with him?" Shad's brown eyes narrowed.

"Yes. It's an old understanding." Friendship would be a better word for it, but Leith didn't want Shad to hear him say it. While it'd be safer to meet Martyn at the canyon rim and away from Shad, Shad wouldn't want him out of sight or earshot. "Walk your horse along the trail your father and his guards left until

167

you're passed that stand of trees up ahead."

Eyes still narrowed, Shad tugged his horse forward. Leith followed, purposely scuffing his feet to kick as much dirt and sand around as possible. He needed to obscure the trail so Martyn wouldn't notice the extra set of fresh tracks.

He spotted a thicket of spruce and firs clumped against the canyon wall. That's where Martyn's camp would be. As they passed the trees, a whuffing snort from Martyn's horse told him he'd guessed right.

On the other side of the thicket, Leith waved Shad over to a stack of boulders that had tumbled from the canyon face at one point. A ledge protruded a few yards above, hiding the spot from the canyon's rim. "Stay here and keep your horse quiet. You'll hear everything we say, but we'll also hear you if you make noise."

Shad placed his hand on his horse's nose. He raised his eyebrows. "I suppose you're going to ask for your knives back?"

"Martyn's going to think something's strange if I don't have them." Leith kept his arms loose at his sides. They'd built something resembling trust in the three days they'd travelled together. But would it be enough?

Something rattled along the trail into the canyon. Shad glanced toward the sound, and his shoulders straightened. He yanked the bundle of Leith's weapons off his saddle and shoved them at Leith.

Leith grabbed them, gripped Blizzard's reins, and tugged the horse into the thicket. On one side, a small puddle collected the water trickling from a crack in the canyon wall. Martyn's dust-colored horse stood beside it, head up, ears pricked in their direction. The remains of a fire piled against the canyon wall where it couldn't be seen from above while Martyn's pack and bedroll lay tucked under a rock shelf next to his horse.

Dropping Blizzard's reins next to Martyn's horse, Leith buckled on his weapons as fast as he could. As soon as the last knife settled in place, he flopped to the ground next to a cedar.

He'd just laced his fingers behind his head as Martyn shoved through the last of the spruce trees. Leith yawned and stretched his arms above his head. If he yawned loud enough, maybe Martyn wouldn't notice the faint dust cloud he'd kicked up. "Took you long enough."

"Don't complain. You enjoyed your nap." Martyn shook dust from his curls, dropped to the ground across from Leith, and lounged on his hands. "I had to do all the hard work of eavesdropping on Lord Segon."

"Learn anything interesting?" Leith's chest tightened. Martyn wasn't acting like he'd overheard anything about Leith, but he still could've learned enough to make him suspicious.

Martyn kicked at a pebble. "No. Not for lack of trying. But they went into the only room in the entire manor without a window and stationed guards in front of the door and the doors of the rooms around it too. I couldn't get anywhere close. Whatever they talked about, it must've been important."

Leith rested his arms on his knees to disguise the way his shoulders sagged in relief. "Must be."

Martyn dug into his pack and pulled out two slices of dried beef. Handing one to Leith, he chomped on the other. "What brings Lord Alistair out this way?"

Tearing a bite from the meat, Leith chewed to give himself some time. "Apparently the trouble the First

Blade and I stirred up in Stetterly got Lord Alistair's attention. He plans to take Lady Rennelda and Lady Brandiline to Walden."

Martyn frowned and gnawed on his next bite. "Why now? If the Resistance was so concerned with their safety, why haven't they taken them away from Stetterly before this?"

Leith shrugged. "King Respen hasn't bothered them until now. And the Resistance wouldn't want to give the impression they were rallying behind Lady Rennelda."

"Does that mean the Resistance is ready to set Lady Rennelda up as queen?" Martyn shoved the last of his meat in his mouth.

Leith swallowed. The meat thumped into the bottom of his stomach. What were Lord Alistair's intentions besides keeping Renna and Brandi safe? Was he planning to rally the Resistance behind her?

The words from the message he'd seen tucked in Lachlan's Bible whispered down his spine. *The Leader is almost ready.* "Guess we'll find out."

Martyn ran his fingers through his hair. "I—"

The sound of a hoof on stone clipped around the clearing.

Martyn planted his hands to push himself to his feet. Leith motioned for him to stay put.

Leith couldn't hear anything over his galloping heart. If Martyn investigated, he'd spot Shad. What would Leith do if his friends tried to kill each other?

Across the thicket, Martyn's horse stared in Shad's direction, ears pricked. Blizzard snorted, shook his mane, and lowered his head to slurp at the puddle.

Leith forced himself to relax. "Must've been a deer or something. Blizzard doesn't sense anything wrong."

Martyn lowered himself back to the ground, but his

eyes flicked from his horse to the trees surrounding them. "Strange. My horse does." He shook his head and narrowed his eyes at Leith. "Blizzard? You named your horse?"

He'd made a mistake. He'd forgotten that Martyn didn't know his horse's name. He rolled one shoulder like it didn't matter. "He seems to like it. Better than calling him Horse all the time."

Martyn cocked his head at him. "Guess so." He shoved to his feet and dusted off his hands. "Better go back to spying. Wouldn't want Lord Segon to do something interesting without me."

Leith scrambled to his feet. "And I can't let Lord Alistair get too far ahead of me."

Martyn slapped Leith on the back, glanced one last time in the direction of Shad's hiding place, and strode towards the trail. Leith gathered Blizzard's reins and led him from the thicket. He listened to the faint clicking of rocks as Martyn climbed the trail.

When he couldn't hear any more sounds and Martyn disappeared over the rim, Leith led Blizzard around the boulder.

Shad leaned against the cliff wall, his horse's reins tight in his fist. "That was close." He kept his voice pitched low.

Leith squinted over his shoulder. "We need to get out of here. Stick to the canyon wall."

They led their horses as close to the cliff face as they could. The trees and fallen boulders hampered their progress, but Leith didn't dare step into the open.

When a good five miles of safety lay behind them, Leith halted Blizzard and sank onto a rock. "Time for a halt."

Shad sagged onto a rock across from him. "Finally. You had a chance to eat, but I was too busy hiding."

While Shad rifled in his pack and pulled out a length of dried beef, Leith unbuckled the knives strapped across his chest. He held them out to Shad. Shad glanced at the knives, finished chewing, and met Leith's gaze. "You keep them."

Leith stared at the knives in his hands, then back up at Shad. "You trust me?"

"Yes." Shad's mouth quirked. "If you'd wanted to kill me, you would've done it long ago, weapons or no."

Leith strapped the knives in place and grinned. Trust had a nice sound to it. Like the sound of friendship. Or freedom.

As soon as camp was set up for the night and supper cooked on the fire he'd deemed them sheltered enough to risk, Leith pulled out the Bible and leaned against the base of a tree.

Shad lounged against a tree a few feet away. "You're actually serious about reading the Bible."

"You didn't think I was?"

Shad shrugged. "I thought you were doing it to make yourself look good. But I've been watching. You're actually reading, and"—Shad leaned over and tapped the page— "no one sticks with reading Leviticus unless they're really serious."

Leith grimaced. "It's kind of confusing." His brain ached with the muddle he'd crammed inside his head.

Shad took the book, flipped a number of pages, and handed it back to Leith. "Try reading the New Testament for a little while. Now that you've read about Creation and how Adam and Eve sinned, you might want to read about Jesus Christ, the Son of God Who came as the redemption from that sin."

Leith cocked his head. "Son of God? Like the person the evil king saw in the furnace with Daniel's three friends?"

"Yep."

At least this part looked easier to read than the section he'd been trying to get through. This book described events just as crazy and impossible as the book of Daniel, yet Leith found he couldn't stop reading and couldn't help but hope it might be true, despite King Respen's insistence that it wasn't.

23

Leith lay on his back and watched the crack of sky above the canyon walls lighten to iron grey veined with shades of indigo.

If he could, he'd stay like this forever and forget he was a Blade. He huffed a sigh that clouded the air above him. Shoving the blankets aside, he sat up. The morning air slithered down his spine.

After shaking out his boots, he tugged them on. As he tied the leather laces, Shad groaned, rolled over, and stretched. His hair frizzed in several directions while his chin wore the shadow of several days' worth of bristles.

Leith scrubbed his hand along his own face. Six days of travel and…nothing. A little scruff on his chin and a couple of bristles above his lip. Maybe. If what he felt was facial hair and not dust and wishful thinking. "We'll reach Stetterly today."

Shad nodded and tugged on his boots. When he finished, he shook out his bedroll, droplets of dew bursting into the air. "So this is where we split up."

"Yes. The First Blade is still at Stetterly." Leith eyed Shad. How much did Shad trust him? Unlike when

Leith talked to Martyn, Shad had no way of knowing what Leith would tell Vane. "I have to report to him."

Shad rolled his blanket. "It'll be a boring report. All you've done is travel to Stetterly all by yourself." A smirk creased his face.

Relief washed through Leith's chest. Shad trusted him, and Shad would convince Lord Alistair to trust him. He reached for his saddle. "You'll have to wait here a day before you can ride into Stetterly to join your father. Martyn knows you weren't with your father when he stopped at Uster."

"All right." Shad flopped to the ground and rested his head on his bedroll. "I need to catch up on my sleep anyways. Blades don't get a lot of rest."

"And lord's sons value rest too much."

Shad grinned and laced his fingers behind his head. His expression sobered. "What are you going to do about the First Blade?"

"Hopefully after I report to him, he'll return to Nalgar Castle and leave me in charge of watching all of you. I'll report to you when it's safe." That was the plan, anyway. Leith wasn't sure what he'd do if Vane stayed to watch while he sent Leith to Nalgar Castle.

He swung his saddle onto Blizzard's back and tightened the girth strap. Blizzard twisted his head around. His ears pressed against his head irritably.

After placing his saddlebags behind his saddle, Leith dug into one and drew out the Bible. He held it out to Shad. "Can you keep this for me? I wouldn't put it past the First Blade to search my saddlebags."

Shad took it, eyebrows raised. "He'd search your saddlebags? Even though he doesn't have any reason to suspect you?"

Leith shrugged. "It's his job to keep the rest of us in line. Rumor has it he even loosened one of the stones in the wall separating his room from the Second Blade's so he could make sure the Second Blade wasn't plotting to take his place."

No one knew if the rumor was true, but Leith had taken to checking the walls of his room for loose stones and peep holes just in case.

He finished saddling his horse and waved as he rode into the gray morning. The canyon's walls echoed with the lonely clip of Blizzard's hooves. The sun rose higher in the sky. Without a breeze, the temperature rose along with the sun in the depths of the canyon.

Mid-afternoon, Leith reached the section of canyon below Stetterly Manor, the stretch of canyon he would've plunged into during that blizzard if he'd missed the manor.

Renna seemed to think that God had a purpose in bringing Leith to Stetterly. Could God have a purpose for him? Most likely Leith was being directed for Renna's good or Brandi's good or Shad's good. Leith could be content with that. It was a nice feeling, thinking that perhaps he was being used to bring good to someone's life instead of only evil.

In a thick clump of spruce, he spotted Vane's camp. He unsaddled Blizzard and tied him next to the other horse. Was Vane watching him even now?

Warily, he climbed a pebbled path and slipped through the prairie grass towards Stetterly. Only the occasional bend in the grass marked where Vane had walked that morning.

"Looking for me, Torren?" Vane's voice slithered from the prairie behind him.

Leith whirled. Vane rose from the grass a few feet away. His eyes cut through Leith, as if he could dissect Leith's head and read every traitorous thought. Leith swallowed. "Lord Alistair has come to Stetterly."

Vane huffed. "I already knew that. Do you know why he's here?"

"He plans to take the ladies Rennelda and Brandiline back with him to Walden." Were the girls all right? Had Vane harmed them?

"Why now after all this time?" Vane turned towards Stetterly as well. He stroked the hilt of his favorite throwing knife, the one buckled on his right hip. "Lord Alistair is a key player in the Resistance, is he not?"

Leith couldn't hide that fact. "Yes."

"And he's been in communication with Abel Lachlan." Vane's mouth twisted. "He plans to set his son up to take the throne. If the younger Alistair were to marry Lady Rennelda, he could claim Acktar's throne. With the backing of the Resistance, he could pose a threat."

Vane's words gave Leith pause. Was that Lord Alistair's plan? Did he intend to have Shad marry Renna so that Shad could claim the throne?

A strange sensation twisted his stomach. Why should it matter to him?

24

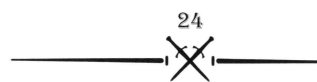

Renna heaved another wet dress onto the clothes line and pinned it in place. Scrubbing droplets of water from her face, she bent to grab the next article of clothing.

With the tension of the past month, they'd gotten behind on laundry. But now with the guards from Uster patrolling the yard, Aunt Mara decided they could risk washing their clothes as long as they finished in daylight.

She skimmed the prairie for a smudge of black and spotted nothing. Her back itched with the feeling of eyes on her, but at least the Blade had kept his distance. If he was out there and not her imagination.

Brandi struggled outside with another basket. She dropped it beside Renna. "That's the last of it."

"Good." Renna swiped hair out of her face with the back of her wrist.

Figures in the distance caught her eye. Several silhouettes on horseback trotted towards their manor. Renna's heart stopped for a second before leaping into her mouth.

The guards halted their patrol and closed in a defensive line. The captain pointed from her to the kitchen door. She placed a hand on Brandi's shoulder. "Let's go inside."

Brandi clenched her fists and nodded. They hurried into the manor, barred the door, and drew the curtain.

Aunt Mara blanched, set down the bowl she was stirring, and reached for the butcher knife resting on the tabletop. "Is the Blade back?"

Renna lifted one corner of the curtain and peeked out. "Riders are coming this way. Six of them." If only Uncle Abel were here. But he'd taken the risk to go into Stetterly. He'd neglected the townsfolk long enough.

Aunt Mara bustled to her side and peered out the window as well. "The guards can handle six men if they're a threat."

Renna squeezed her hands together. At least there didn't appear to be any Blades among the riders.

The horsemen drew closer. As they entered the yard, the guards surrounded them, swords drawn.

One of the riders nudged his horse forward. Grey streaked his brown hair at his temples, but his beard remained thick and untouched by grey. He wore muted, green and brown clothing under a leather vest with matching leather gloves. After a few minutes, the guards gave half-bows and sheathed their swords.

The man swung down from his dark bay horse. Renna sagged against the windowsill. Lord Alistair. He'd come in response to Uncle Abel's message. But why had he come in person? Why hadn't he just sent guards the way Lord Segon of Uster had?

Aunt Mara relaxed and hurried to the door. She swung the door open before Lord Alistair even had a chance to knock. "Henry, we're so glad you came. Please come in and sit down after your long journey."

"Glad I arrived in time." Lord Alistair bowed and stomped the mud from his boots as he entered.

Aunt Mara closed the door and waved him to a seat. "Something to drink?"

Renna tiptoed away from the window and slipped onto the bench. What was Lord Alistair doing here?

"Water would be fine." Lord Alistair perched on a bench and leaned his forearms against the table.

Brandi grinned, pranced to the table, and plopped onto the bench across from Lord Alistair. "I'm Brandi."

Lord Alistair grinned back at her. "You were only knee-high to my horse last time I saw you."

"You let me pet him. I remember." Brandi bounced on the bench and cocked her head towards Aunt Mara. "May I go see the horses?"

Aunt Mara opened her mouth, but the door slammed open. Renna jumped and inched her hand toward the knife on the table. Uncle Abel stomped inside and hung his cloak on the peg. "Henry, it's good to see you again."

"I wish it was on better circumstances." Lord Alistair took the glass of water from Aunt Mara and drained it in a few gulps. "I need to speak with all of you."

Lord Alistair's tone chilled Renna's arms. What he had to say couldn't be good.

Lord Alistair pushed to his feet, stepped out of the door, and called over his guards. After positioning three in front of the outside door, he directed the other two men to guard the inside door leading to the rest of the manor. Renna shivered. What did Lord Alistair have to say that would warrant such caution?

When the guards were in place, Lord Alistair returned to his seat. Uncle Abel and Aunt Mara also slid into seats around the table. Aunt Mara toyed with her apron while Uncle Abel rested his elbows on the table.

Lord Alistair's gaze flicked between all of them. "Six days ago, I received your message, but I was delayed in translating it because the Bible I keep hidden in my study was missing. After searching for it, I eventually translated the message with another Bible. As I was finishing, a Blade broke into my study, returned the missing Bible, and claimed he wanted to spy for the Resistance."

Renna dug her fingers into her palms. What trick were the Blades playing now?

Brandi smirked as if she'd already guessed what was going on. "Leith must've really wanted to read more about Daniel."

Lord Alistair raised his eyebrows at her. "Yes, so he told me. He said he'd been the Blade you helped a month ago, and he had the scar to prove it."

"Where is he now?" Uncle Abel half-turned to the door.

Lord Alistair steepled his fingers. "Supposedly he followed me here from Walden. Shadrach went with him to keep an eye on him. I haven't seen either of them since I left."

A squirrely feeling skittered through Renna's stomach and chest. Was Shadrach all right? Six days alone with a Blade. A lot could happen in six days.

And if nothing had happened, then would both the Blade Leith Torren and Shadrach Alistair show up here? Something squeezed at her chest. Not fear, exactly. Something else she didn't dare name.

"You want to know if he's telling the truth about joining the Resistance." Uncle Abel scrubbed his jaw.

Aunt Mara rested a hand on his arm. "Leith Torren was a sight better than the Blade watching us now. He was polite and respectful. He never threatened the girls and never did anything untoward to either of them, not even when he was with them alone during that blizzard. I'm not sure if that makes him trustworthy, but I wouldn't be scared to feed him a meal if he were to show up on our doorstep again."

Uncle Abel nodded, lines framing his mouth. "I've risked my life on his word before. I'd be willing to risk it again."

But what about her life and Brandi's life? Was Uncle Abel willing to risk their lives too?

Brandi slapped her palm on the table. "This is ridiculous. Of course he's telling the truth." She rolled her eyes. "The First Blade being here proves it."

"How so?" Lord Alistair tapped his beard. His eyes glinted as if he really considered what Renna's thirteen-year-old sister had to say.

Brandi crossed her arms. "Well, if Leith had told King Respen everything he knew about us, then the king would've sent the First Blade to kill us. The First Blade didn't kill us. He just spied on us for a month and stole our Bibles, which would've been completely unnecessary if King Respen already knew all about us." She shrugged. "If Leith told the truth about hiding what he knew, then it makes sense he'd tell the truth about this too."

Why did everyone but Renna think that Blade was trustworthy? Yes, he'd been better than the First Blade, but that was like saying a mountain lion was better than a rattlesnake. Both could be deadly given the chance.

Lord Alistair swung his gaze towards her. "He said all he told Respen was that he was saved by a man named Daniel."

Brandi's grin widened until it extended nearly from ear to ear. Renna clenched her cold fingers. Another trick? The First Blade had toyed with her for the past month. Was the Third Blade doing the same thing?

Lord Alistair turned his gaze back to Uncle Abel. "If Leith Torren's information is to be believed, Respen is preparing for a major strike against those who oppose him."

Aunt Mara clapped her hand over her mouth. Uncle Abel put his arm around her shoulders. "And the girls?"

"He won't let them live a second time. According to Leith, the First Blade will be sent after them."

Renna reached under the table and gripped Brandi's hand. Would this fear never end? "When?"

"In three weeks or so." Lord Alistair's voice lowered. "I'd like you and Brandi to come back with me to Walden. I have soldiers and will better be able to keep you safe."

Renna gulped. "Leave?"

Brandi glanced at Aunt Mara and Uncle Abel. "You'll both come too, won't you?"

Uncle Abel and Aunt Mara shared a look. They clasped hands, and Uncle Abel turned back to Renna and Brandi. "We're needed here. I can't leave the congregation here without a pastor."

Aunt Mara reached out and grasped Renna's other hand. "We can't protect you. You and Brandi need to go to Walden where you'll have a chance to be safe."

"Even Walden might not be safe for long." Lord Alistair leaned closer. "But, the Resistance has gained strength. If worse comes to worse, I can take the girls out of Respen's reach."

"Thank-you." Tears brightened Aunt Mara's eyes.

"We won't be coming back to Stetterly, will we?"

Aunt Mara and Uncle Abel shared another look. Uncle Abel shook his head at Renna. "No. Not while Respen is in power. He can't afford to let you live, so you'll be in constant danger even if Lord Alistair can protect you from this current threat."

Renna gripped Brandi's hand tighter to disguise her shaking. All she wanted to be was safe at home. Why couldn't Respen just leave them alone? She'd promise to never get married, never have children, if that's what it took.

"Will we get to ride horses?" Brandi bounced in her seat.

"Yes, you will. I brought a horse for each of you."

Brandi grinned. "Which one is mine?"

"Whichever one you want." Lord Alistair smiled at Brandi. Her happiness blasted away the gloom of the past few minutes. "I'm sure Renna won't mind if you have first pick."

Renna nodded, but she didn't speak. She didn't care if she rode a beautiful mare or a work-roughened mule. Either way, her heart would tear in two when she was forced to leave home.

25

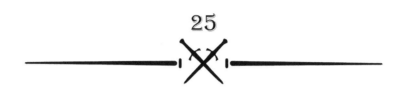

Shadrach Alistair stood in her kitchen. Renna halted in the doorway, her hand resting on the door frame. Her heart pattered through her chest. Her memories had been of a sixteen-year-old boy.

But he'd grown into a man with broad shoulders carrying his bow and quiver, scruff bristling across his square jaw, and a feet-planting, long-legged stride. His dark brown hair shagged into eyes the color of the canyon walls after a rainstorm.

Her legs wouldn't move. She should smile. Or at least say something. Anything besides the strained gurgle that burbled from her throat.

Shadrach's mouth quirked as he stepped forward. "It's good to see you again, Renna."

"I..." Her voice withered like midsummer grass. Footsteps pounded the hallway behind her. She slid her feet two steps out of the way as Lord Alistair strode into the room at a pace that would've been a run had his dignity allowed it.

Lord Alistair gripped Shadrach's shoulders, blinked, and bear-hugged him. Shadrach stiffened, his arms at his side. Perhaps it was as awkward for him as it was for Renna as she pressed her back against the wall. Or maybe his quiver was jabbing him in the back, which was a painful possibility considering how tightly Lord Alistair squeezed him.

"I'm fine." Shadrach thumped his father's back. "I can take care of myself, you know."

Lord Alistair returned his grip to Shadrach's shoulders. "I know. I..." He shook his head and dropped his arms to his sides. "Let's call the guards so we can talk."

When he'd stationed guards outside both of the kitchen doors and Uncle Abel, Aunt Mara, and Brandi had joined them, Shadrach slid onto the bench near the table. Uncle Abel remained standing while Aunt Mara lifted the frying pan from its hook on the wall next to the fireplace.

Brandi breezed across the kitchen as she fetched eggs from the lard barrel. Lord Alistair perched on the bench across the table from Shadrach.

Renna's feet felt mired in snow as she tottered across the kitchen. She yanked plates from the cupboard and slid them onto the table. Did her hair look all right? She'd twisted it into a braid, but she hadn't been expecting Shadrach.

Lord Alistair leaned both elbows on the table. "So what happened? Did the Blade give you any trouble?"

Renna reached for one of their glasses. Her hands trembled so much the glass slid in her fingers. Blades outside, Shadrach Alistair inside. Both things squiggled through her chest.

Shadrach rested his arms on the table. "No trouble. Far from it. He went out of his way to prove himself."

"Is it a trick?" Lord Alistair's question echoed the buzz in Renna's head.

She dipped a glass in the water bucket. As she set it in front of Shadrach, he smiled at her. Her hand bobbled. Water sloshed over the rim, across her fingers, and onto the table.

His hand darted forward and steadied the glass before she dumped the rest across his lap. Her face heated. He must think her a clumsy girl who couldn't even handle a glass of water.

"Thanks." He tugged the glass from her grip. She dropped her hand and backed away. Shadrach turned to his father. "Not a trick. I trust him. He's sincere."

Brandi smirked. "Told you."

Shadrach winked at her. "I bet you did. Leith told me all about your stories."

The smell of frying eggs turned Renna's stomach. She held her breath as Aunt Mara passed her, carrying the frying pan in a cloth-wrapped hand.

"Where is he now?" Uncle Abel dragged the curtain aside with a finger and peered out.

"To keep up appearances, Leith had to meet the First Blade yesterday morning. Both of them are out there somewhere. Leith will find me when the First Blade leaves." Shadrach leaned backward to give Aunt Mara room to place an egg on his plate. "Thanks. I haven't had a hot breakfast in almost a week."

Aunt Mara's smile lifted her cheeks and sparkled in her blue eyes. "You're welcome. There'll be more when you finish that."

Uncle Abel dropped the curtain and leaned his shoulder against the wall. "What makes him think the First Blade will leave?"

Lord Alistair scrubbed at his beard as Aunt Mara placed an egg on his plate. "Leith Torren claimed the First Blade only had orders to stay here two weeks, but we can't be sure the First Blade will leave once he sees we've arrived."

Shadrach shrugged one shoulder. "Leith seemed confident he could convince the First Blade to leave."

"Let's hope so." Lines formed across Lord Alistair's forehead.

Renna twisted her hands in her skirt. Would the First Blade leave? Or would he send Leith Torren back to Nalgar Castle instead?

She'd rather both Blades returned to the castle, but if she had to pick a Blade to stick around, Leith Torren was the better of the two.

Leith sprawled on his stomach in the tall grass, overlooking Stetterly Manor. What was Shad telling Lord Alistair?

Vane lay a few feet away, still as a hunting mountain lion. "Seems I was correct. Lord Alistair does intend to use Lady Rennelda to claim the throne."

Leith spread his fingers in the sand. If that was Lord Alistair's plan, would Renna go along with it?

He tensed and eyed Vane. "King Respen will have to be informed of this development."

"You will report to the king." Vane stared at Stetterly Manor like a hawk studied a prairie dog hole. "I'll remain here."

Leith dug his fingers into the sand. Grit scraped under his fingernails. Vane couldn't stay here. "King Respen will want his right-hand Blade to counter this latest plot. Besides, they'll return to Walden in a few days, and Walden is my mission."

He held his breath. King Respen had ordered Vane to return to the castle in two weeks. It made no sense to send Leith when Vane had to return in a week anyways. But Vane didn't always listen to sense.

Vane's mouth curled. "You wish to challenge me? You want to become First Blade?" His hand inched toward his throwing knife.

Leith met those pale eyes and forced confidence into his muscles. "You know I have no wish to be First Blade."

Vane's gaze pierced him for a moment before he snorted. "No, you're right. You don't have that kind of ambition. Never did as a kid. You could've been the Second Blade had you gotten the guts to kill earlier."

"Nor do I want anyone else to think I'm usurping your position now." Leith didn't dare glance at Vane for fear he'd give himself away. "If I returned to confer with King Respen, the other Blades might think I was trying to undermine your position. Spying on Walden or Stetterly, that's a job for a lower Blade. But planning King Respen's countermove? That's a job for the First Blade."

A few feet away, crickets chirped and bounced between blades of grass. A bird swooped low above them, its wings thumping the air. Something skittered in the grass by Leith's knees.

Vane remained still, his tawny clothes fading into the sand. "I'll return to Nalgar Castle. You'll remain here to follow Lord Alistair and the ladies Rennelda and Brandiline to Walden."

Leith didn't allow himself to relax. "Very well."

"And, Torren," Vane's voice dropped into the icy danger of a blizzard wind, "The ladies Rennelda and

Brandiline are mine."

Leith dredged up the familiar cold. "Your targets are yours to kill."

He touched the hilt of his knife. Renna and Brandi were Vane's to kill…and Leith's to save.

26

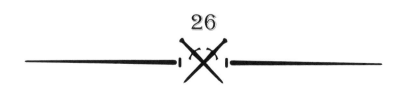

Renna curled her fingers in the smooth fabric of her Sunday dress. A few of the other girls spoke to her as they hurried out of the way so the men could arrange the tables and benches in the ballroom for the Sunday dinner between services.

Renna managed to smile at them, but her gaze kept drifting upward to the curtains draped across the balcony. Shadrach told them Leith Torren had reported to him three days ago that the First Blade had left. Was the Third Blade in that balcony now, spying on the service as he had that Sunday last time he was here?

Across the room, Michelle Allen all but draped herself against Shadrach as he talked with the other young people in their congregation. Renna eyed him. Would he look for her? Was he hoping she'd join them? She stared for several minutes, but he never so much as glanced in her direction.

"Excuse me. Could you move?"

Renna jumped and stumbled backwards. One of the boys from their congregation hefted one end of a bench, his brother straining on the other side. "Sorry." She backed away, turned, and fled the ballroom.

She should help Aunt Mara in the kitchen. But her feet turned towards the back stairway before her mind caught up. Nothing lately was her decision. She'd been told she had to leave her home. She'd been told about the danger from King Respen. And now she was being told this Blade was trustworthy.

Perhaps she couldn't change the decision to leave her home, but she could make up her own mind about Leith Torren. And to do that, she needed to talk to him.

Her shoes clipped. The wood popped and creaked with her footfalls. When she reached the top, silence cloaked the upper gallery. The curtain blocked the light from the windows below, and the far end of the gallery disappeared into a gray dusk.

She stepped forward, her heart pulsing in her throat. If Leith Torren had lied, he could attack her now that she was vulnerable and he had his strength. Or the First Blade might still be here, waiting for another chance to torment her.

But she had to know the truth. If either of those things happened, she'd force herself to scream. Her scream would warn Uncle Abel and Lord Alistair that the Blade was tricking them. They'd keep Brandi safe.

"I know you're up here." She peered into the semi-darkness. "I need to talk to you."

She wrapped her arms around her stomach while she waited for the Blade.

A shadow moved along the wall. The sparks of sunlight filtering through the curtains glinted on the knives strapped across his chest and to his waist. He kept his hands at his sides, palms up. "Are you all right?"

"No." She blinked at the curtains instead of his

green eyes. "I've been stalked by the First Blade. King Respen is planning to kill me. I'm being forced to leave my home, and I don't even get a say about it. I'm not all right. I haven't been all right since the night you helped kill my parents."

The words strengthened her spine. She was tired of being helpless, of not making her own choices. But being here, facing him and speaking her mind instead of swallowing the bitterness of words she didn't dare say, felt better than holding a dagger to his chest.

"I'm sorry." His voice cracked on the last word. "You probably don't believe me, but it is the truth."

She peeked up at him. He hadn't moved, his eyes peering at her through a fringe of black hair. If he didn't look so vulnerable, she might've found more words to stab at him.

Instead, she leaned against the wall, slid to the floor, and hugged her knees. She waited for fear to prickle along her skin as it had when she'd been alone with the First Blade. But it didn't.

She squared her shoulders and met his gaze. "Why didn't the First Blade kill me?"

He slid to the ground several feet away. "You and Brandi are the First Blade's only failure. He's become obsessed with the idea of killing you. Since he can't kill you until King Respen gives the order, he's going to torment you instead. I'm sorry I couldn't stop him."

She hugged her knees tighter. "And when King Respen does give the order?"

The Blade rubbed a hand along one of his knives. "I'll do my best, but I can't face the First Blade alone. He's better than me."

Voices babbled in the ballroom below. Had anyone

noticed she was missing? Had Shadrach noticed? Would he come looking for her? Would Shadrach be able to protect her from the First Blade? "Did you really hide what you learned from King Respen?"

"Yes." The Blade rubbed at a scuff on his boot. "Seeing your courage made me want to be brave too."

"I'm not brave." She rested her chin on her arms. If she were brave, she'd go up to Shadrach and talk to him instead of cowering up here. If she had courage, she wouldn't be so helpless all the time. He didn't know her, not really, or he'd know he was wrong.

"You saved me when it would've been easier to let me die. You hid me when it would've been safer to let the sheriff kill me." A hint of a smile creased his mouth and puckered into dimples in his slim cheeks. "You're here confronting a Blade when it would've been wiser to remain in the ballroom."

She flapped a hand at him. "You're not going to hurt me. If you were, you'd have done it long before now."

He wasn't going to hurt her. She still didn't trust him, but he was safe in a way the First Blade wasn't. She wasn't sure what trick he was playing, but he wasn't going to hurt her just for the enjoyment of it.

"Don't discount your type of bravery." He shrugged, his eyes swerving everywhere but at her. "It takes more courage to help someone who doesn't deserve it than someone who does."

His words settled into her like water filling cracks in sunbaked ground. Was she brave? Even a little bit?

Footsteps tromped on the stairs. Renna jumped and glanced at the Blade. He scrambled to his feet, cocked his head, and relaxed.

Brandi hopped up the last few stairs and dashed

across the gallery. "Leith!"

The Blade barely had time to brace himself before Brandi plowed into him. He smiled, the dimples in his cheeks deepening, as he hugged her.

Renna found herself unable to tear her gaze away. With his green eyes twinkling, he didn't look like a Blade. He looked like...a boy.

More footsteps pounded the stairs. Shadrach stepped into the gallery, balancing a tray heaped with plates and steaming dishes.

Brandi spun on her heels. Her smirk crinkled her nose. "See. I told you they'd be up here."

Shadrach set the tray on the ground in front of Renna. "Good thing we brought enough food for four."

Brandi flopped to the floor across from Renna while Shadrach folded his long legs and sat to Renna's left between her and Brandi.

Renna stared at the open spot next to her. Brandi patted the floor. "Come on. Sit. I'm hungry."

The Third Blade tiptoed away from the wall and eased to the floor. This close to him, she could see the scattered bristles on his chin. The tips of his black hair brushed his tanned forehead. Shafts of light winked on the hilts of the knives strapped to his chest.

She waited for fear to prickle along her skin or dance down her spine. Her stomach growled. Her scalp itched.

Was he right? Did she have a shred of courage buried deep down? She toyed with her skirt and peeked at him. "Thanks...Leith."

A smile twitched his mouth as he ducked his head. Were his ears turning red? She couldn't tell in the half-light, but she smiled too. Saying his name was better than a dagger or angry words.

27

Leith leaned against a tree near the edge of the Spires Canyon. Behind him, Blizzard lipped at a tuft of grass. An owl's harrooo shivered through the darkness.

A large animal rustled the prairie grass coming towards him. Blizzard huffed a breath and cropped at the grass once again.

Dark shapes moved closer, but Leith didn't reach for his knives. The starlight gleamed against the prairie enough for Leith to make out Shad's face as he halted a few feet away, his horse lowering its head to graze. "I was just getting used to sleeping in a real bed."

Leith grabbed Blizzard's reins and elbowed Shad. "Four days and the lord's son goes soft."

Shad slugged Leith's shoulder. "And the Blade is jealous. Now let's set up camp and get some sleep. My father is planning to leave early."

Leith turned towards the town instead of the path into the canyon. "Before we set up camp, there's someone I need to talk to in Stetterly. I'd like you to come with me."

"To keep my father from misunderstanding?"

"And to prevent the man from killing me."

Leith swung onto Blizzard. They rode in silence across the stretch of prairie between the manor and the village. At the edge of town, Leith ground-hitched Blizzard. Shad also dropped his horse's reins.

Together, they slipped into the dark alleys between the buildings. Reaching a house near the edge of town, Leith's stomach tensed when he noticed a candle still shone in the window. "Could you knock? He won't step outside if he sees me."

Shad crossed his arms, but his mouth twitched in a smirk. "Who am I going to be luring outside for your nefarious scheme?"

"He's the town sheriff. Last time I was in Stetterly, the Twenty-Second Blade kidnapped his daughter. The sheriff accidentally killed him and hunted me. I need to warn him."

"All right." Shad walked to the door and knocked. Leith pressed his back against the wall of the house. The shadows wrapped around him.

The door opened. The sheriff poked his head out. "Shadrach Alistair. Would you like to step inside?"

"It'd be better if you came outside."

The sheriff strode out and closed the door behind him. "What's this about?"

Leith moved between him and the door. "I need to talk to you."

The sheriff whirled. He pawed at the dagger stuffed in his belt. "You don't scare me, Blade."

Leith held up his palms. "I came to warn you."

The sheriff's gaze shifted from Shad, then back to Leith. "It seems I don't have a choice. I'm listening."

"When I returned to Nalgar Castle, I didn't tell King

Respen about Renna and her family. But, I had to tell the king something so I told him you hunted me."

Leith's fingers itched to touch his knives. He clasped his hands behind his back. "The king leapt to the conclusion that the Twenty-Second Blade's death was part of a Resistance plot."

The sheriff's face paled in the uncertain light. "He'll have me killed."

Leith nodded. Another family he'd endangered. "He has other plans at the moment, but he won't forget about you. If I were you, I'd leave Stetterly as soon as you and your family are able."

Shad stepped forward. "Make your way to Walden. We can get you and your family somewhere safe."

"Thank-you." The sheriff bobbed his head towards Shad. Turning back to Leith, he eyed him. "Why would you come back to warn me?"

Leith wasn't sure. Something had been unfinished until tonight.

The sheriff's eyes narrowed. Leith wiped his palms on his shirt. He couldn't hide his involvement with the Resistance, not after he'd shown up on the sheriff's doorstep with Shadrach Alistair at his side.

As long as King Respen or Vane never got a hold of the sheriff and interrogated him, Leith would be fine.

"Thank-you." The sheriff gave Leith a nod and retreated into his house.

Shad raised his eyebrows. "You could've told me it was a Resistance mission."

Leith shrugged. "Would you have believed me?"

"Of course." Shad clapped him on the back as they crept between the buildings. "Now let's set up camp and get some sleep before dawn."

28

Renna hugged Aunt Mara and breathed in the warm scent of bread and sage. A dove chittered overhead and landed on the peak of the manor roof where it woo-cooed long and low.

Aunt Mara stepped back first. "We'll visit Walden as soon as we can."

Brandi shoved between Renna and Aunt Mara. "Will you be there for my birthday? It's only a month away."

"We'll try." Aunt Mara hugged Brandi, but Renna spotted the tear slipping down Aunt Mara's face.

Renna rubbed her fingers along the leather of her divided skirt, an ache building in her chest and rising into her throat. Aunt Mara hadn't promised anything. She didn't know when—or if—she and Uncle Abel could come to Walden. Renna might never see them again.

She wrapped her arms around Uncle Abel's neck and pressed her face against his shoulder. He rubbed her back as he'd done when she'd cried for her parents' deaths.

How was Renna going to survive at Walden without Uncle Abel and Aunt Mara? She needed their solid shoulders, their unmovable faith. Her faith drifted as wispy as a cloud strung across a summer sky.

"You'll be all right." Uncle Abel patted her back.

No, she wouldn't. But she couldn't tell him that.

Courage. Leith thought she had it. He and Shad were out there somewhere, watching over her and Brandi every step of their journey. Maybe she wasn't brave, but could she at least pretend?

She straightened her spine and bit the inside of her cheek until the lump cleared from her throat. "We'll miss you both."

A guard led a brown horse over to her. He knelt, and she used his knee as a stepping block to reach the stirrup and heave herself into the saddle. She settled a large brimmed hat onto her head to protect her face from sunburn.

After snatching final hugs, Brandi scrambled onto her palomino. Her hat flopped against her back by its string, her hair already frizzing from her braids.

Lord Alistair led his horse over. He and Uncle Abel spoke in low voices for several minutes before Uncle Abel gave a half bow. Lord Alistair settled into his saddle and motioned to his guards. They swung onto their horses almost in unison and closed around Renna, Brandi, and Lord Alistair.

Lord Alistair nudged his horse forward, and Renna's horse eased into a walk without her urging. Brandi twisted in her saddle and waved her entire arm as if warding off a swarm of mosquitoes.

Aunt Mara's chin trembled as she waved back. Uncle Abel waved, but lines dug into his face around his mouth.

Renna forced herself to wave back. Aunt Mara, Uncle Abel, and Stetterly Manor's tan stones blurred. She blinked, and twin tears burned down her cheeks, curled around her chin, and dried on her neck.

Would she ever see Uncle Abel and Aunt Mara again? What would King Respen do to them once she and Brandi were out of his reach? At least the guards from Uster remained behind to ensure their safety.

Brandi trotted her horse next to Renna's. "I'm going to name this horse Sunshine."

"What? A name that actually matches its color?" Renna's voice cracked, but she managed to smile.

"It seems to fit him." Brandi patted the horse's neck, but Renna caught the wet gleam in Brandi's eyes.

When they reached the edge of the Spires Canyon, Renna craned her neck and spotted the gray slate roof of the manor peeking above the rolling prairie hills, its four chimneys poking at the hard, blue sky.

She watched until her horse started down the trail into the canyon and the horizon swallowed the tips of the chimneys.

Leith read the pages of the Bible intently, so absorbed with the story unfolding in its pages that Blizzard could've run over him and he wouldn't have noticed.

His stomach churned. The main character, the Son of God called Jesus, knelt in a garden, pleading with His Father to be spared what was coming. The scene echoed deep in Leith's bones. He understood a father's silence.

A betrayal. An arrest. A trial. The pages shook. Leith took three tries to turn the page. Surely Jesus wouldn't die. He'd performed many miracles throughout the book. He had the power to stop what was happening to Him even if His Father wouldn't step in to save Him.

But He didn't. His death punched Leith's stomach. No miracles this time. He wasn't spared the way Daniel's three friends had been spared from the fiery furnace. He'd actually died. God had forsaken His own Son.

Someone nudged Leith's boot. Leith dropped the book and had his hand halfway to his dagger before he noticed Shad. "He died." Leith closed the book and stood. "He actually died."

"Who died?" Shad's eyebrows scrunched. His hand rested on his sword's hilt.

"Jesus. He was nailed to a cross and died." An ache ground into his chest. Why was this such a big deal? It was just a story. But, he'd expected happy endings from this book. Daniel and his friends survived some awful things. He'd thought Jesus would do the same.

Strangely, Shad smiled as if he was happy. "Yes. Yes, He did."

Shad walked over to his horse, leaving Leith stumped by his cryptic answer. Shaking himself, Leith headed for Blizzard, placed the Bible in his pack, tightened the girth strap, and swung into the saddle.

Shad led the way, following the trail that Lord Alistair's party had left in the pebbled ground. Leith directed Blizzard to follow him. They rode in silence for several minutes.

Leith gave up. He nudged Blizzard to move alongside Shad's horse. "If Jesus was the Son of God like He said He was, then why did He let Himself be killed like that?"

Shad leaned onto his saddlehorn. "The answer to that question is the basis of my faith. All of humanity is evil at its heart. This evil is like a debt to God that we can never hope to pay. All of our sins add to this evil."

Leith hunched his shoulders. He deserved death for each of the killings he'd done, yet he couldn't die several deaths to pay all the spilled blood even if his life could be considered worth the same as the lives he'd taken.

"But God chose to pay this debt for His people. He sent His Son Jesus to pay the full amount of our sins. Man could never pay it, but Jesus could. It's this punishment that He bore on the cross." Shad's eyes searched Leith's face.

Leith shuddered. He wanted no part of this God. No father should sacrifice his son for someone else's debt. "Jesus still ended up dead."

Shad grinned, as if he knew a great secret that Leith had yet to discover. "You didn't read the next chapter. Jesus didn't stay dead. He rose from the dead three days later. He returned to Heaven in glory."

"Really?" Leith couldn't help the hope that crept into his voice. The story didn't have a sad ending after all. Questions pressed on his tongue too firmly for him to ignore. "How do you become one of God's people?"

"God chose His people before He even created the world. The Holy Spirit works in their hearts and draws them to God and belief in Him." Shad sneaked a glance at Leith before turning his gaze back to his horse's ears.

Leith hunched further in his saddle. His knives weighed on his chest and waist. God wouldn't choose him. He was too evil. He'd done too many bad things, killed too many people. His own father hadn't wanted him when he'd done nothing wrong. God surely wouldn't want him after he'd done everything wrong.

Shad halted his horse and stared at Leith, his brown eyes somber. "God's choice isn't based on our actions. We're all completely evil. God chooses us because He decided in His good pleasure to love us. That love isn't dependent on our actions or our choices. God can choose, and has chosen, anybody, no matter their past actions." He opened his mouth but snapped it shut as if deciding he'd pushed Leith far enough.

The idea pounded at Leith's temples. The God he'd read about in the Bible was a majestic, glorious God. Why would the God with the power to create the world even take notice of despicable humans on this earth? What would love from a God like that be like? So huge, so enduring, so powerful that no mere human could ever comprehend it.

If he could trust it. Could he trust a God who'd forsake His own Son? Leith didn't want to trust, only to have that trust ripped away when God changed His mind. His father had taught him exactly how painful that could be.

Still, God wouldn't choose Leith. Leith had done too much. He'd been a slave to King Respen for too long. The most Leith could hope for was a slight mercy if he helped the ones that God did love. At the very least, Leith's conscience would rest a little easier.

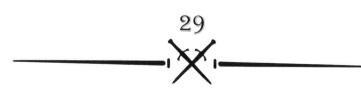

29

Renna had never been more thankful to see civilization when they crested the hill overlooking Walden. The two wings of the gray stone manor formed an L around a hedged garden while trees bordered the manor's yard.

To the north, the town sprawled along two roads, much larger than Stetterly's single line of wooden buildings. Would she still remember every path in the garden from the times she'd dashed through it when she'd visited Walden with her parents?

As their horses trotted down the hill, eager with the smell of home flaring their nostrils, she gritted her teeth and clung to the saddlehorn.

She ached down to her bones. Every muscle in her body was stiff while her hips were so bruised from sleeping on the ground that she could barely walk. She hated touching her scratchy hair while her dress and body stank. At least Shadrach followed at a distance with Leith, so neither of them was close enough to see how bad she looked.

Her horse stopped without her urging beside the others in front of Walden Manor. Brandi was off

Sunshine and unbuckling her saddlebags before Renna managed to ease down from her horse. She fumbled with the buckles on her saddlebags.

Brandi skipped to her side. "Here. I got it."

Renna stood back and allowed her little sister to unstrap the saddlebags and swing them over her slim shoulder. Renna should've reached for her saddlebags and carried them herself, but her arms hung at her sides, and she wasn't sure she could coax them to move.

Lord Alistair led the way up the bluestone stairs and through the double, oak doors into the grand entry hall. A broad staircase marched to the second level directly in front of them, a red carpet flowing down the center.

Over the staircase landing hung a large painting of King Brian Eirdon on his dappled horse driving back the Surrana raiders to found the country of Acktar.

When she was nine, she'd stood before that painting and asked her father about it. He'd placed his arm around her shoulder and told her the story, his deep voice echoing down the stairs like a drum calling for battle. *And King Brian drew his sword and nudged his steed into battle. The warriors found courage at the sight of their king riding before them...*

"Welcome!" Lady Alistair swept down the staircase. Her sleeves formed a series of puffs down her arms while her juniper green skirt billowed around her feet and trailed on the stairs behind her. A gold chain wove through hair the color of polished walnut. Her mouth curved into a smile too large on her delicate face.

She gave Brandi a hug. "Brandiline! You've grown so much." When she turned to Renna, her smile never faded, and she hugged Renna despite the dirt and smell. "We've missed both of you so much these last few years."

Lady Alistair stepped back as a young lady glided down the stairs. She wore a blue dress the color of twilight sky while her brown hair, several shades lighter than her mother's, flowed over her shoulders. Renna blinked. Was that Lydia? She'd been eleven the last time Renna had seen her, frizzy braids flying as they dashed through the garden to annoy Shadrach while he practiced his archery.

Lydia smiled and performed a poised curtsy. "Welcome to Walden, Renna."

Renna opened her mouth, but she couldn't force her mouth to form any words.

Another girl flounced down the stairs in a pink and lace dress with fluttering sleeves. Before she had a chance to reach the bottom, Brandi dropped the saddlebags onto the floor and flung herself into a hug. "Abigail!"

Abigail returned Brandi's hug. "It's so good to see you again, Brandi."

"Papa!" A flurry of brown hair and light blue dress dashed down the stairs, brushed past Renna and Brandi, crashed into Lord Alistair, and clung to his legs.

Lord Alistair tousled her hair. "And this is Esther. She was only a baby the last time you saw her."

Renna nodded and swallowed. Her family had visited Walden a few weeks after Esther had been born. Renna had cradled the baby close, watched her tiny mouth pucker and her delicate lashes brush against her cheek, and decided that babies were the most beautiful things in the world.

But that was before King Respen killed her family and stole the possibility that she'd ever marry and have a family of her own.

Another set of footsteps tromped in a halting rhythm. A twelve-year-old boy turned the corner and started down the final set of stairs. He eased down one stair at a time, his eyes glued to the pages of a leather-bound book he held in one hand. The other hand trailed down the banister, only leaving to turn a page.

Lady Alistair motioned towards him. "And this is Jeremiah." A stern tone sharpened the edge of her voice. "Jeremiah, welcome our guests."

The hand on the banister lifted in what might've been a wave.

Lady Alistair turned back to Renna. "Let's show you to your rooms. Abigail, would you like to show Brandiline her room?"

Brandi grabbed Abigail's arm and half-dragged her up the stairs. "Come on!"

Renna grimaced and picked up the saddlebags Brandi had discarded on the floor. Lydia swept to her side. "Let me help with those." She picked up one the saddlebags and draped it over her arm, holding it away from her skirt. "The servants will fetch the rest. "

Hugging her saddlebags to her stomach, Renna followed Lady Alistair up the stairs and to the right, Lydia at her side. Lady Alistair opened one of the doors along the corridor and stepped inside.

A rosy pink paint covered the walls and matched the rose pattern twined in the rugs on the floor. A cream dressing table and chair stood next to a matching wardrobe along one wall while a four-poster bed with gauze drapes and pink bedspread took up the other wall. Across the room, a window overlooked the garden.

"I thought you might like the Rose Room. You and Brandi always shared it when you visited." Lady

Alistair rearranged the pillows on the bed, eyed them for a moment, and turned away with a nod. "Brandiline is in the Violet Room next door."

The room her parents' had always had. Renna blinked and focused on the sound of Brandi's and Abigail's voices drifting through the doorway. Would Brandi remember? If not, Renna would have to tell her. Anything to keep their parents close.

"Hot baths are being prepared and will be sent up to your rooms. Supper will be served in the dining room in an hour." Lady Alistair put a hand on the latch. "If there's anything else you need, please let me know."

When Lady Alistair had slipped from the room, Renna dropped her saddlebags on the floor near the wall, her shoulder cramping from the weight. She'd unpack later.

Lydia placed Brandi's saddlebags beside Renna's. "We usually spend evenings in the parlor, if you'd like to come. You can read or work on a new dress or play Raiders, though don't play against Shad. He's pretty much unstoppable at that game."

"I remember. We used to play Raiders a lot." Renna found herself smiling. Perhaps they hadn't outgrown the friendship they'd had as children.

"I'd better let you get settled in." Lydia left the room with the same graceful stride as her mother.

Would Renna have learned to be as graceful and poised as Lydia if her mother had lived?

She snorted and shook her head. No, definitely not. Her mother had been like Brandi, moving through rooms with the grace of a tornado. When it rained, she dragged them all outside to jump in the mud puddles. Her father had been the serious one, warning about the danger of catching a cold or the discomfort of soaked clothes, right before their mother yanked him outside.

But Renna wasn't like either of them. They'd been as flinty as the rocky columns in the Sheered Rock Hills the night they'd been killed. All Renna ever did was run and hide. She'd never have the courage to turn back and sacrifice herself, no matter what Leith thought.

She shuddered and stared out the window looking south towards Stetterly Manor. Were Uncle Abel and Aunt Mara putting themselves in danger, like her mother and father had, to buy Renna and Brandi more time to escape?

When her bath arrived, Renna scrubbed the prairie dust from her hair and changed into the mostly clean dress she'd stuffed in her saddlebags. The skirt remained crinkled, but she didn't have time to press the wrinkles out before supper.

At supper, she sat between Lydia and Lady Alistair. She squirmed. Her wrinkled, cotton dress stuck out between their silks and flounces.

Lydia leaned closer. "Tomorrow you can raid my wardrobe. We're close enough to the same size. The bodice on my dresses might be a little big, but I think we can lace them tight enough to fit you."

"Thanks." Renna lowered her eyes to the beef roast on her plate. Her cheeks heated. Lydia had noticed the state of her dress. At least Shadrach hadn't shown up for supper so he wouldn't see her like this.

As soon as supper finished, Lord Alistair excused himself from the room. Lydia stood next to Renna's chair. "Would you like to join us in the parlor?"

Renna squeezed her gritty eyes shut. Slide under the pink covers and rest her head on the fluffy pillow or stay awake and try to be sociable? She opened her eyes and caught sight of Lydia's hands twisting in front of her and the eager expression tightening her eyes. "For a little while. Can I borrow a book to read?"

"Sure. They're in Father's study."

Renna used the table to drag herself to her feet. "I know where it is. I'll join you in the parlor in a minute."

While Lydia, Lady Alistair, Brandi, and the rest of the family crossed the hall to the parlor, Renna tiptoed through the entry and into the corridor on the other side. Her shoes sank into the green rugs while candles in wall sconces lit the corridor. Halting, she knocked on one of the paneled doors.

When it opened a few inches, Renna caught her breath. Shadrach peeked his head through, his hair still dusty, several days of scruff covering his chin and cheeks.

She scrubbed her hands along her skirt. "Shadrach. I…I hadn't…realized you were back. You're all right?"

Renna bit her tongue. Of course he was all right. He was standing right in front of her. She sounded as silly as she had when she'd been thirteen and so infatuated with him that her tongue spoke before her brain could catch up. She backed away from the door. "I just wanted a book, but I'll come back later."

"No, come on and pick a book. It's fine." Shadrach stepped aside and opened the door wide enough for her to step through. As soon as she was inside, he closed the door behind her.

She halted. Leith sat in one of the chairs in front of Lord Alistair's desk. He jumped to his feet, his green eyes widening. Lord Alistair slid to his feet and nodded at her. "Feel free to pick out any book you like."

"Thanks." She darted to the bookshelf. Silence

pressed into the corners of the room and tightened along her muscles. Her back prickled with three pairs of eyes watching her. Of all nights to skip ironing her dress. Did they have to stare?

She grabbed a book off the shelf, a book of legends she'd liked as a child. Bobbing a curtsy at Lord Alistair, she rushed to the door. "Thank you."

She whipped the door open, whirled through, and clicked it shut behind her. She leaned against it, her heart thudding like a fist in her chest. Now they all must think her a ninny.

As she hurried back to the parlor, she couldn't decide what was worse: Shadrach Alistair's raised eyebrows or Leith Torren's green eyes.

30

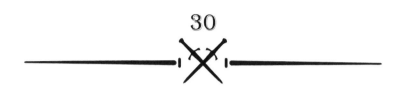

Leith watched Renna dash from the room. He'd scared her. He hadn't meant to. Then again, what did he expect? That their talk in the gallery had made her like him? He was a Blade. The blood of her parents and cousin stained his hands. She wouldn't forgive him any more than her God would.

"Now, where were we?"

Leith wrested his gaze from the door. Lord Alistair had already regained his seat behind his desk. Would he listen to Shad and trust Leith? They only had two weeks until Leith had to return to Nalgar Castle. He had no more time to waste.

"You were telling me how you convinced the First Blade to return to Nalgar Castle."

Leith shrugged. "He left, and I waited a couple of days before I sneaked into Stetterly and told Shad it was safe. You know the rest."

Lord Alistair steepled his fingers. "Let's say I trust you. You claim Blades are stationed at eighteen towns in preparation for mass assassinations. What should I do with your information?"

"Fight back." Leith rubbed the hilt of one of his knives with his thumb. Was the Resistance ready to fight back against King Respen? *The Leader is almost ready.* Was Lord Alistair the Leader? Or someone else? Leith didn't dare ask.

Shad rested a hand on the hilt of his sword. "We should send messengers to warn them."

Leith shook his head. "King Respen has one of your messages. I have no way of knowing if he's figured out your code. If you send out messengers, the Blades will intercept several of them and King Respen would figure out that I gave information to you."

Leith shuddered, picturing Zed's body writhing against the chains as the Fourth Blade slit his throat. One mistake was all it would take for Leith's blood to join Zed's.

Lord Alistair tapped his chin. "We could have the riders memorize verbal messages."

"The Blades would torture them for information. One would crack, and we'd have the same problem."

Shad paced two strides before spinning on his heels. "We have to warn them somehow. We can't let Respen kill them just because we can't safely warn them. Is there anyway a messenger can get through?"

"If a messenger were carrying an innocent message, something the Blade could slip into camp and read one night and find nothing suspicious, he might get through." Leith gripped the edge of the leather seat.

"An invitation." Shad's pacing quickened. "We invite all of the nobles here and warn them in person."

"Wouldn't that alarm Respen and cause him to kill everyone sooner? Perhaps while they're travelling and vulnerable?" Lord Alistair leaned his elbows on his desk.

"Not if no one knows the invitations are for a big gathering. We send out each invitation like it's a personal invite to spend a couple of days at Walden. The nobles—and the Blades—won't know it's a large gathering until everyone's here." Shad turned to Leith. "It'll work, won't it?"

Leith cocked his head and grinned. So Shad had been paying attention. "It might. Even if a few Blades take the time to report to King Respen and the First Blade, it might not rouse too much suspicion. But how do I explain why I didn't notice anything?"

Lord Alistair's beard bobbed as a grin spread across his face. "Lydia turns sixteen in four weeks. Why shouldn't I host a gathering to celebrate my eldest daughter's birthday? It would only be natural, given the significance of a sixteenth birthday, for me to host such a party."

What was so special about a sixteenth birthday? Leith glanced between Lord Alistair and Shad.

Shad crossed his arms. "Means she's old enough to be courted. Respen will know that and won't think it's odd if Father invites a bunch of nobles with sons and daughters around Lydia's age to a party. Celebrations like that used to be common a few years ago."

"I see." Leith churned the scenario in his head. If the Blades didn't think anything wrong until they arrived here, there wouldn't be time for them to ride back to Nalgar Castle to ask for instructions. The Blades didn't dare take action on their own, so they'd all simply observe the nobles until told otherwise. If no one reported to Vane as they passed the castle, Vane might not even show up. "I think it could work."

"Once the Blades realize this is a big gathering,

THE BLADES OF ACKTAR

won't Respen order all the nobles killed on their journey home?" Shad stopped pacing and rested his hand on his sword's hilt.

"As Blades, we have three rules. Never fail. Never disobey orders. And never be late for a Meeting of the Blades." Leith ran his finger over one of the knives strapped to his chest.

He'd broken two of them in the last few months, but even he didn't dare break the third. "The next Meeting is two weeks from this coming Sunday. If you have the celebration two evenings before, the Blades will have no choice but to return to Nalgar Castle instead of following the nobles."

Lord Alistair stroked his beard for several minutes. "What do we do if something does go wrong? What if a Blade does report to Respen, and he gives the order to assassinate us while we're all together?"

"I don't think he will. Even if he suspects it's a Resistance meeting—which he will if a Blade reports to him—he can't send the Blades to kill everybody during the celebration. Too many people and guards gathered in one place. Too many things to go wrong."

Leith traced the length of his knife's leather sheath. "But he will use the meeting to his advantage. When he gives the assassination order, he'll claim you were plotting rebellion and he's justified in killing all of you. After all, he won't want the remaining nobles getting restless. Not all of them are active supporters."

Leith tapped his toes against the pine green rugs covering the stone floor. Lord Alistair placed a lot of confidence in Leith's judgment of the king's character. What if he was wrong about King Respen?

His shoulders slumped. This was the best plan they

had. If they did nothing, everyone would die anyway. They had nothing to lose, and over twenty lives and his freedom to gain.

"Now that we have a cover story for the meeting, we need a cover story for you." Lord Alistair cocked his head. "You'll need an excuse in case a Blade ever does catch you talking to me or Shad. It won't stop all the suspicion, but it could buy you time."

Shad grinned so broadly his cheeks and eyebrows squinched his eyes to slits. "The back vegetable garden still needs to be plowed and planted."

"You want me to plant a garden?" Were they crazy?

"With so many people fleeing to Walden for safety, no one will notice an extra farmer. And if any of the Blades ask, you can tell them you chose the disguise to get close to the manor to spy better." Shad scratched the scruff on his chin.

Leith hunched in his chair. Shad made way too much sense.

"It really would be an ingenious way to spy on us. You'd have the run of the town and the servants' quarters of the manor. You can wander into places you aren't supposed to without getting into too much trouble. And you can eavesdrop on all sorts of conversations. Actually, I really hope none of the other Blades have tried this."

Leith shrugged. "Most of them would rather hide in the grass all day watching than get their hands dirty working in a garden. Besides, none of us has any idea how to plow or plant."

Lord Alistair leaned back in his chair. "I like it. Keeps you where we can watch you."

Shad's jaw shook as he tried to hold a fake serious

expression. "So what do you say? Can a Blade handle learning how to plow?"

Leith sagged against the back of his chair. He sensed the next two weeks were going to make six days of hard riding look like a pleasure trip. "I can handle a plow if a lord's son can handle learning to knife fight."

"Deal." If anything, Shad's grin grew wider.

Of course it would. Leith grimaced. Shad was getting the better end of that bargain.

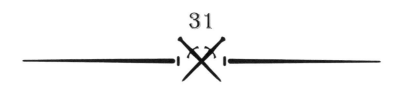

31

Leith gritted his teeth as he pushed the plow blade into the ground. The ground was barely thawed from the long winter, the dirt hard as the rocky crags of the Sheered Rock Hills. Each jolt sent shocks up his arms into his shoulders.

Although the sun had barely inched above the horizon, sweat soaked the homespun shirt and trousers he'd been given. As he turned to make the next furrow, he grimaced. His furrow was as crooked as the Ondieda River splashing its way down the mountains.

"Not easy, is it?" Shad smirked as he leaned against the manor wall.

Leith scowled at him. "How would you know? Have you ever done it?"

"Actually, yes." Shad laced his hands behind his head and closed his eyes. "Father assigned me the job when I turned twelve. Told me it'd build the muscles I needed to train with a sword. This probably would've been Jeremiah's job this summer if you hadn't volunteered."

Great for Shad's little brother. Not so great for

Leith. He maneuvered the mule into the next furrow. He could tough this out. Under Respen's training, he'd spent days without food, learned to tolerate cold and heat, and trained with his knives for hours each day. He could handle this.

After a few hours, Leith's arms and legs shook with the strain of plowing. His back ached, and blisters formed on his palms.

Shad left to drill the guardsmen, but he returned at noon, stepped over the furrows, and slapped Leith's back. "Time to break for lunch."

Leith unhitched the mule and led it back to the stable, where a stablehand took over. Leith returned to the back of the manor to find Shad leaning against a tree, bread and water spread out beside him.

Leith collapsed next to him. He picked up a glass and drained the water in two gulps. When he reached for a piece of bread, Shad raised his eyebrows.

Leith froze. In his hunger he'd forgotten the routine they'd developed on the trail. Leith clasped his hands and closed his eyes. He listened while Shad offered a quick prayer. When Shad was finished, Leith grabbed the piece of bread and dug in. He polished off the slice in a few bites.

Shad finished his lunch and glanced at the sky. "Better get back to work. That plot needs to be plowed by nightfall."

Leith gave himself the luxury of a groan as he pushed himself to his feet.

Renna sat on the end of Lydia's bed. Lydia whipped open the door to her wardrobe, sleeves and skirts bursting out once unconfined. "I have a couple that should work well for you. Here, this pink one will be perfect. It was always too light on me." She tugged a pink cotton dress draped with lace along the bodice and sleeves. She held it out to Renna.

Taking it, Renna held it against herself. "Thank you so much for letting me borrow some of your dresses."

"No problem. Really. I have way too many." Lydia pulled several more dresses from her wardrobe and piled them on the bed. She drew out one last dress, a deep blue velvet edged in gold trim. The ends of the trailing sleeves flowed in ripples. "And you can wear this one at my party."

A lump tightened Renna's throat. She'd never had a sixteenth birthday celebration. She didn't have a father to present her to the other nobles.

A spark heated her chest, but she doused it quickly. It wasn't Lydia's fault. Lydia had every right to be excited. "It's beautiful."

"Let's see if they fit." Lydia helped her into the pink dress. As she'd guessed the bodice hung on Renna's slim body. Tightening the bodice strings helped. Not a perfect fit, but Renna wasn't going to complain about the soft fabric swishing against her skin.

Lydia dressed in a rich, green dress and reached for her jewelry box. Pulling out a simple chain with a silver cross dangling from it, Lydia clasped it around her neck. Her fingers lingered on the cross. "Your mother gave me this necklace for my tenth birthday. She had a way of always giving the right gift."

Renna's mother had given her a similar necklace on her tenth birthday. A lump filled her throat. Brandi didn't have one. She'd been nine when her parents died.

Lydia perched on the bed next to Renna. "I miss your

parents too. Your family was here so often and our fathers were so close…losing your parents was like losing an aunt and uncle."

Renna stared at her hands in her lap. How could she ever measure up to someone like her mother? Her mother gave so fearlessly to everybody.

"My father doesn't laugh the way he used to. I remember when your family would visit, and my father wouldn't stop grinning or laughing the entire time." Lydia's sigh wafted air across Renna's fingertips. "I miss it."

"Me too." Renna widened her eyes to stop the gathering tears. An ache built in her chest, but she couldn't give in to it now.

Lydia straightened her back, her shoulder bumping into Renna. "I just thought you should know that I wish your parents were here to celebrate with us too."

"Thanks." Renna smiled at Lydia. Perhaps Lydia hadn't changed that much after all. So many years had passed since Renna had had a friend, but maybe it wasn't too late to remember how a friendship worked.

And maybe, while she was at it, she'd be able to recapture a hint of the laughter they'd once had in this manor. Standing, she held a hand out to Lydia. "Come on. We're supposed to be helping your mother plan this celebration."

They hurried down the stairs and headed for the parlor. Through the open door, Renna spotted a pile of ribbons and lace spilling from the end table, Brandi chatting with Abigail more than sorting, and Lady Alistair shuffling through a stack of thick paper.

Lord Alistair exited the room, smiled at Lydia, and touched Renna's arm. "Rennelda, could I speak with you for a moment?"

Lydia brushed past her father into the parlor. Renna clenched her fingers in her skirts. What would Lord Alistair have to talk to her about?

He closed the parlor door and glanced around as if checking they were alone.

When he faced her, a frown dragged at his beard. "As I mentioned in Stetterly, Leith Torren has informed me that he believes Respen is planning a major strike against any of the nobles he thinks might be a part of the Resistance."

Renna focused on the candelabra holding a single candlestick on the wall next to the parlor door. The flame pulsed and swayed in the wispy drafts trailing through the corridor. What other danger did Lord Alistair have to tell her about now?

"When the other nobles arrive here for Lydia's celebration, I'm going to call a meeting after the supper to warn them about the threat." Lord Alistair's brown eyes demanded her attention. "As Lady Faythe, I'm going to ask you to attend."

Renna clenched her fists in the soft, pink fabric of her skirt. Lady Faythe was her mother's title. Renna had never claimed it, even though it was her inheritance.

It wouldn't be fully hers until her eighteenth birthday in a few months, but Lord Alistair was asking her to claim it now, to take her place among the other nobles. Could she do it? Stop hiding and start leading? Like her mother and father had?

"What do you want me to do?" Her voice scratched through her throat.

"All I'm asking is that you come. You won't have to say anything. Just be there and show where Stetterly stands."

She nodded, slipped past Lord Alistair, and hurried down the corridor. She didn't stop until she burst out the door to the back garden.

Letting her feet carry her along the paths she'd run years ago, she collapsed on the stone bench facing the tiered fountain in the center of the brown beds waiting the green of summer. The fountain remained silent and empty of water.

Lady Faythe. Could she wear her mother's title? Could she take her father's place in Lord Alistair's gathering?

She closed her eyes and tipped her face towards the sun hanging in the southwestern sky. Songbirds chittered in the hedge surrounding the garden.

Somewhere close by, a mule or donkey scraped a bray. The clatter of the town drifted over the manor, deepened with the rumble of the sawmill and flourmill beyond the town along the Ondieda River.

If not for her mother's birth as princess of Acktar, Lord Alistair wouldn't even bother with her. While all the lords of Acktar had equal rank, the real power was land and commerce. Stetterly had a little land and some timber, but nothing compared to towns like Walden, set against the vastness of the Sheered Rock Hills.

The mule brayed again. It sounded like it was going to burst through the hedge. Renna slid to her feet and eased around the shrubs. Crossing under an arched trellis, she halted in front of a patch of ground by the kitchen door.

Half of the patch curled in jagged furrows. In the middle, Leith tugged on the mule's halter. The mule brayed and dug its hooves in deeper, refusing to plow another step.

Leith had his back to her, his homespun shirt damp between his shoulder blades. His black hair stuck to the back of his neck. He'd rolled his sleeves up to his elbows, and sinewy muscles flexed in his forearms.

Gripping her skirt, she forced herself to step closer. "I think you need Brandi's help. That mule doesn't look like it's going to move any time soon."

He dropped the mule's halter and tugged on his right sleeve, as if checking to make sure the fabric covered his marks.

When he glanced up, his face relaxed, though his stance remained wary. "Brandi's help would be appreciated. If anyone could get this mule to move, she could."

The kitchen door opened, and Shadrach strode towards the garden, a pitcher in one hand, two pewter cups dangling by their handles in the other. His brown eyes shot to Renna, and he grinned. "What brings you out here? Shouldn't you be with Mother and the girls filling out invitations?"

"I..." She should say something. Brandi would've come up with something funny, like how she'd come to see who was torturing that mule over here, but Renna couldn't force her mouth to move.

Both Leith and Shadrach gaped at her, and the longer they stared, the hotter her neck and face burned. "You have a Blade plowing your garden."

Leith stiffened and swayed onto his heels. His eyes dropped to his boots.

Shadrach's grin didn't change. He nudged Leith with his elbow. "And you enjoy it so much, don't you?"

"Sure." Leith's gaze swiveled back to the mule as if

facing the stubborn animal was better than facing her. Renna fisted her fingers. She'd said the wrong thing. Should she apologize? She wasn't exactly sure how she'd offended him. Should she pretend she didn't notice his discomfort? Why did she always have to say such mindless things when Shadrach and Leith were around?

"What will you plant?"

"Corn, beans, potatoes. Lei—" Shadrach paused mid-word and cocked his head. "We never did come up with a name to go with your cover story."

"Daniel. I can be Daniel." Leith's eyes flicked towards her before returning to the mule.

"All right. Daniel." Shadrach waved towards Leith with the pewter cups. "Lady Rennelda, this is Daniel, our new gardener from…Where do you want to be from?" He cocked his head towards Leith.

"Blathe." Leith nudged a clump of dirt with his boot. The clump crumbled into a pile. "I was born in Blathe."

Renna focused on that pile of dirt by Leith's boot. What would've it been like growing up as Lord Respen Felix's servant? It couldn't have been pleasant.

"This is Daniel of Blathe. Obviously, his skills don't lie in plowing, but he learns fast." Renna glanced up as Shadrach jabbed at her with the pitcher. Water splashed over the rim and fell onto the grass at the edge of the plowed area. "Daniel, this is Lady Rennelda Faythe of Stetterly. She and her sister are visiting us for a while."

Leith—alias Daniel—gave her a stiff bow. "Lady Rennelda."

"Daniel." Even though it wasn't necessary, she curtsied, as if she were meeting a nobleman instead of a peasant.

When she straightened, she met Leith's gaze. The breeze toyed with his long, dark hair. His green eyes tossed her stomach. Her mouth got that urge to spout something mindless, but this time she snapped her teeth shut before she made a fool of herself.

A rustling from the flower garden behind her grabbed her attention. She whirled as Brandi waltzed under the trellis. "There you are, Renna. Lady Alistair sent me to find you." She halted and a grin burst across her face. "L—"

Renna caught her elbow. "Daniel. His name is Daniel while he's here."

"Oh, I see." Brandi's eyes got that knowing twinkle, and Renna let her go. More than likely, her sister did see what was going on much clearer than Renna did.

A smile returned the dimples to Leith's face. "Actually, your sister was just telling me I should ask you to help me with a little problem I'm having with that mule." He pointed a finger at it. "It won't move."

"You just have to ask it nicely." Brandi skipped over the furrows to the mule. Running her fingers over its nose, she crooned to it.

Shadrach poured water into the pewter cups he still held and handed one to Leith. They both turned to watch Brandi as she coaxed the mule to take a step, then another.

Renna had been forgotten. Instead of standing around awkwardly, she gathered her skirts and backed toward the flower garden. She needed to return to the parlor before Lady Alistair worried about both her and Brandi.

As she tiptoed under the trellis into the flower garden, she glanced back one last time. Brandi had the mule moving. Shadrach walked away, carrying the empty pitcher and pewter cups back to the kitchen.

As he looped the reins around his back and gripped the handles of the plow once again, Leith looked up. For a moment, his eyes met hers. Her breath caught. Why couldn't she look away?

He looked away first, snapped the reins, and the mule threw itself against the harness. After stumbling against the trellis, Renna whirled and dashed through the flower garden without another backwards glance.

32

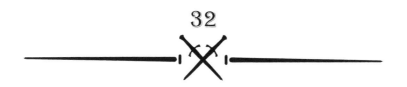

After supper in a corner of the servants' quarters, Shad snagged Leith and led him down the corridor and up a back stairway. Leith's legs wobbled as they reached the landing.

Why had he made the deal to train Shad after plowing? He barely had the strength to stand, much less spar with Shad. But he'd made a deal, and he'd stick by it. Besides, Shad needed to know how to fight a Blade. It could save his life.

Leith tottered in Shad's footsteps down the corridor. Near the grand staircase, Shad opened a door and waved Leith inside.

Leith stepped past him into the room. A four-poster bed dominated one wall, its oak posts as thick as the beams supporting the ceiling. A mountain lion skin covered the floor while a rack along the wall held arrows in various lengths and stages of completion.

Shad closed and locked the door behind him. "This is my room. We'll be safe to practice here without anyone asking questions."

They'd have to roll up the rug so they didn't damage

it with their scuffling, but the room had the open space they needed and no windows where they could be observed. "What's below us?"

"The dining room. No one's in there now that supper is done and cleared." Shad knelt and rapped the floor with his knuckles. "This floor is solid oak, tightly fitted in two layers to prevent sagging and bouncing. No one can hear us talk, and our fighting won't be noticeable besides a thump or two."

Leith helped Shad roll the animal skin and place it on the bed. Shad drew the bundle of Leith's weapons from under the bed and handed them to him.

He fingered his weapons. After so many years, it was strange how quickly he grew used to being weaponless.

He pulled a knife from its sheath. "A number of the Blades are good at throwing knives. I'm not, and most aren't. It's a skill that takes years to master, and most of us had better things to do than chuck knives."

Shad nodded, but his face and shoulders drooped. "So you aren't going to teach me how to throw knives?"

"No. But you'll need to watch for it. Especially if the First, Second, Fifth, or Seventh Blades happen to be around. You'll need to alert those nobles and their guards to be extra careful."

"What do you look for?"

"Keep an eye on the hands, the wrists. Here's how I'd grip the knife if I intend to fight with it." Leith gripped the knife firmly around the hilt. He switched his grip so that he pinched the knife between two fingers. "Now I'm about to throw it. Depending on the distance, the place I'm holding might change, but it'll always be pinched between my fingers instead of gripped in a fist."

Shad studied his grip, eyes narrowing. "I take it they can switch between fighting and throwing so fast, I'd probably be dead before I spotted the difference."

"Something like that." Leith changed his grip back to a fighting stance. "They'll only try to throw a knife if they have some distance. Get in close, and they'll opt for fighting. Your best chance, if they're standing back and appear to be toying with their knife, is to have your bow ready and shoot them. But don't take too long. The minute they see an arrow on your string, they'll throw."

Shad touched the arrows in his quiver. "I can do that."

False confidence, but Leith didn't correct him. Leith handed half his knives to Shad and strapped on the rest.

Drawing a knife, he balanced on the balls of his feet. The blisters on his heels and toes burned. His calves cramped. He faced Shad. "I'm going to come at you. Try to block my thrust."

Shad drew one of the knives. "Aren't we going to train with poles or something to start?"

You'll learn quick or you die. Respen had said as he pressed a knife into Leith's hand for the first time. *I've no time to train weaklings.*

Leith lifted a shoulder in a shrug. "This is how a Blade trains. Don't worry. I won't stab you."

Shad's face remained tense as he bent his knees, knife in front of him like he was holding a sword.

Leith lunged forward, arm tucked close to his body, the knife ready to thrust into Shad's stomach. Shad tried to swipe away the knife as if parrying with a sword, but the move extended his arm too far from his body.

Leith side-stepped, pinned Shad's arm behind his back, and pressed the tip of his knife against Shad's stomach above his sword belt.

Shad glanced down at the knife, then up at Leith. His jaw set. All traces of humor fled his brown eyes. "If I'd been facing any Blade but you, I'd be dead. That took what, two seconds?"

Leith stepped back. He'd made his point. "That's the first move a Blade's going to do. For most swordsmen, it works just as it did with you. If you can live past that first move, you might have a chance of fighting the Blade off. Maybe. You've at least bought yourself a few more seconds for help to come."

"That's my best option? Delay until help arrives?"

"Yes." Leith met Shad's gaze. "Respen is going to send First Blade Harrison Vane here to kill Renna and Brandi. Even I can't face the First Blade alone."

"Then we'll face him together." Shad grinned and returned to his fighting stance. "He won't stand a chance against the two of us."

Leith hoped so. Shad was becoming a friend, and Leith didn't want to see him killed in the fight that was coming.

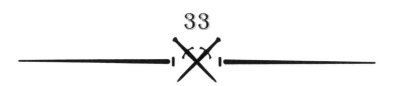

33

Leith gritted his teeth as the blisters on his hands popped against the rough wood of the hoe. He chopped at the clumps of dirt, softening it into fluffy mounds. Pausing, he rubbed at the taut muscles cramping his neck and shoulders.

The kitchen door creaked open. Shadrach balanced a tray on one hand. Sweat marked his shirt under his arms and across his chest.

Leith grasped the hoe and trudged from the garden. Propping the tool against the manor, he collapsed to the ground. "How did training go?"

Shad flopped to the ground next to him, somehow keeping the tray steady. "Well enough. The men were confused when I showed them the defensive moves you showed me, but some got the idea eventually."

"Good." Leith reached for a cup, filled it with water, and drained it in a few gulps. He polished off his hunk of bread and cheese in a few bites.

After popping his last bite in his mouth, Shad turned his empty glass over in his hands. "So, do you think Renna likes me?"

Leith's stomach dropped. Did Shad like Renna? "Uh, no. I don't think so. You're asking me for girl advice? I'm a Blade. I don't talk to girls." He rested his forearms on his knees, tightness moving from his throat to his chest. "Why do you ask?"

"Well, Jolene Lorraine is coming with her mother, and I...like her. But I happen to know Renna used to like me back when we were kids." Shad scratched his toe in the dirt. "I don't want to hurt Renna. Should I tell her about Jolene?"

The tension in Leith's chest vanished. "Probably."

"Would you?" Shad raised his eyebrows.

Leith leaned his head against the warm stones of the manor. The sun soaked into his shirt. "Not a chance."

Shad scowled and elbowed him. Leith scrambled to his feet and grabbed the hoe. "I need to get back to work." He hurried to the garden before Shad came up with any more questions involving girls.

In the heat of afternoon, the chatter of party plans drove Renna from the parlor. Now that she knew the truth about Lydia's celebration, she couldn't hold on to her excitement.

Gathering her courage, she fetched two glasses, filled a pitcher with water, and tiptoed through the kitchen and out the back door.

As she stepped outside, Leith swiped his sleeve across his forehead. His eyes caught on her, and he paused in his work. Shadrach strolled over to her.

"I brought water." Her face flushed. Of course she'd spout the obvious. She held up the glasses and pitcher to hide her burning face. She filled a glass and handed it to Shad. "Here."

"Thanks." Shad gulped down the water. Renna tried to keep her attention on Shadrach, but her eyes strayed to Leith. He'd returned to his work, chopping the clods of dirt.

Drawing her shoulders straight, she tiptoed towards the garden. The smell of rich, wet earth wrapped around her. Her heart pounded. "Would you like some water?"

Leith straightened and rubbed at his lower back. His hands left dark smudges on his shirt. As he strode toward her, she caught a whiff of sweat and dirt. With trembling fingers, she poured water into the glass and held it out to him.

His dirt-covered fingers closed around the glass and brushed her fingers. She jumped, but she managed to stop herself before she snatched her fingers away.

He drained the glass in a few swallows, and she refilled it without asking. When he'd finished his second glass, he handed it back to her. "Thanks."

She tucked a strand of hair behind her ear. She should say something, but her jaw locked. A chorus of starlings jabbered as they swooped overhead, the thrum of a thousand wings vibrating the air. A cool breeze ruffled Leith's hair and trickled down Renna's neck. "How did you like church yesterday?"

Leith's gaze swiveled from the ground to the manor roof behind her. "It was different sitting with everyone else."

She hadn't been surprised to see him there yesterday. She hadn't even been surprised when Brandi plunked onto the bench next to him and Renna had no choice but to sit on Brandi's other side. He'd had a Bible, though she could only guess where he'd gotten it, and Brandi had eagerly shared her songbook with him. After some whispered urging from Brandi, he'd even tried to sing along, though his voice faltered.

Was it possible he was sincere?

"I'm glad you were there." Her thoughts and words jumbled in her head. She needed to get out of there before she said something stupid.

Backing away, she turned and came within inches of running into Shadrach. "Sorry! I—" She stopped herself. She'd forgotten he was still standing there, but saying so seemed rude.

Shadrach took the empty pitcher and glass from her and set them on the ground. "Can we talk?"

The tone in his voice mixed into dread in her stomach. What did Shadrach have to say to her? She nodded, unable to speak, and followed as he led her under the trellis into the flower garden.

The dead stalks of last years' flowers filled the beds along the stone paths, but green stems poked from the ground. In another week or two, their blossoms would fill the garden with color and the air with scent. Newborn leaves curled on the branches of the indigo brush hedges.

Shadrach slowed his pace. Renna eased next to him, her mouth dry. Something had to be wrong. Shadrach's jaw didn't knot like that unless he didn't like what he had to say.

He halted next to the empty fountain. "We spent a lot of time in this garden when we were little."

Renna glanced at the section of hedge where she and Lydia had once crouched, giggling, as they'd spied on Shadrach and the other young guardsmen training. That was the day Renna confessed to Lydia that she liked Shadrach. She wasn't sure what to say to him now. "Yes, we did."

"You remember that last summer you spent here?" His voice lowered, and his gaze focused on the fountain rather than on her. "Lydia told me what you told her back then."

Renna's mouth fell open. "You knew? She told you?" Her heart sunk into her toes. This whole time, Shadrach knew she'd been infatuated with him back then. Her face heated. What did he think of her now? Was he as embarrassed as she was?

"Don't blame her. She was eleven and thought it'd be cool if her brother and her best friend someday..." He trailed off as a red tinge crawled up his neck.

"Both of us were young." Renna scrubbed her damp palms on her skirt. The heat from her face moved into her chest and across her skin. Why couldn't he drop this?

"I know. And people change when they grow up." Shadrach rubbed at the back of his neck and finally turned to her. His brown eyes searched her face. "Jolene Lorraine has been here a lot when her mother comes to speak with my father. And I...and we..."

Renna stared at the manor, the light brown stones, the ledge that ran beneath the arched windows of the second story, the chimneys that puffed smoke into the pale, blue sky. She'd made a fool of herself yet again. Why had she even thought Shadrach liked her that way? He'd only ever acted as a friend. Or a big brother.

A burning lump settled in her throat. She couldn't cry in front of him. She'd only make more of a fool of herself. If her mother was alive or Aunt Mara here, she'd at least have a shoulder to cry on, but she was alone. She couldn't tell Brandi or any of Shadrach's family.

Drawing in a deep breath, she faced him and forced a smile onto her face. "Jolene was always nice when her family visited when we were little. Will she be coming to Lydia's party?"

Shadrach's shoulders relaxed. "Yes."

At least he had the decency to tell her before Lady Paula Lorraine and her daughter Jolene arrived for the celebration and secret meeting. She stumbled towards the trellis. "I'd better return to the parlor."

Turning, she dashed under the trellis, scooped up the pitcher and glasses, and hurried to the kitchen door. As she juggled the pitcher and glasses to free one of her hands, a dirt-encrusted hand reached past her.

She met Leith's green eyes as he tugged on the latch. Her mouth was too dry to form words, her brain too muddled. Managing a bob of her head, she brushed past him into the manor, more confused than ever.

34

Leith poked his finger in the ground, dropped a seed of corn in the hole, and covered it once again. Moving forward a couple of inches, he repeated the process.

For once, his efforts were growing something. These seeds would grow into plants that'd feed Shad's family and the servants that lived in Walden Manor. Up until now, Leith had only ever planted bodies six feet down, soaking the earth with blood.

Now, he had honorable dirt on his hands, the ache of labor in his back, and the contentment at the end of each day that he'd accomplished something worthwhile.

Tonight he'd have to return the Bible, the rough work clothes, the peasant's lifestyle. He'd put on his black clothes and return to a campsite in the forest. Tomorrow, the first of the nobles would arrive, and Leith would once again be a King's Blade.

He speared the ground and dropped in another seed. He had to be a Blade only a little longer. Once he'd stopped Vane from killing Renna and Brandi, he could collect on Lord Alistair's promise. He'd be free to leave the Blades and disappear into the Sheered Rock Hills.

Why did that ache in his chest? He wasn't reluctant to leave the Blades. Was it his friendship with Martyn, a friendship he'd have to sacrifice to leave? Or was it knowing he'd disappear and leave Renna, Brandi, and Shad behind in Walden?

"Hey." Brandi plopped onto the grass outside the garden. "How much more do you have to go?"

Leith waved at the two feet of dirt that separated him from the edge. "Looks like two more rows." He glanced at the shadows cast by the sun. A few hours left. So little time, and he couldn't even tell Brandi he was leaving. "How's Blizzard?"

"Good. I've been giving him apples and brushing him every day." She bounced on her heels and leaned forward to peer at the hole he'd poked in the ground. She stilled, her eyes darkening. "I'm going to miss him when you leave."

He halted, one finger buried to the second knuckle in the dirt. She'd guessed he'd have to leave soon. "Blizzard will miss you too. As will I."

This time, she didn't ask him why he had to leave. Perhaps she better understood the knife's edge he walked.

When she didn't speak for several long minutes, he brushed off his hands and sat next to her. She had her knees tucked against her chest, the toes of her boots peeking from under her skirt. "Will Uncle Abel and Aunt Mara be all right?"

He rested his forearms on his knees. "They'll be fine. There isn't even a Blade stationed at Stetterly."

"I know, but we have you to protect us and they don't have anybody." Brandi stared south, her eyes wet.

His chest ached with knots. What could he say to reassure her without sugarcoating the truth? She was thirteen, the same age he'd been when he'd become a Blade. She could handle the danger. "Respen won't send a Blade after them this time. He can't without taking a Blade away from more important targets."

She nodded and swiped at her eyes. He patted her knee. "You look after your sister, all right? She's going to need you to be brave."

Brandi straightened her shoulders, her jaw stiffening.

Leith returned to work, and Brandi kept him company, handing him seeds and chattering as if she'd never been worried.

When he finished planting the garden and Brandi left for supper, he grabbed a quick meal in the kitchens, retrieved his weapons from Shad's room, and sneaked Blizzard out of the stables. Hiding his horse in the trees behind the flower garden, he changed into his black clothing.

As he strapped on his knives, the hair along his arms and neck rose. He touched one of his knives and scanned the trees around him. Was it his imagination or instincts?

Crickets squeaked in the prairie grass. The breeze stirred the scent of churned earth and whined through the branches, dropping powdery buds onto Leith's hair and shoulders. Nothing seemed out of place.

He sneaked past the guards, though the flower garden, and slipped over the windowsill into Lord Alistair's study. The dry scent of paper wrapped around him even in the alcove.

Shutting the windows, he jammed a knife through the latch. After a moment's consideration, he dragged the cushions from the windowseat, exposing the stone ledge underneath.

Pressing against the wall, he eased around the end of the curtain in the shadows next to the wall instead of striding through the center where the light inside the room would silhouette him against the window.

Shad had his hands pressed against Lord Alistair's desk, speaking in a low tone Leith couldn't hear. Lord Alistair leaned back in his chair, fingertips pressed together, eyes hard as the manor's walls.

Leith cleared his throat and stepped into the candlelight. Shad whirled, his hand reached for his sword, before his gaze rested on Leith. He grinned, and his hand dropped from his sword. "I'd forgotten what you looked like as a Blade."

"Me too." His knives bumped against his ribs and weighed down his boots. For two weeks, he'd been able to forget that he'd only been playing a role. He wasn't Daniel, a wandering peasant. He was Third Blade Leith Torren, and his past couldn't be put aside as easily as his knives.

"Let's go over the Blades' missions again." Lord Alistair waved at the map on the wall. "Don't leave anything out. Any detail, no matter how tiny, could be crucial."

Leith straightened his shoulders, strode to the map, and tapped the town of Sierra. "The Second Blade is stationed here. He's good at throwing knives, but he has a tendency to rush if he's cornered."

He shivered at the cold tone of his own voice. Without meaning, he'd slipped into the same voice he used when reporting to King Respen.

He pointed at each town and recounted everything he could about each Blades' fighting style and mannerisms. Behind him, only Lord Alistair and Shad's breathing filled the room. They couldn't chance writing anything down.

Leith hesitated. His finger rubbed against the carved divot that marked Uster on the map. What if his information got Martyn killed? Did he want to be responsible for his friend's death?

But if he didn't tell Lord Alistair about Martyn, Martyn would murder Lord Segon and his family. "The Sixth Blade is stationed here. He can't throw knives, but he's good at tracking. He..." Leith's voice cracked as he turned to face them. "He's my friend."

"We'll ask Lord Segon to do his best to drive the Blade off without hurting him." Shad gave him a slow nod.

Leith's shoulders relaxed. Shad understood.

"And you and the First Blade will be sent here." Lord Alistair tapped his fingers against his beard. "What if King Respen decides to send only the First Blade here and send you somewhere else? Isn't it a waste to send two Blades?"

A valid question. Leith crossed his arms. "I don't think so. You have a large family. Nine people are too many targets for one Blade, even the First Blade. If Respen should send me elsewhere, I'll ignore my target and come here anyway."

"And if the First Blade is sent elsewhere?" Shad raised his eyebrows.

Leith snorted at that. "The First Blade is so obsessed with Renna and Brandi. I don't think even Respen would dare take them away from him."

"So Respen fears the killer he's created." Lord Alistair stroked his beard. "He has to give the First

Blade what he wants."

Leith touched his knives. How much did Respen actually trust Vane?

Shad leaned on the desk. "We came up with a plan to corner the First Blade when the two of you return."

Leith stepped closer. A sketch of the first floor of Walden Manor spread across the oak.

Lord Alistair tapped on the curved line that designated the study's window. "You and the First Blade will come in through here. We'll leave the corridor outside the study free of guards, but we'll have guards armed with bows stationed in the far room here and the entry here. Once you have the First Blade in the corridor, shout for Shadrach, and he and the guards will block both ends of the corridor. The First Blade will be trapped. Hopefully, he'll surrender."

Vane would fight, but Leith didn't try to correct them. Better to let them think they were planning Vane's capture, not his death. Leith inched his hand to his knife. When the time came, he'd kill Vane before he had a chance to hurt Renna and Brandi. "And if he tries to get past you?"

"We thought we'd send the women and children into the Sheered Rock Hills until the danger was passed."

Leith shook his head. "Vane is too good at tracking. If he can't kill Renna and Brandi here, he'll track them down even if it means risking being late to the next Meeting of the Blades."

"In that case, the upper corridors can be well-guarded, and everyone instructed to lock their doors to delay any attempt to enter." Shad traced the staircase on the sketch. "We'll be prepared."

Lord Alistair leaned back in his seat. "We won't

know the exact day of the attack, so we'll have to put the plan into action the day after the next Meeting of the Blades. I assume we won't have long to wait. If Respen wishes to make these attacks appear to be retaliation for my gathering, he'll act immediately."

Leith waved in the direction of the garden. "Shad and I worked out a system. I'll leave a pile of rocks at the northwest corner of the vegetable garden. I'll try to slip into Walden the night before the attack to warn you if I can."

"Good." Lord Alistair tapped his chin for several minutes before he bowed his head. "May the Lord bless our plans."

Leith's muscles tensed. But would He? So much trust to rest on nothing but faith. Leith couldn't see how they managed it. He turned to Shad. "I left the Bible in your room. Thanks for letting me borrow it."

Shad clapped him on the shoulder. "We'll keep it here for you when you return. After Respen's plans fall apart, he'll know you gave information to us. But don't worry. We'll get you out of here."

Freedom. Leith tried to capture the taste of it, but he couldn't. What would it be like to ride away from Nalgar Castle knowing he'd never return?

A pang shot through his chest. Before he could be free, he'd have to face Vane. "Do you think God would give me courage if you asked for me?"

Leith hadn't meant for his words to come out sounding so vulnerable. He straightened his shoulders and faced them.

Shad held his hands out, palms up, as if speaking to a spooked horse. "You could ask for courage yourself."

The longing cascaded over him like the waterfalls on

the Ondieda River. "I can't. God would never want me."

He stared at the pattern his scuffing toe made in the green rug. "I prayed for courage, once. When I faced King Respen after Renna healed me and I wasn't sure what I was going to tell him. I prayed for courage, and I think He gave me some for Renna and Brandi's sake."

Shad's eyebrows lowered over his dark brown eyes. "The only reason God listens to our prayers is for the sake of His Son, Jesus Christ, not for the sake of sinful human beings. For Christ's sake, God listens to every prayer given by one of His own."

Leith's thin thread of hope snapped and flew away on a blizzard wind. God would never grant him courage, not even for Renna's sake. He was truly hopeless.

Shad held his arms out, as if he wanted to beg Leith to understand. "You don't see it, do you? You said God gave you courage. You're already one of His people."

Leith shook his head. He couldn't have heard Shad right. "God wouldn't choose me. Look at what I've done."

"That's the point. God doesn't look at what we've done. He looks at what Christ did." Shad glanced at Lord Alistair as if pleading for help.

Lord Alistair leaned his elbows on the desk. "He forgives us. Like a father."

"Like a father?" Why did they have to keep pushing this? Couldn't they see how much he wanted to grasp it?

But it was impossible. They didn't know—couldn't know—what stood in the way.

Leith crossed his arms and hung his head. "I could never be good enough to please my father. He hit me when I didn't bring him his whiskey mug fast enough. When he got sick of feeding me, he sold me to Lord Respen to pay his gambling debts. I know what I was worth to my father. One night at the card table."

"Your father *sold* you to Lord Respen?" Shad's voice rose an octave. Of course he wouldn't be able to understand. With a father like Lord Alistair, he wouldn't be able to comprehend the mixture of ache and anger that filled the spot in Leith's chest that should've been filled by his father.

"My own father didn't want me. What makes you think God would be any different?" The long ago taste of blood, sweat, and stale whiskey coated his tongue. His head spun with the memory of hitting the floor, ears ringing, the cracked bone in his arm screaming, though he hadn't dared voice his pain and risk another blow.

"You can't compare God to your father." Lord Alistair's voice softened. "We earthly fathers are only pictures of our Heavenly Father. If we're good fathers, it's only because we're on our knees every night asking God to grant us the strength and wisdom to be better pictures for our children."

Lord Alistair's gaze fixed on Leith, but Leith sensed his words were meant for Shad as much as for him. Shad's sword thunked against the desk as he shifted.

"Your father made you a slave to Respen." Leith could picture Lord Alistair steepling his fingers and leaning back in his chair. "And your slavery to him only increased the more you did. Because of sin, we're all slaves of evil, binding ourselves tighter with each sin."

Respen owned him. Leith had sold his soul for him, drenching himself in blood, binding himself with loyalty to the Blades. At least Respen had been better than his father. Leith had pleased King Respen, had earned the marks on his arm, and heard the king tell him *well done* thirty-five times.

"But God had a plan all along. He sent His Son to die to purchase us from our slavery."

Leith's head reeled with heat. "So your God is just like my father. He sold His Son to pay someone else's debts."

Shad's eyes widened, but Lord Alistair didn't flinch. "You were unwilling when your father sold you, but Jesus volunteered to die on the cross. In His sacrifice, God's people were adopted as God's sons and daughters. So He wasn't dying for strangers. He was dying for His brothers and sisters."

"Sometimes the eldest son, as the firstborn, has to risk himself for his brothers and sisters." Shad leaned against the wall, his gaze focused on Lord Alistair.

Could Leith be one of God's people? It didn't seem possible. He clenched his fists, as if he could hold what they were telling him, but he didn't dare.

He stepped away from the desk, turning his back to them. He had to reconstruct all the walls that had crumbled in the last few weeks. When the other Blades arrived, he couldn't be weak like this.

Letting out a long breath, he turned around. Steel closed around his heart. "If that's all, then I'd better get going." He pushed through the curtains, replaced the cushions on the windowseat, and yanked his dagger from the lock.

Easing out the window, he slipped into the darkness surrounding Walden Manor.

As he crept through the garden, a voice oozed from the darkness. "You've become very cozy with the lord of Walden and his guests."

Leith froze. How much had Vane overheard? Could he have heard Leith's conversation with Lord Alistair and Shad just now?

No, Vane couldn't have. Leith's dagger had been jammed in the lock as he'd left it, and any attempt to dislodge it would've sent it clunking onto the stone windowseat. Vane had to assume Leith was spying on Lord Alistair as ordered.

Vane was fishing, and Leith's hesitation was giving him the information he searched for. Vane must've spied on him earlier in the day and saw Leith with Shad and Brandi.

Leith glanced through the darkness, but he couldn't spot Vane. "I got a job as a peasant farmer so I could get close to them."

"Clever." Derision dripped from Vane's voice.

Leith resisted the urge to pick at the dirt crusted underneath his fingernails. He wasn't ashamed of the hard work he'd done in the last few weeks.

"It must be satisfying, knowing you'll see the pain of your betrayal on their faces when you kill them."

Was Vane testing him? Or was he reveling in the coming bloodshed? Leith couldn't afford to disagree either way. "Yes."

A rustle whispered in the darkness, and Vane appeared beside him. Leith followed him along the hedge, past the guards, and into the trees. Retrieving Blizzard, Leith fell into step with Vane as they hiked across the prairie towards the Sheered Rock Hills.

When the rolling hills screened them from the manor and town, Leith turned to Vane. "What are you doing here?"

Vane's teeth glinted in the light of the crescent moon hovering above the horizon. "The Twelfth Blade reported that Lord Alistair was gathering a number of his friends to a celebration. The king sent me to investigate."

Leith worked to keep the grimace from his face. Of course Twelfth Blade Quinten Daas had reported it. He was stationed at Aven, only a day's ride from Nalgar Castle, and he never missed a chance to get in Respen's good graces.

"What're the king's orders?" Leith gripped Blizzard's reins. Had Respen given Vane orders to attack at the celebration?

"We're to observe who the lord of Walden invited. Nothing more." Vane's mouth curled into a frown.

Leith couldn't show the relief that eased the muscles in his shoulders and neck. Cold stars dotted the sky high above him, though a line of purple clouds stretched across the western horizon.

The prairie rustled with the breeze dancing through the grass and gorging itself on the scents of dust, dry grass, and the wet promise of rain. In the hollow, the first mosquitoes of the year buzzed his ears.

Would anyone miss him tomorrow? Brandi might. Would Renna?

He couldn't think about them. Not tonight. Not tomorrow. For the next few days, he had to be a Blade and nothing more.

35

Rain splattered Renna's window and drooled down the manor's stone exterior. A lousy day for a party. A gust peppered the panes with raindrops, sounding like a handful of pebbles rattling the glass.

Was Leith out there in this? He'd disappeared last night, and she could only guess he'd resumed his role as the Third Blade. She rubbed at her chest where a dull ache had formed. Did she miss Leith? A strange thought, but what else could explain it? Perhaps the gloom outside clouded her thinking.

A loud stomping and jabber of voices drifted up the staircase and through her open door. Renna touched her braid and smoothed her skirt. Time to face the guests. She trudged from her room and peered over the railing.

In the entry, Lady Alistair hugged Lady Paula Lorraine. Lady Lorraine's straight, blond hair hung down her back, contrasted against the dark blue of her cloak and dress. Faint lines weaved around her eyes and roughened her hands, but her hair remained free of gray. Although Lady Alistair stood a half a foot taller than her, Lady Lorraine's back remained straight, her head held high, in a manner that made her appear taller than she was.

Next to her, Shad helped Jolene Lorraine remove her dripping, green cloak. Her blonde hair and lithe form mirrored her mother. Lydia greeted both of them, smiling.

Renna sank to her knees. Shad's rich, brown eyes focused on Jolene, a smile toying with his mouth. His hands flapped at his sides, as if he wasn't sure what to do with them.

At least he'd been honest with her. She couldn't fault him for her clinging to childhood fantasies for too long.

Gathering her last shards of courage, she tiptoed down the stairs and stood next to the newel post. After several minutes, Lady Alistair turned. "Oh, Rennelda, there you are. Lady Paula Lorraine and her daughter Jolene have arrived."

Renna bobbed a curtsy as Lady Lorraine swept forward. Renna blinked. Even she stood a few inches taller than Lady Lorraine. Lady Lorraine grasped her shoulders. "Rennelda, it's wonderful to see you again. I'm sure you remember Jolene?"

Jolene glided forward and smiled. "Hello, Renna." Behind her, Shad rocked back and forth on his heels, his hands clasped behind his back.

Renna swallowed the lump in her throat and forced a smile. Her mother would've expected her to be gracious. No reason to treat Jolene badly on account of her own misplaced feelings. "You look soaked. Would you like to head to my room to change into something dry? I don't have much, but I'm sure Lydia can find something that might fit."

Shad's shoulders relaxed, and he gave Renna a slow

nod over Jolene's head. The stiffness in Renna's chest vanished. A genuine smile eased onto her face.

Jolene picked at her skirt, water droplets flinging into the air. "I'd appreciate it. Even the dresses in my pack are soaked."

Renna led the way upstairs while Lydia turned to the next group of guests stumbling in from the rain. Inside Renna's room, Jolene finger-combed her hair. "Do you have a brush I can borrow? I forgot mine."

"Sure." As Renna turned to fetch her brush, she caught sight of the silver cross dangling from a chain around Jolene's neck. Renna didn't have to ask to know her mother had given it to Jolene, just like she'd given one to Lydia.

After handing the brush to Jolene, Renna opened her jewelry box and dug her own silver cross from the bottom where she'd shoved it four years ago. Her fingers trembled, and she struggled to work the clasp.

"Renna?"

Renna turned. Jolene touched her silver cross. "I know what it's like. My father was killed just before my sixteenth birthday."

When Renna met her gaze, she could see her own ache mirrored there.

She touched the cross resting against her bodice. *Do not be afraid. Only believe.* That was her mother's favorite verse, and the one she'd repeated when she'd given the cross to Renna. Her mother had always acted like faith was that simple. Don't fear. Just believe. Trust and take courage.

As Renna picked out a dress for Jolene, and they fixed each other's hair, Renna grasped at the laughter warming her chest and tingling in her fingers. For so long, she'd clutched that one faint hope because she hadn't dared dream for anything else.

But now? Did she have the courage to look for a future?

The mud squelched through Leith's shirt and slicked along his chest. Water squished through his toes in his boots.

His cloak and hood had shielded him from the rain initially, but even the lanoline in the unwashed wool failed to completely shed the rain and now made his cloak smell like he'd been wrapped in wet sheep.

The rain heightened the rancid stench of unwashed body wafting from several of the Blades sprawled in the grass along the hill with him. At least the rain provided the first bath they'd had since starting their missions a month ago.

Throughout the morning, seven of the Blades had joined him and Vane on the hill overlooking Walden. The Second Blade had been the first to arrive. He lay a few feet away to Leith's right.

Another group of riders approached Walden from the southeast, their faces shielded by the hoods of their cloaks. Leith pulled his cloak tighter around his neck. As the riders dismounted, Martyn nodded at the Second Blade and plopped into the mud beside Leith. "Hey."

"Finally came to join the crowd?" Leith had to force the teasing tone into his voice. Would Martyn notice anything different about him?

Martyn glanced at the other Blades lying in the mud and grass. "I thought only a few guests had been invited to this gathering. But I see I was wrong. What's Lord Alistair up to?"

Leith shrugged as cluelessly as he could. "Don't

know. As far as I could tell, he planned a celebration for his daughter."

Martyn dragged a hand through his hair, causing the blond curls to stick out in odd directions. "Well, something's up. That's plain to see."

Vane appeared in the grass between Leith and the Second Blade. Even in the mud, Vane hadn't made any sound loud enough to hear over the drumming rain.

The Second Blade waved a finger towards the manor. "They'll be huddled inside. Nothing for us to see up here. It might be better to post a watch here and let the rest of us get out of this rain."

Vane's mouth curled, as if he considered the suggestion weak. But he nodded. "Very well. Assign a two-man watch. Rotate every hour."

The Second Blade pointed at the Fourth and Thirteenth Blades. "Keep watch. The rest of us will head into the Hills to find shelter. Torren, you were stationed here. Any good spots?"

"There's a hollow not far into the foothills north of here." Leith shoved himself to his elbows, mud slicking his shirt to his chest. What he wouldn't give to be dry and warm in Walden Manor.

"All right. Meet there." The Second Blade snapped his fingers at the other Blades.

One by one, the Blades slid down the hill and wandered towards wherever they'd left their horses.

Leith wiggled below the crest of the hill. Mud squooshed between his fingers as he shoved himself to his feet. Cold water sloshed inside his boots.

After hiking through the knee-high, wet grass, he reached the hollow. As the other Blades arrived, they constructed makeshift shelters of pine branches, gathered the semi-dry deadfalls sheltered by spruce trees or the lee of the cliffs. Martyn coaxed a flame from the damp wood.

Leith checked on the horses in a nearby meadow bounded by trees and rocky outcrops. Blizzard munched on the rain-soaked grass, his mane slicked to his neck, water clumping the hair along his back.

More Blades straggled in until all of the Blades, except the two left at Nalgar Castle and the two on watch, huddled in the hollow. They perched on rocks and fallen logs like large, silent crows. Leith's skin prickled.

Vane glided to his feet. "Lord Alistair has called half the nobles to Walden. He claims he's hosting a celebration for his daughter."

"Obviously a diversion for his real plan." The Second Blade scratched at his pointed chin. "All of them are known to be a part of the Resistance or potential allies should the Resistance prove it can succeed."

"But why did he call only the nobles we're following?" The Fourth Blade crossed his arms.

Leith's stomach clenched. Of course they'd noticed that coincidence. He didn't speak for fear of drawing attention to himself.

"We're following the ones that're the most likely to cause trouble." Martyn shrugged. "I guess this confirms that the king's suspicions were correct."

No one argued. The Second Blade tapped his mouth with his thumb. "I find it suspicious that Lord Alistair brought Lady Rennelda to Walden a few weeks ago and immediately gathered these nobles to Walden."

"Should we send someone to Nalgar to inform the king?" The Twelfth Blade leaned forward, as if eager to volunteer.

"Our orders are to watch." Vane rested his hand on his knife. "Torren and I will sneak into Walden. The rest of you will stay here."

The Twelfth Blade scowled, and the Fourth Blade crossed his arms. But the Second Blade nodded and glared at the other Blades. "Too many of us will attract attention."

Leith met Vane's eyes. "I can get us into the manor where we can spy on the party."

In the distance, a pack of coyotes yipped their hunting call. A wild light pranced in Vane's pale eyes. His thin smile revealed a row of white teeth stained red with firelight. "Excellent."

36

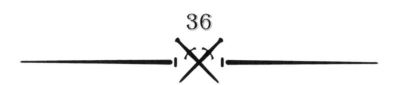

Renna stabbed at the steak on her plate. A few seats away from her at the head of the table, Lord Alistair chuckled at something Lord Spencer said. How could he pretend to be so carefree when he knew he'd be calling a meeting to discuss resistance to King Respen as soon as supper finished?

The chatter in the crowded dining room increased as more of the guests finished eating and began talking. Renna's skin heated with the warmth of so many bodies packed into the windowless room.

Lord Alistair stood and clinked his fork against his glass. "Thank you all for coming to celebrate my daughter Lydia's sixteenth birthday."

Lydia ducked her head, her cheeks beaming red, her brown eyes dancing.

"There will be desserts and further festivities in the parlor. I would like, however, the heads of all of the noble families to remain here for a while longer."

Lady Alistair rose to her feet. "Please follow me."

The room emptied as the sons, daughters, and wives that had come for the celebration headed for the parlor until only eighteen nobles remained.

Shadrach was the last to leave. As he closed the door, he nodded at Lord Alistair and his hand reached for his sword's hilt. Renna didn't have to be told that he'd be standing outside the door, protecting this meeting from Blades.

Renna squirmed in her seat, a rush of cool air shivering the hair on her arms. She was the youngest lady present, though Lady Amber Dawson of Hender was only two years older having inherited her title three years ago when her parents had been killed by Blades. Lord Philip Creston of Arroway was a year younger. His parents had died at the castle the night King Respen and the Blades took over.

One of the lords seated about halfway down the table slapped his pudgy hand on the wood so loudly that Renna squeaked. "What is this all about, Henry? I hope it's important enough to drag me all the way from Calloday. I had to ride four whole days to get here."

Renna imagined the sarcastic eye-rolling Brandi would give that statement. The two of them had ridden six days, and *they* weren't complaining about it.

In a patient tone, Lord Alistair nodded in the lord's direction. "Lord Doughtry, I understand that many of you have come a long way on nothing more than my word that it'd be worth your while."

He paused and leaned forward. Many of the others around the table straightened in their seats. "I've heard from a reliable source at Nalgar Castle that King Respen plans to assassinate all of us sitting in this room in the next few weeks, possibly as soon as next week."

The gasps of shock drowned anything else Lord Alistair might've said. Renna hunched in her seat as several of the lords pounded their fists on the table. Lady Dawson swayed her in chair, perhaps terrified at the news that a Blade was hunting her as her parents had once been hunted.

"That is absurd!" Lord Doughtry's cheeks jiggled with the force of his words. "King Respen wouldn't send a Blade against me. I've never done anything against him."

Lord Alistair's gaze turned icy. "I know. The church in Calloday has suffered without your protection."

"I'm still a Christian. I just don't believe in sticking my neck out where it can be hurt." Lord Doughtry attempted to cross his arms over his bulbous stomach, but he only managed to tuck his hands against his chest.

"Perhaps King Respen has decided to kill all of the Christian nobles at once instead of one at a time." Lord Spencer frowned and rubbed the balding patch on the top of his head.

Lord Segon shook his head. "That can't be Respen's only reason. You all know my particular beliefs don't match yours."

"Beliefs we've debated over the years." The corner of Lord Alistair's mouth quirked upward.

Lord Segon tilted his head in Lord Alistair's direction. "And I look forward to many more such debates. If Respen has decided to kill us, then he must see us as some kind of threat, whether it's because we're actively a part of the Resistance, a Christian, or simply someone who has tried to remain neutral."

"King Respen knows I'm not a threat to him!" Lord Doughtry pounded the table, the motion sending a wave through the fat stretching his doublet. "It's preposterous!"

"I agree!" Another lord shouted, and the lord sitting beside him shouted back. Around the table, other lords yelled at each other. A few stood up, their fists clenched as if to punch each other. Was a brawl about to break out in the room?

Lady Paula Lorraine gracefully rose to her feet. She tapped her water glass with the gold ring on her finger. The sound pinged through the room. The lords froze. She glared at them down her long, straight nose. "Really, ladies and gentlemen. Surely we can behave with more decorum than that."

A few of the lords shifted guiltily while some of the ladies blushed. Lord Doughtry harrumphed and folded his hands on his ample belly.

Regaining her seat, Lady Lorraine faced Lord Alistair. "Henry, I mean no disrespect to you, but I believe we would like to know if this information can be trusted. It does seem to be a drastic measure."

Lord Alistair stroked his beard. "I understand your concern. If I didn't know the source of my information, I'd question it as well. In fact, I did question it until my source proved himself."

Renna sat up straighter. She hadn't heard Lord Alistair declare Leith trustworthy before. What had changed his mind?

"Well, what is this source?" Lord Doughtry's scowl traced lines through his drooping jowls.

"One of the Blades has joined the Resistance. More than that, I cannot say."

As she'd expected, the chaotic pounding, yelling, and demanding explanations burst around the room once again.

Renna squeezed her hands together. She was the only one here besides Lord Alistair who'd met Leith. Should she stand up and back Lord Alistair? Her fingers trembled.

She closed her eyes and rubbed her fingers against the soft velvet of the royal blue dress Lydia had given her. Did she believe Leith was trustworthy? He was better than the First Blade, but he was still a Blade.

Her fingers stilled. A Blade. That's what she always went back to, as if his past made him incapable of change, as if she believed he was beyond hope.

But he had changed. She'd seen the vulnerability in his green eyes when he'd promised he'd do his best to protect her from the First Blade, a promise that could get him killed.

He was willing to die for her.

A part of her ached like the pain of new skin growing beneath a scab. Her muscles relaxed in a way they hadn't in four years, as if she'd been pulled taut by the wind but now released to float on the breeze.

When she opened her eyes, Lord Alistair's eyes questioned her. Renna's stomach shriveled. She couldn't stand up in front of all these people. Her words would twist on her tongue. Her knees would buckle. She couldn't do it.

Her father wouldn't hesitate. He probably would've led the meeting. Her mother would've been by her father's side, serene, but flinty. Renna had neither her father's courage nor her mother's steel. She touched the silver cross hanging from her neck. *Do not be afraid.*

If Leith was willing to die for her, then surely she could stand up for him here. Pressing her palms to the tabletop, she wobbled to her feet. No one noticed her in the chaos.

Lady Lorraine pinged her ring against her glass again. The arguments died.

Renna twisted her hands in her skirt. "You all know

I have as much reason to hate the Blades as any of you sitting around this table." She drew a deep breath and took in the solemn nods. "I've met this Blade. He..." She didn't know how to describe Leith. His dark, tousled hair. His green eyes. The dimples around his mouth when he smiled. "He's trustworthy. I've forgiven him."

She sank into her chair, leaned against the back, and soaked in the cool rush washing her heart. Lord Alistair nodded at her, a silent *well done*.

Lord Farthen of Keestone spoke for the first time. "We must assume this information is valid. It'd be unwise to do otherwise."

"Thank-you." Lord Alistair steepled his fingers and leaned back in his chair. "Respen assigned a Blade to each of our towns to watch us for the past month. These Blades have been learning our movements and our guard patterns so they can kill us when Respen gives the word."

One of the ladies at the far end of the table shifted. "I thought I felt watched."

Her words gained a few nods. One of the men added, "I saw a black speck on the horizon a couple of times."

Renna shuddered, the memory of the First Blade's low tenor whispering in her ear. But she wasn't about to speak again. She'd used her last shred of courage.

Lord Farthen rubbed his smooth jaw. "What do you suggest we do?"

"When you return to your towns, don't change the number of guards or their patrol patterns outside. Inside your manor, keep several guards with you at all times, especially at night. When the Blade attacks, you'll have to overwhelm him with numbers. Arrows work best."

"What? You mean, fight the Blades?" A nobleman dressed in lavish red silk bolted upright.

"Preposterous!" Lord Doughtry huffed.

Lord Hector Emilin ran a hand through his blond hair. "I've never done anything to provoke King Respen except maintain a quiet, underground church." He glanced at Lord Alistair. "It's wrong to rebel against the government."

Lord Alistair raised his eyebrows. "Even a government that has made it a point to destroy our faith? Even a government that's a rebellion itself?"

Lord Emilin sighed as if he'd had this conversation with Lord Alistair one too many times. "I know King Respen isn't the best king, but he is the king that God has placed over us. I won't rebel against him."

A few of the other noblemen nodded. Renna hunched in her seat. Was King Respen the government God had placed over Acktar? King Respen had gained his position by rebelling against her uncle and murdering whole families. Was that the government that God wanted them to obey? Or should they fight back to preserve their faith and lives?

It didn't matter what she thought. She was under Lord Alistair's roof, and he'd decided to fight back. Whether that was right or wrong, Renna couldn't help but be grateful. She and Brandi would be as safe as Lord Alistair, Shadrach, and Leith could make them.

Lord Alistair stared at Lord Emilin, lines creasing his forehead and around his eyes. "If you don't fight, you'll die, and your family with you."

Lady Lorraine waved a hand. "I, for one, do not intend to sit back idly while a Blade kills me."

"I'm glad to hear it since the Second Blade has been

assigned to you." Lord Alistair rubbed his beard. "He's skilled at throwing knives."

Lady Lorraine's calm nod amazed Renna. How could the lady be so calm when the Second Blade would be ordered to kill her?

Lord Alistair met Lord Emilin's gaze. "What if an heir to King Leon still survived?"

Lord Emilin glanced at Renna. "Lady Rennelda can't inherit the throne unless we stretch the inheritance laws."

"Which the Council of Nobles has changed in the past so women could inherit estates." Lord Farthen crossed his arms.

"Or Henry might have plans to marry her off to his son and claim the throne for himself." Lord Doughtry rolled his bulk to lean his elbows on the table.

Was that all Renna was to the nobility in this room? A gateway to the throne? She'd never be able to rule Acktar. She could barely speak in front of this small gathering.

Lady Lorraine arched an eyebrow at Lord Doughtry. "If you'd used your eyes earlier this evening, you would've seen that Shadrach Alistair has interest only for my daughter."

Lord Doughtry harrumphed. "He's an obedient son. He might have interest in your daughter, but he'd place his affections elsewhere if Lord Alistair demanded it."

Renna's face burned. If only she could leave.

Fire flared in Lord Alistair's eyes. "My son's personal business is his own. I have no designs on power. Only justice. My immediate concern is in saving your lives and that is the only plan I have."

Renna folded her hands on her blue skirt. Lord

Alistair didn't have any plans to marry her to Shadrach, nor would Shadrach allow it even if he did. Yet, what plans did Lord Alistair have for her? Did he intend to place her on the throne?

37

Leith hunkered on the floor and peered through the railing into the entry hall of Walden Manor. Chatter, laughter, and music poured from the parlor.

Shad stood in front of the door to the dining room, his bow strung and an arrow set on the string. Three other guards paced the hall, preventing Leith and Vane from sneaking any closer. If Vane tried, Shad would put an arrow into him in seconds.

Perhaps that was the answer. If Leith alerted Shad, they could take Vane out now.

No, it wouldn't work. The Second Blade wasn't as decisive as Vane. He could be swayed into attacking in retaliation by the other Blades. If things went wrong and Vane survived, he'd lead all the Blades in an attack that would leave many nobles and Blades dead.

"Are you sure there's no other way into that room?" Vane hissed by Leith's ear.

Leith drew back and faced Vane. "That's the only door. With the guards patrolling as they are, we can't even get close to a wall."

Vane scowled, his blue eyes paling to the color of a

mid-winter sky. "Lord Alistair is canny. Let's see if we can find a bedchamber above the dining room."

They slipped down the upstairs corridor. Leith opened the door to Shad's room. Vane ghosted into the room on his heels. He held his breath as Vane shoved the mountain lion skin aside and pressed his ear to the floor.

Kneeling, Leith pressed his ear to the floor as well. The voices below were the indistinct tone of thunder on the other side of the mountains. Exactly how it'd been when he and Shad tested it.

Leith forced a grimace on his face as he sat up. "Trust the Alistairs to put in solid floors."

With a curse, Vane pushed himself upright. "Split up. Surely one of the guests has something worthwhile."

Leith hated letting Vane wander Walden Manor by himself, but he had to agree. It'd be suspicious otherwise.

Leith slipped through several rooms. He rifled through a few papers some of the noblemen had left on their desks, but he didn't find anything that'd be worth mentioning to Vane. Or anything worth not mentioning.

As he exited one of the guest rooms, he heard a babble of voices in the entry hall below. He peered through the railing. The noblemen and women exited the dining room. Most headed for the parlor, though some turned towards the stairs.

Leith's breath caught in his throat as he spotted Renna. A deep blue dress hugged her body while her long, blond hair fell around her shoulders, free of the tight braid she normally wore.

Pounding footsteps on the stairs jolted him. He slipped into a linen closet, holding the door open a fraction. Lady Alistair passed him, supporting a blond woman whose shaking rattled the pins from her hair. A portly nobleman waddled up the stairs and lumbered down the hall.

After the bustle died down, he eased from the closet and padded down the hallway. By the door to Renna's bedchamber, he paused. He heard voices.

Renna yawned as she shut her door behind her. The dark shadows in her room closed around her.

Shivering, she rubbed her arms. The goosebumps on her forearms scratched against the palms of her hands. All that talk of Blades and assassinations had gone to her head.

She tiptoed across her room to her dressing table. Pausing in front of it, she reached for her necklace clasp.

A shadow, blacker than the night around her, filled the mirror behind her. Before she had a chance to scream, a hand pressed over her mouth. The blade of a knife stroked her exposed throat.

In the mirror, she met the First Blade's pale blue eyes. His teeth glinted as he smiled. "Soon. Very soon."

She trembled in his grip. Not again. Why did the First Blade have to keep tormenting her like this?

He can't kill you until King Respen gives the order. Leith's words echoed in her head. Her heart still pounded, her body still seizured with shaking, but she could think and thinking told her that Vane wasn't going to kill her this time.

She eased her hand towards the heavy jewelry box on the corner of the dressing table. She needed a distraction. Wiggling her mouth free, she didn't have to fake the quaver in her voice. "Don't hurt me."

He leaned closer, his breath hot on her neck. "Your mother only pleaded for her children. Touching, perhaps, but I like my targets whimpering for mercy. It's so much more satisfying when I don't give it to them."

Images of that night tore through her. Her mother's last kiss. The knowing, sad look in her eyes. The moment the Blade dragged his knife across her throat and met Renna's gaze with a promise. He'd kill her someday.

Her fingers closed around the jewelry box. She drew in a deep breath and steeled herself to smash the box into the side of the First Blade's head.

"First Blade." Leith's voice snapped from the darkness behind them. "Let her go. You'll get a chance to kill her soon enough."

Her heart stopped at Leith's words. Would the First Blade realize why Leith was protecting her?

The First Blade gave a small laugh and tossed her away from him. She slid to the floor, the jewelry box clutched in her hand.

"She'll tell Lord Alistair about this."

She peeked at Leith. He crossed his arms. For a fraction of a moment, his eyes darted her way. She saw a brief softening. Perhaps worry? The flicker had been too quick to tell.

"More of a challenge." With one last glance at Renna, the First Blade sidled out the door.

Leith reached for the door handle to follow.

"Leith." His name whispered from her before she'd given it much thought. But before he left, before he returned to the darkness of Nalgar Castle, she had to tell him what she'd realized during that gathering.

He halted and turned towards her. Her heart pattered a strange rhythm, so loud and aching she barely heard her own words. "I trust you."

His green eyes widened, and he dipped his chin. As he disappeared out the door, something clunked to the carpet.

When her room remained silent and her shaking drained into the floor, she picked up the object he'd dropped. The sheathed knife gleamed in the moonlight pooling on the floor. She traced the initials *LT* inscribed on the hilt, a silent promise that he'd protect her.

Her fingers closed around the hilt. When the First Blade returned, she'd be armed with more than just a jewelry box.

38

Renna meandered the stone paths through the red columbine and pink trefoil, the thick, sweet smell of the blooming flower garden hard to breathe.

Brushing through the vines covering the white trellis, she stopped at the open area Leith had transformed into a vegetable garden. Rows of seedlings burst from the ground.

Renna knelt and touched one of the small stalks of corn, a lump curling in her throat. After all his work, Leith didn't even get to see the results.

A weed sprouted next to the corn, already towering over it. In another few days, the weed would overtake the small stalk and snuff it out. She yanked the weed from the ground and tossed it aside.

Dirt pressed under her fingernails. She let herself simply move, not thinking, not feeling, as she worked her way down the row. Here she didn't have to be Lady Faythe or a possible heir to the throne or a pawn in anyone's strategy.

"You don't have to weed. I'm sure we can find someone else to do it."

She started and nearly toppled onto a corn stalk. She gulped in a deep breath and glanced at Shadrach. "I enjoy it. It gives me something to do."

Shadrach knelt a few feet away and plucked the weeds. An easy silence fell around them. Somewhere in the distance she could hear Brandi's voice chattering to someone. A stablehand. Or Abigail.

The sun warmed her back, and if she closed her eyes, she could smell the plants growing, green, bursting with the hope of life for one summer.

She sneaked a glance at him. "Jolene and her mother leave safely?"

A red tinge splotched the edges of his face as he concentrated intently on pulling a weed from the ground. "Yes."

"Jolene's nice. She helped me do my hair for your sister's party." She smoothed a stalk's tiny leaf between her thumb and forefinger. "She's good for you."

A grin shot across Shadrach's face. "Thanks."

That word settled on her with a sweet finality. But that was all right. He was a friend and always would be. Perhaps someday she'd visit Walden Manor so her children could play with his as her parents had once done.

A smile tugged at her mouth. "Did you see the eyes Lydia was making at Lord Creston at her party?"

"What? She's not even sixteen yet." Shadrach glared at the weed in his hand.

"She will be in two weeks." Renna restrained herself from a Brandi eyeroll. "He's her age. And already the lord of Arroway."

Shadrach muttered and yanked at another handful of weeds. Renna grinned and continued weeding.

When she reached the end of the row, she paused.

Rocks piled at the corner of the garden with a single rock placed on the western side. "What's this doing here?"

Shadrach's mouth pressed into a thin line. "Leith piled the stones like that to let me know the Blades had left. When they move, I'll know Leith has returned."

He didn't have to explain further. When Leith returned, he'd be under orders from King Respen to kill Lord Alistair. If the First Blade was with him, he'd be unable to warn them in person. A pile of stones was their solution.

"Do you think he's all right?" The question burst out before she could stop it. She wasn't sure why she worried about Leith. Surely he could take care of himself. Still, she couldn't banish the niggling flurry in the pit of her stomach.

Shadrach glanced in the direction of Nalgar Castle. "Depends if Respen believes him or not. Pray for him. He is going to need the wisdom of Solomon and the courage of Daniel when he faces Respen to give his report."

Renna nodded. Prayer was one thing she could do.

39

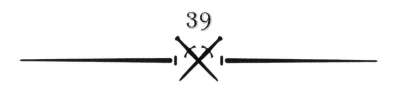

He slipped across the room. On the bed, Brandi slept, basking in a pool of moonlight. Her hair spread out on her pillow in wild abandon. As he reached the side of the bed, her eyes fluttered open. She glanced up, and smiled.

Her smile froze, changing to confusion when she saw the knife he gripped in his hand. She was too confused to even scream as the knife plunged down. Only then did her eyes fill with pain, her blood pumping onto the blankets.

He turned to the next bed. Renna was already awake. She didn't scream, though her eyes fixed on her sister's body. Her expression was resigned, as if accepting that her death was inevitable.

He raised the knife. Moonlight glinted on blood.

Leith bolted upright, shaking and sweating. Another nightmare. The darkness clawed at him, seeking a crack to fill his body. He fumbled to light the lamp. The flame flared, banishing the darkness to the corners.

He swung his legs over the edge of the cot, leaned his elbows on his knees, and fought to keep his stomach where it belonged. He touched his side, feeling the ridge of his scar through his shirt. If he hadn't been wounded and stumbled onto their doorstep, he might've killed them. Even if he didn't kill them with his own hands, he wouldn't have prevented the Blade that did.

Leith heaved a long sigh. He wasn't ready to sleep. That Bible from Walden would've been a nice distraction.

He bowed his head. Why had his first thought been that Bible? He should go down to the common room. Surely he could find a practice fight to join even at this time of night.

He didn't belong here anymore. More than that, he didn't *want* to belong here anymore. If he could, he'd pack his things, saddle Blizzard, and ride away, never to return.

But if he did that, his blood would stain the castle walls in a slow death, and he'd be unable to help Lord Alistair, Shad, Renna, Brandi, and everyone King Respen would kill to maintain his power. He had to stay. Soon Lord Alistair would help him leave. He only had to survive until then.

If he had the courage to do so.

What had Shad told him about courage? True courage came from God, and God only granted it to His people.

Could Shad be right? Had God chosen him? Loved him? Adopted him as a son? Leith didn't dare reach for it, only to find it was a dream that his hand passed through like mist. His father's love had been like that.

You can't compare God to your father.

He rubbed his hand on the forearm he'd once broken. He'd come at it from the wrong direction all along. He'd compared God to his father when he should've compared his father to God.

A comparison his father failed.

If God wasn't like his father, then what? It seemed impossible that God could forgive the things he'd done, but he'd thought it impossible that Renna would forgive him, and she'd done it.

Could Leith trust? Did he dare?

He did dare. He wasn't sure when he'd decided, as if his decision happened between heartbeats. One moment he was hesitating and the next he was sure.

How could he hesitate? If God had chosen him and already worked in his heart, there was nothing left for him to do. No reason to hesitate or wait for the right moment.

Leith had nothing to do at all.

He leaned against the wall beside his bed. The darkness of the room didn't go away. But he didn't fear it. Blowing out his lamp, he lay back in bed, closed his eyes, and slipped into a peaceful sleep.

40

Leith woke with his stomach twisted in knots. If he were in Walden, he'd join the church service this morning. He might even attempt to sing along.

Did Respen purposefully pick Sunday to meet with his Blades? It was as if he'd claimed the Lord's Day as his own, turning the day of worship into a day of death.

At five minutes to eight, Leith joined the other Blades as they filed into the meeting room. Darkness prowled the corners beyond the meager light of the candles. Its musty breath brushed against the back of Leith's neck. His hair prickled. *God...Father...grant me courage.*

Forcing his hands to remain steady, Leith hung his weapons on his peg near the door and slid into his seat. The other silent shadows slid into their seats around him. No one spoke, and, once seated, no one moved.

Leith resisted the urge to shift in his seat. Did he stand out like one of the candles amid the darkness of this room?

The door soundlessly swung open. Respen glided inside like a wraith of death.

Leith rose with the other Blades. Respen claimed his place at the head of the table and intoned his greeting. Leith thumped his hand over his heart with the rest of the Blades. As he mumbled "my king," Leith focused his eyes above the king's head.

Leith sat with the rest of the Blades. Leith listened as each of the Blades made their report. They felt they knew each town inside and out, and that confidence could be their downfall.

The Fourth Blade finished his report on the layout of Flayin Falls and eased to his seat, his blood soaking into his right sleeve.

"Third Blade Torren." Respen's voice rolled across the room and echoed in the darkness.

Leith stood and strode to the head of the table. He knelt. He should've been trembling, but calm lingered in his chest.

"What is your report?"

Leith met Respen's eyes. He outlined the guard schedule and the layout of the Walden Manor, including which bedroom belonged to each person of the family.

When he'd described the layout, he gave a quick summary of the events of the past month. "The First Blade and I slipped into Walden the night of Lord Alistair's celebration, but he had the dining room too well guarded for us to overhear anything."

King Respen nodded, his eyes staring over Leith's head without seeing him. His fingers stroked the arms of his throne. Leith remained silent. Respen shook himself. "You have done well, my Third Blade."

Leith pushed up his right sleeve. Respen swiped his knife across Leith's arm only a few inches above his elbow. His thirty-sixth mark. Hopefully his last.

Leith let go of his sleeve, stood, and returned to his seat. As he slid onto the hard wood, he had to bite the insides of his cheeks to stop a smile. Respen was blind to what Leith had left out.

The Second Blade gave his report, followed by the First Blade. Because Leith had told the truth—minus a few details—to the king, his story matched Vane's, leaving no discrepancy for Vane or the king to question.

When Vane returned to his seat, Respen swept his dark eyes over the room. "You are prepared for the mission I have for you."

Leith tensed. His thirty-sixth mark seeped blood into his shirt, throbbing in time with his drumming heart. What if he'd guessed wrong? What if King Respen chose a different plan than the one that Leith had so confidently told Lord Alistair? All of their counter-measures would be in error.

"Acktar is growing restless. The nobles who supported Leon Eirdon are growing bold as they conspire against me."

Around the room, the Blades sat in silent agreement. Leith tapped his fists against his knees.

"I will send a message that will shock my enemies into submission. I will show them they are not strong enough to withstand my power, my Blades. I tasked you with watching eighteen noblemen and women. Those eighteen nobles and their families will die."

Leith couldn't feel relieved that his guess had been right. Too many lives were threatened. Even with all their preparations, some of those men and women might still die.

He risked a glance around the room, lingering for just a moment on Martyn. Due to his planning, some of the Blades, perhaps many of the Blades, could be killed. Blood would be shed either way.

"You will have one week. On the fourth night, sneak into the manor and kill them."

Leith nodded along with the rest of the Blades. Respen didn't want a smattering of attacks spread out across a long period of time. He wanted to show his utter control over life and death by having eighteen of the most prominent families die on the same night all across the country.

"My lord," Vane cut in. "I have a request to make. Allow me to kill Lady Rennelda and Lady Brandiline. Their deaths will add to the shock and will prevent them from becoming a rallying point for your enemies."

Respen's eyes narrowed. Was that suspicion Leith glimpsed? "Of course, my First Blade. It was the task I had for you all along. You will work with the Third Blade since your targets are at Walden Manor."

"As you wish, my king." Vane bowed his head.

"Execute your orders, My Blades." King Respen stood and clasped his right hand over his chest.

Leith stood with the rest of the Blades and fisted his right hand over his chest. He mumbled the pledge with the rest of the Blades, but the words tasted bitter on his tongue.

He waited, but Respen didn't stride toward the door. Instead, he waved his hand. "Dismissed."

Leith shoved his chair out of the way to join the other Blades in claiming his weapons, but Respen's voice halted him. "Third Blade Torren. Stay a moment."

Leith froze. What did King Respen want?

Martyn eyed him, frowning, as he grabbed his weapons and left the room. Vane glared, lingering until all the other Blades had left before he too claimed his weapons and slipped out the door, closing it behind him.

Respen tapped his fingers against the throne's armrest. "You neglected to tell me everything in your report."

A chill sliced through Leith's fingers. Did Respen suspect him? Could Leith reach his knives before the king killed him?

The tapping continued. "What really happened when you sneaked into Walden the night of Lord Alistair's celebration?"

Leith swallowed and faced Respen. "The First Blade and I slipped into Walden Manor. Lord Alistair had guards posted around the dining room where he met with the nobles he'd gathered. When we couldn't listen at the door, we found a room above the dining room, but the floor was too thick to hear anything. The First Blade ordered me to split up to search for anything suspicious in the guest rooms."

Respen's fingers halted. "You split up? You weren't with the First Blade the entire time?"

"No." The muscles at the back of Leith's neck eased. Respen suspected Vane, not Leith. "I didn't know where he was until I found him talking with Lady Rennelda." Threatening her, but Respen didn't need to know that.

Respen stood and clasped his hands behind his back. "It has been nine years since I rescued you from your father, has it not?"

"Yes, my king." Was that how Respen saw it? Rescue? More like trading one owner for another.

"And so far you've never made me regret that action." Respen's dark eyes speared him. "Vane may be the First Blade, but you were my *first* Blade."

Without waiting for a reply, Respen swept from the room.

What had that been about? Leith shook the shivers from his skin, collected his knives, and left the room.

As he reached the fourth floor, he found Martyn waiting for him. Martyn slapped him on the back. "Hey, good luck."

Leith returned the gesture. "You too."

Martyn turned away. He'd leave in less than an hour, and if things went wrong, Leith would never see him again.

"Martyn." Leith gripped his arm. Martyn turned back to him, forehead scrunched. Leith swallowed. His mouth burned with a warning. His actions could lead to Martyn's death. "Be careful. If the nobles are planning something, they'll be wary."

Martyn clasped Leith's shoulder. "In that case, you'll be in more danger than me. The lord of Walden is a leader in the Resistance. He'll be well-guarded."

Leith dropped his hand. It was the most warning he could give his friend.

Martyn strode away and disappeared around the curve of the corridor.

Leith reached for the latch on his door. A shadow flickered at the edge of his vision. He whirled and reached for his knife.

Vane bashed Leith's fingers against the doorframe. Pain shot through his bones, and his knife clattered to the stone. He twisted his body to grab another knife.

Pain pricked Leith's stomach in the soft flesh below his ribcage. Glancing down, he spotted Vane's knife prepared to thrust underneath his ribs and up into his chest. Each ragged breath pressed his stomach harder against the tip of the knife.

Was Vane going to kill him? He couldn't die. Not now.

In the light of the torches lining the corridor, Vane's teeth gleamed with the reflected flicker of orange and red. "Remember, Torren. I've always been better than you."

Vane released him, sheathed his knife, and slipped into his own room.

Leith sagged against his door. When he touched the aching spot on his skin, his fingers shone with blood.

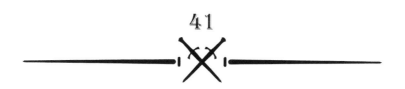

41

Grabbing a fresh roll from the kitchen, Renna exited the back door and checked the first row of corn for weeds. The tiny stalks waved at her in the morning breeze. At the end of the row, she touched the pile of stones. So far they hadn't moved.

Shadrach strolled along the edge of the garden, as if he were pretending he'd happened along at the right moment instead of tailed her from the kitchen to guard her. At the east corner, he knelt, touched the stones, and started weeding. "Still nothing."

"How soon do you think they might return?" Her stomach churned. How long did she and Brandi have? Weeks? Days? Hours? Was the First Blade on his way to Walden now?

Shadrach tossed a handful of weeds from the garden. "I have no idea. It's been five days. Enough time to ride to Nalgar Castle and back. Any day, I'd guess."

A tremor racked her body until she thought her bones might rattle apart with the force of her shaking. She didn't want to die, not by a Blade's knife. She could picture it, slicing through her chest, the pain exploding outward until it encompassed her whole body, her screams choked by her own blood.

Shadrach touched her arm. "It's going to be all right. You'll be protected. And God is in control."

He meant to reassure her, but Renna didn't find those words comforting. God's control didn't necessarily mean safety. He didn't stop the bad things from happening. In fact, He'd planned for them to happen. What if His plan involved her death? Or Brandi's?

Some of her thoughts must've shown on her face. Shadrach's eyes grabbed hers. "God is God, right?"

"Yes." She flicked a clod of dirt from her skirt.

"Is He good?"

Renna picked at another smear of dirt. "Yes."

"And does He love His people?"

Her shoulders sagged. What else could she say besides the correct answer? "Yes."

"Since God is God, He is in control. Since He is good, everything He does is good, including His control. Since He loves His people, He controls everything that happens for their good." Shadrach shrugged and pulled another weed. "It's as simple and as hard as that."

Renna hung her head. She was such a weak Christian. People like Shadrach trusted God even through bad times, but Renna wavered like the prairie grass blown in the wind. What could be good about death and bloodshed?

Do not be afraid. Only believe. She bowed her head and touched the silver cross on her necklace. She had to trust God no matter her doubts. After all they'd been through, surely God wouldn't take Brandi now.

Renna waited for a feeling of peace to come over her. But nothing happened.

Shadrach climbed to his feet. He held out a hand to her. "Come on. Let's find my father and go over the plan one last time. Then, you can spend some time with Brandi."

Renna took his hand and let him pull her to her feet. She needed to hug her sister tightly. She'd write to Uncle Abel and Aunt Mara to let them know how much they meant to her.

If something did happen to her, there'd be no regrets, nothing left unsaid. She wouldn't make that mistake a second time.

42

When the prairie wallowed in the blackness of full night, Leith and Vane slipped from their campsite in the Sheered Rock Hills and hiked across the prairie, leading their horses.

Something itched at Leith's spine. He couldn't put his finger on it, but something felt wrong. Maybe it was the moonless darkness that ached against his eyes. Or the sly smile that twitched Vane's mouth.

They crested the hill overlooking Walden and padded through the grass toward the town, circling to enter the trees lining the edge of the manor's property. When they reached the trees, they dropped their horses' reins onto the ground.

Leith crouched at the base of a large cottonwood tree. Vane hunkered a few feet away. Leith tracked the progress of the guard walking the edge of the estate.

As he turned the corner, the next guard stepped into view around the far corner. Leith suppressed a smile at the normality of the routine. Lord Alistair was doing a good job of keeping up the appearance.

Lights remained lit in the manor. Leith spotted the

candle flickering in the window of Renna's room. Someone snuffed out the candle in Brandi's room, the one next to it.

Vane glanced over his shoulder and grinned at Leith. Only his teeth flashed in the faint light of the stars. He, like Leith, had held the blades of his knives over their small fire, burnishing them with a dull layer of smoke to prevent them from glinting and giving away their position. "Let's get closer."

Leith's back tightened. Why did Vane want to get closer? They'd observed enough. They couldn't risk alerting the guards before tomorrow night, the night King Respen had ordered them to complete their mission.

Leith could do nothing but nod. Perhaps he'd have a chance to slip away from Vane and move the rocks at the edge of the garden. He watched from cover as Vane slunk across the open space and into the safety of the hedge before the next guard rounded the corner.

For several minutes, Leith waited. What was Vane doing while Leith remained stuck here? The guard paced slowly along the edge of the property. He paused by the gap in the hedge, inspected it, and continued on his way.

When he was several yards past him, Leith slipped from the cover of the trees, crossed the open space, and slithered through the gap in the hedge. The cloying scent of the hedge's flowers choked him. Inside the hedge, he froze, listening for signs the guards had heard him.

Vane crouched next to him. "We're carrying out our orders tonight."

"What?" Leith gaped at Vane. A buzzing sound filled his ears. They were supposed to go tomorrow night. He was supposed to have time to warn Shad tonight so they'd be ready. "Our orders are to kill them the fourth night."

Vane's eyes glinted. "It won't matter if we're a day early."

Leith should've realized Vane's eagerness to kill Renna would make him bend Respen's orders. Only the First Blade could get away with such actions.

No time to warn Shad. Leith couldn't call out to the guards. They were too widely spaced outside to succeed in stopping Vane.

Leith's heart pounded faster as he followed Vane through the flower garden. He swiped his palms against his trousers, trying to keep them dry.

After they reached the window, Vane slid his knife between the wooden frames and lifted the latch. Leith gripped the hilt of his knife. He should stab Vane in the back before he had a chance to enter Walden Manor. It was the smart thing—the Blade thing—to do.

But it wasn't right. He let his hand fall from his knife. He'd have to stick with the plan and help trap Vane inside.

The window swung open without a sound. Leith climbed over the sill first. The cushions of the windowseat huffed out air at his weight. Rolling from the windowseat onto his feet, Leith stepped out of the way as Vane came over the sill.

After peeking through the curtains, Vane brushed them aside and strode through the room, the thick rugs muffling his footsteps. He slid a knife from its sheath.

Leith drew one of his knives and rolled the leather grip against his palm. As soon as Vane stepped into the corridor, Shad and his guards would surround him.

Vane would fight back. Leith would never get another chance to try to talk to him. He couldn't allow Vane to be killed without talking to him first. Perhaps God would work in Vane's heart. Leith was, after all, the proof that God could touch any heart, no matter how hardened.

Perhaps it was foolish. But he could still hear thirteen-year-old Vane's hissed words the night Leith had met him. *I saw my mother die.*

Vane was nearly at the door. Leith called out in a soft voice, "Don't make another move."

Vane turned, and a smile wormed across his mouth. "I wondered how long it would take you to show your true colors."

Chills trickled down Leith's arms and legs. "What are you talking about?"

"I saw how friendly you were with these people. I knew you were up to something, but I never had enough proof to go to the king. Nor could I with you turning him against me."

At least Vane hadn't told Respen. Leith tightened his grip on his knife. "That's why you decided to carry out our orders tonight."

"Of course," Vane's pale eyes glowed in the starlight filtering through the curtains. "I couldn't let you warn your friends."

"These are good people. They shouldn't be murdered like this." Leith stepped closer. He kept his gaze locked on Vane's eyes. His heart thumped in a steady rhythm. He should call for Shad. But, he'd lose his chance to try to reach Vane before it was too late.

Vane scowled at Leith. "You've gone soft. Either that or you're daft. We have orders to kill them. What does it

DARE

matter what kind of people they are?"

"Murder is wrong. God is the One who holds the power of life and death." Leith took yet another step closer. "God worked in my heart. He saved me from my slavery to sin and Respen."

"So you have become the Alistair lapdog. You're spouting their nonsense."

"It isn't nonsense." It had taken Renna, Brandi, and Shad weeks of patience before the seed of faith sprouted. With Vane, he had only seconds. "It's the truth of the gospel. Jesus died for the sins of His people. His blood washes away the blood from our hands."

"You're a fool," Vane growled. "A weakling to listen to their stories."

Leith had no response. Maybe he was a fool. But he was a fool saved by grace and freed from the darkness that still held Vane in its chains.

The door rattled. Vane glanced at it, his eyes widening. Leith had run out of time. "Shad!"

Vane hurled his knife at Leith.

Leith threw himself to the ground as the knife whistled through the air above him. The study door burst open. As guardsmen spilled in, Vane dashed across the room and shoved aside the curtains.

Leith pushed himself from the floor and sprinted after Vane. An arrow zipped by his head and sliced through the curtains beside him.

Leith slammed through the curtains and dove out the window. Rolling to his feet, he glanced around the garden, searching for a dark figure.

A scratching sound made him look up. Vane was partway up the brick face of the manor, using his knives to help him scale the building.

303

"Renna!" Leith yanked out a second knife. He jammed a knife into the mortar between the bricks and wedged his toes in the space between bricks.

He scaled the bricks, moving the opposite hand and foot at the same time. Had Shad heard him? Leith wouldn't reach Renna in time. No matter how fast he climbed, no matter how much he hurried, he couldn't get to Renna's room before Vane.

Partway up the wall, Leith's arms and shoulders burned. The insides of his arms cramped from gripping the hilts of his knives. He glanced upward. Vane gasped for breath as well, slowing his pace as he pulled himself up another few feet.

Vane reached the ledge that ran along the base of the second floor and pulled himself up. Standing, he padded along the ledge.

Leith forced himself to pick up the pace and reached the ledge a minute later. He hooked an elbow on the ledge and tried to pull himself up. With the outward angle, he couldn't get a good grip with his toes.

His feet slipped, and his arm slid from the smooth surface. His stomach lurched as he fell.

Leith's downward motion jerked to a stop, wrenching his right arm. For a minute, Leith dangled by his one-handed grip on his dagger.

The metal bent at the strain of holding his body's weight. The ground swayed twenty feet below him. His head spun as if he were already falling.

He curled his body towards the wall and latched his toes in the cracks between the bricks. He clung to the wall and gulped in several lungfuls. He couldn't afford to panic now. When his wrists stopped shaking, he reached for the ledge again.

This time, he crammed his toes into higher holds and shoved upward with his legs. He managed to get most of his body onto the ledge before his toes slipped.

He rolled onto the stone ledge, panting and shaking. He left his bent dagger where it was, jammed into the bricks below the ledge.

A scream tore the night. Its echoes drifted on the clear air. *Renna.*

Leith scrambled to his feet as another shriek poured from Renna's bedchamber. He'd promised her he'd protect her. He couldn't fail. Not with her.

He dashed as fast as he dared along the foot-wide ledge. The muscles in his arms and shoulders still ached from climbing, his right hand cramping. Leith flexed his fingers, trying to loosen his muscles.

He skidded to a halt in front of Renna's window. Inside, a black figure stood over the bed, knife raised for the killing blow.

43

Renna jerked awake. Her door rattled under a heavy pounding. "Lady Rennelda, open the door. Lord Shadrach says you must come quickly."

She rolled to her feet and pulled the knife Leith had given her from under her pillow. Since she'd slept in her dress, she didn't have to change.

Dashing to the door, she fumbled with the key. It slid from her slick fingers and plunked onto the carpet. Scooping it up, she tried to insert it in the lock.

Her window creaked, and something heavy landed on the carpet. She whirled as the First Blade stalked across the room towards her. She darted away and pointed the knife at him. If he came any closer, she'd use it.

He sidled past her and jammed his knife into the keyhole. "There. Now no one will disturb us."

He rushed at her and swept her dagger aside as if it were nothing more than a minor annoyance. The back of her legs hit the edge of her bed, and she stumbled. He pinned her hand to the bed and raised his knife.

She was going to die. The truth wracked her body

until each limb convulsed. She fought to draw in air past her thundering heart. She had to scream. She wasn't going to survive, but maybe she could warn Brandi. She put all the strength in her body into another scream.

A black shape dove through the window and rolled over the windowseat. The First Blade's mouth curved into a taunting smile. "Perfect timing, Torren. You get to watch her die."

She couldn't wait for Leith to save her. She'd be dead before he crossed the room. Gathering her strength, she lashed out with her foot. She missed the sensitive area she'd been aiming for, but she managed to kick the First Blade's thigh hard enough to send him stumbling backwards.

Rolling to her feet, she swiped at the First Blade with her knife. The tip sliced along his cheek.

She stared at the blood dribbling down the First Blade's face. She'd hurt him. Her fingers trembled so much she nearly dropped the knife.

The First Blade touched his cheek and held his fingers in front of his face, as if he were as shocked as she was. When he looked up, his eyes blazed. He raised his knife again.

Leith rammed his shoulder into the First Blade. Both of them tumbled to the floor. They rolled, each of them seeking to pin the other down.

An icy claw raked at her chest. Leith's words from the gallery at Stetterly Manor haunted her. *I can't face the First Blade alone.*

Leith needed Shadrach's help. Renna dashed to the door and yanked at the knife embedded in the lock.

It didn't budge.

Smashing the hilt of his knife into Vane's jaw, Leith scrambled to his feet. With a snarl like an enraged mountain lion, Vane rushed at him.

Even in his anger, Vane didn't aim high for Leith's chest like an amateur but came in low, his knife poised to plunge into Leith's stomach and rip into Leith's chest underneath the ribcage.

Leith sidestepped, grabbed Vane's wrist, and twisted it away from his body. With his other hand, Leith blocked a chop at his neck.

Vane grabbed Leith's wrist and wrenched his arm backwards. Leith stepped to the side to relieve the pressure and twisted Vane's other hand.

For a moment they wrestled, trying to either free themselves or get the other off balance. Out of the corner of his eye, Leith caught glimpses of Renna leaning her weight against the knife jammed in the lock.

Vane reeled back, turning as he did. The move launched Leith forward. Rather than fight it, Leith used the momentum to yank his wrist free from Vane's grasp. Leith pivoted and gained a few feet of space between them.

They eyed each other warily, waiting for the other to make a move. Leith tightened his grip on his knife, ignoring the bitter taste sticking to his tongue. He needed to remain sharp to outwit Vane. He couldn't outfight him.

Vane rushed Leith again. They grappled, knives close to skin, breath hissing over each other's faces.

With a snarl, Vane hurled Leith away from him. Leith stumbled and fell against the far wall. His head clunked against the top edge of the wood paneling.

Black spots burst across his vision, splinters of pain creasing his skull.

Vane turned towards Renna, the tip of his knife pinched between his thumb and forefinger.

Leith scrabbled at the paneling, trying to pull himself to his feet. His head was clearing, but not fast enough.

Renna faced Vane. Her body shook, but she raised her chin a fraction. Her trembling fingers closed on the latch. With a swift motion, she jerked the door open.

Shad stepped inside, bow in hand, an arrow already nocked to the string.

As Shad drew back the arrow, Leith's stomach tightened. Shad wouldn't get off the shot before Vane threw. Leith lunged from the floor and hurtled into Shad. Shad stumbled a pace but stayed on his feet.

Something heavy struck Leith. His back slammed against the door jam and slid down the wall. As pain tore through his body, Leith watched Shad steady himself and draw the bow back the rest of the way.

Vane reached for another knife. Leith could see the next seconds play out. He'd seen it before. Vane would dodge and throw his knife as soon as Shad released the arrow. The arrow would fly through the air where Vane had been. Vane's knife wouldn't miss.

Leith opened his mouth to warn Shad, but the words stuck in the pain closing his throat and squeezing his chest. He could only stare helplessly as Shad let the arrow fly.

44

A meaty thunk filled the room. Renna clapped a hand to her mouth as the First Blade staggered. Blood pumped around the arrow buried in his chest halfway to its fletching.

His hand wavered. He tried to throw the knife, but it slipped from his fingers. His eyes met hers, their depths going dark, then blank. His body crumbled to the floor, his hand still twitching.

He was dead. No more tormenting. No more danger. Renna leaned against the wall. For the first time in months, she was safe.

Guards peeked their heads into the room. Shadrach jumped to block their view of the room. "Danger's over. Fetch my father."

Leith. She sprinted across the room. Leith leaned against the wall next to the door, eyes closed, chest rising and falling. A knife stuck from his left shoulder. He pressed his right hand against the wound, his fingertips red with blood.

She pressed her hand against the wound as well. Blood dripped between her fingers, hot and wet, while her forefinger touched the knife, its metal warmed with the heat of his body. He turned his face towards her and opened his eyes. "I knew you were brave."

She glanced at the knife she'd left beside the door. She'd been brave. Like her mother, she'd faced the First Blade and fought back.

Shadrach knelt beside her. Leith's mouth quirked at the corners. "You remembered your lessons. Good thing you realized he'd try to dodge."

"A snap decision. Thankfully the right one." Shadrach bowed his head. Renna caught a flash in his eyes. Was it regret? Or lingering fear? She couldn't tell.

Leith twitched his fingers towards Shadrach's bow. "I'm sorry you had to be the one to do it."

"One of us had to." Shadrach shrugged, but his voice scratched rough and low. He turned to Renna. "What do you need?"

She tipped her head towards the leather satchel on the floor next to the dressing table. "I'll need my medical kit, boiling water, and a fire started."

The door flew open. Brandi skidded to a halt a few steps into the room, her eyes and mouth widening as she stared at the First Blade's body.

"Sorry, sorry. I should've covered him." Shadrach staggered to his feet. He ripped a blanket from Renna's bed and tossed it over the body. It formed a grotesque sort of tent, the arrow a middle pole, the blanket draping down over most of the body. Only the First Blade's boots stuck out.

Brandi's gaze swiveled from the body to Renna's direction. "Leith!" She shrieked, shoved past Renna, and crashed to her knees.

Leith's face lacked color, but he still managed a

smile as he nudged Brandi's knee. "I'm still alive. Hurts less than that arrow your sister yanked from me."

Shadrach placed her medical kit beside her, hurried to the door, and shouted a few more orders to the guards outside.

Renna yanked a linen square from her kit, nudged Leith's hand aside, and pressed the linen against the wound next to the knife. She could feel the rhythm of his heart, the warmth of his chest, the shudder of his breath beneath her hand. "I need you to lie down."

His mouth skewed in a tight line, Leith eased himself away from the wall and onto the floor with her and Brandi's help. Renna did her best to keep her hand pressed against the wound, and she felt more than heard Leith's gasps of pain.

She lifted the linen. The knife stuck from one of the straps that crossed his chest and looped over his shoulders. The leather hadn't stopped the knife, but it'd slowed it so the knife had only gone halfway to its hilt. A bad wound, but not life-threatening.

Unbuckling the leather straps, Renna and Brandi helped Leith ease the straps off until only the knife pinned them to him.

Renna handed a fresh linen to Brandi. Brandi nodded, her eyes shiny, the tip of her nose red. If only Aunt Mara were here so Renna didn't have to put Brandi through this. It had been bad enough when Leith had been a stranger, but now that Brandi saw him almost like a brother…Renna shook her head to clear it.

She counted to three under her breath and yanked the knife from Leith's body. He moaned in the back of his throat.

As soon as the knife was clear, blood welled from the

wound. It wasn't spurting nor was it forming bubbles, the lack of both of those things a good sign.

Brandi pressed the linen onto the wound and leaned her whole upper body onto his shoulder to increase the pressure. Leith's fingers formed fists while his face blanched, but he didn't cry out.

"Shadrach, I need more light." Renna flipped open the leather top of her satchel as Shadrach scrambled to light all the lamps and candles in the room.

The door opened again, and Lord Alistair stepped inside. His gaze swept the room before he strode to Renna's side. "How bad is it?"

"Not as bad as it could have been." Shadrach set a lamp next to Leith's head. "The First Blade was aiming that knife at my chest."

Lord Alistair's gaze flickered between the knife and Shadrach. Lines wrinkled his forehead.

"It was my fault Vane got to Renna's room. I messed up our plans." Leith shook his head. "I tried to talk to him, but he wouldn't listen."

Renna paused, her vial of laudanum in her hand. Why had Leith tried to talk to the First Blade? About what? The skin between her shoulder blades crawled. The First Blade's dead body still sprawled behind her.

Lord Alistair cleared his throat and rested a hand on Shadrach's shoulder. "No matter. You stopped him. Well done. Both of you."

Renna uncorked the vial, but Leith's hand closed around hers. "No. Not yet."

"Why not?" She needed to clean and stitch his wound. No need for Leith to be awake and in pain while she did so. Not this time.

"I need to be alert." Leith's gaze switched to Brandi,

and he patted her hands. "Brandi, I left Blizzard in the trees beyond the flower garden. He and the First Blade's horse should be taken into the stables before morning. If Lord Alistair can spare a few guards to go with you, do you think you could take care of them for me?"

Brandi glanced at Lord Alistair, her eyebrows lifting. Lord Alistair's gaze met Leith's, and he nodded. "I know just who to send with you."

The two of them strolled from the room, Brandi chattering up a storm. Shadrach took Brandi's place pressing the linen to the wound.

"Thank-you for that." Renna laid a hand on Leith's arm. She should've realized from Brandi's silence that she needed to get out of there.

His mouth quirked, though his eyes remained shadowed. "If I had a little sister, I'd want her to be just like Brandi."

Setting aside the laudanum, Renna peeled the linen and his shirt away from his wound. When she'd pulled the collar of his shirt open and exposed his mark-free left shoulder, she washed the wound with the warm water and rag Shadrach handed her.

Renna reached for her bag to find her needle and thread to stitch the wound. Leith gripped her wrist. She jumped. "That wound needs to be stitched closed."

He shook his head, his mouth tightening into a grim line. "I'm returning to Nalgar Castle."

"What?" Shadrach thumped onto his knees beside Renna. "Why? Why would you return now? We can get you out of there."

"This isn't going to end here. Respen will retaliate." Leith's green eyes stared at the ceiling. "A war has started, and you're going to need me to help fight it."

A war? Renna squeezed her fingers into fists. No Blades had been sent after Uncle Abel and Aunt Mara this time, but would they still be all right if Respen started a war? Would he ignore Stetterly since Renna and Brandi were at Walden or would he attack Stetterly anyway?

"But how can you return? Respen will know you were the one that betrayed him." The pitch of Shadrach's voice rose, as if he was desperate.

"Not if I convince Respen that the First Blade was the traitor." Leith bobbed his head in the direction of the First Blade's body. "Only a few of your guards know a Blade was killed here. If we hide his body, I'll tell Respen that the First Blade is still alive and working for the Resistance. Respen was already suspicious. It won't take much to convince him."

Shadrach heaved a sigh. Renna could've sighed as well, but arguing only delayed her healing. "What does this have to do with stitching your wound?"

"When I return to the castle, Respen has to believe I was wounded and forced to flee. I would've tended this wound by myself." He glanced down at his shoulder, then back up at her. "I wouldn't be able to stitch a wound like that closed."

She frowned. She could see his point. Not only would he be unable to see what he needed to stitch, but it'd be impossible to stitch it closed with one hand. Even if he managed a few stitches, they'd look nothing like her neat ones. "What do you suggest?"

He drew in a deep breath. "I'm going to have to cauterize it."

Renna slammed her mouth closed against a gasp. She'd seen her Aunt Mara cauterize wounds before. It involved getting a piece of metal hot and burning the flesh so it no longer bled. The patients usually screamed and thrashed when the metal was applied to their skin.

"Clean off my knife and stick it in the fire. I'll do it myself. Might as well be able to tell Respen the truth."

Renna nodded and hurried to do as he asked. While the knife heated, she prepared cold water to press against the burns afterwards, a poultice of herbs, and the bandages.

She choked on the bile rising in her throat. She couldn't even give him laudanum to dull the pain because he needed to be alert to press his knife to the gash.

Shadrach handed Leith a piece of leather. Leith clamped it between his teeth while Shadrach pinned Leith's left shoulder and arm down to keep them steady.

Renna drew the knife from the fire, wrapping its hilt in a cloth to keep from burning herself. The blade glowed with a hint of dull orange, the same color as the coals puffing in the fireplace. Swallowing hard, she handed it to Leith.

He hesitated for only a fraction of a second before he touched the hot metal to his skin. A cry gurgled from his throat. His back arched while his left arm stiffened in Shadrach's grasp.

He dabbed the knife against the wound two more times before he dropped the cooling knife to the floor. When he squeezed his eyes shut, tears leaked from the corners.

Tears burning the corners of her own eyes, she pressed the damp cloths to his shoulder, hoping the coolness would take some of the sting from the burns. Applying the poultice, she wrapped his shoulder with bandages.

When she'd finished, she picked up her vial of

laudanum again. "Now will you let me give you laudanum?"

Leith gave a short nod and spit out the piece of leather. A half circle of white marks marred its surface. Lifting his head, she gave him a spoonful of the painkiller.

By the time she had cleaned her hands and picked up her supplies, Leith had slipped into sleep, though his jaw remained clenched, his chest shuddering with each breath.

Shadrach slumped onto his heels, his face nearly as ashen as Leith's. "Father and I will move him to a room where he can rest."

Nodding, she swiped at a strand of sweaty hair that had fallen across Leith's forehead. What would she have done had Leith not stumbled into their kitchen during that blizzard?

Trust. She hadn't trusted in God's control when she'd saved Leith, but saving him had saved all of them.

Something shifted in her chest. Something deep. Powerful. More than admiration for his courage. More than the safety he provided. She wasn't sure what it was, but her heart already ached with Leith's leaving.

45

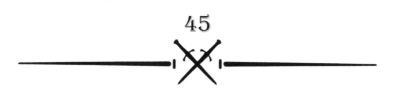

Sunlight warmed Leith's face. Blankets weighed on his legs and chest. He would've been comfortable except that his shoulder was hot...too hot. No, it burned, spiraling deeper and deeper. Coals touched his skin.

He jolted and pressed a hand to his shoulder. Blinking, he stared at the small room around him. He lay on a narrow, brass bed, a tiny window beaming a square of light onto the wall by his feet. No rugs covered the wooden floor.

How had he gotten here? He couldn't remember anything after pressing his glowing knife to his shoulder...the searing agony...the swirling blackness beckoning him.

How long had he slept? His tongue stuck to the roof of his mouth, but his head only pounded a little behind his eyes. He must've slept off most of the effects of the laudanum Renna had given him.

The door latch lifted. He glanced around the room but couldn't find his weapons. He tensed and prepared to launch himself at whoever stepped through that door.

Brandi skipped through. When her gaze locked on

him, she grinned. "I guessed right. I told Renna you'd wake up soon. Do you want breakfast? Sausage? Eggs? Toast?"

He relaxed onto the pillow. "All three."

"All right." She spun on her heels but skidded to a halt as Lord Alistair stepped inside. "Leith's awake. I'm fetching him food."

When Brandi disappeared down the hallway, Lord Alistair closed the door and sank onto the wooden chair beside the bed. Lines radiated from the corners of his eyes while dark circles pooled beneath.

A pang shot through Leith's chest. "It's my fault the First Blade got so close to Renna. I shouldn't have tried to talk to him. I knew it was useless. I should've stuck to the plan."

Lord Alistair bowed his head. "You have nothing to apologize for. The nobles were right. I have become wrapped up in planning and forgot that we're fighting a war of resistance, not of rebellion. We're fighting to worship God freely and share His Gospel freely. If we fight only to save our lives, then we're missing our true cause."

Lord Alistair was apologizing to him? Leith shook his head. What kind of strange dream did he wake up in?

"Shadrach tells me you intend to return to Nalgar Castle." Lord Alistair pressed his fingertips together and leaned back as much as he could in the wooden chair. "Our original deal still stands. I can claim both you and the First Blade were killed last night, and I can get you to a place where you'd be safe. You could leave the Blades like you wanted."

Leith could ride into the vastness of the Sheered Rock Hills, guided to the safety of whatever secret hideout the Resistance maintained. Without the First Blade, Leith stood a good chance of disappearing

But he'd known he had to go back the moment he'd watched Vane die. This assassination attempt would be paltry compared with Respen's retaliation. And Leith had come too far and done too much to walk away now. He was in this to the end, whether that meant his death or his eventual freedom.

It didn't matter which. He'd already found the freedom he'd been looking for, and that freedom wasn't going to leave him when he returned to Nalgar Castle.

He met Lord Alistair's gaze. Leith didn't know what the Resistance might have planned or who its Leader might be, but he trusted Lord Alistair, and that was enough. "Yes, I'm going back. You need me there."

Lord Alistair clapped him on his good shoulder and held out a sealed letter. "Then please take this to Respen. Tell him I forced you to take it before we let you go, which is true enough."

The thick envelope rustled between Leith's fingers as he took it. Was it a threat? An ultimatum?

Lord Alistair tapped the letter. "As you reminded me, the Resistance is fighting for our freedom to worship. We don't want to become a rebellion, even if what we've started turns into a war. This contains our requests for peace. I've outlined our beliefs and why we must be allowed to worship freely. If Respen continues to fight us rather than reconcile, that is up to him."

Leith placed the letter in an inner pocket of his shirt. "I'll make sure he gets it." How would Respen react? Especially when Leith delivered it on the heels of the news of Vane's supposed betrayal?

The door burst open again, and Brandi twirled

through, somehow not dumping the tray she balanced on one hand. "Here's breakfast."

Lord Alistair patted Leith's shoulder one last time before he left the room. Brandi claimed his spot. "Want company?"

A laugh shook Leith's chest. He groaned and pressed a hand to his shoulder. Brandi leaned forward. "Are you all right?"

Leith forced himself to grin. "Just hungry." He wiggled upright but kept his left arm tucked against his chest. Even with that precaution, shafts of pain radiated from his shoulder.

Brandi plopped the tray onto his lap, and he dug into the food. He finished the buttered toast, eggs, and sausage topped with maple syrup in a few bites.

After he handed the tray back to Brandi, Leith settled down in the covers. Tonight he'd have to leave, and he might never see Brandi again. He needed to tell her he'd be all right even if the worst happened. "I think it's my turn to tell you a story."

Her eyebrows lifting, Brandi perched on the edge of her seat. "All right."

Leith closed his eyes. "Once there was a Blade who found himself wounded and lost in a blizzard. When he thought he was going to die, these two girls rescued him. One of them told him stories that touched his soul. The other gave him kindness that touched his heart. Because of them, he couldn't go back to the life he'd been living so he joined the Resistance. But even that wasn't enough."

Leith opened his eyes. Brandi gripped the edge of her seat, leaning forward, a huge grin on her face. Movement dragged his gaze to the doorway where

Renna stood, her hands clasped in front of her. Her cheeks reddening, she ducked her head.

Swallowing, Leith tried to ignore increasingly loud thump of his heart. "Their words wouldn't leave him alone. One night in the darkness of Nalgar Castle, God showed him why their words were so powerful. The Blade found courage and a peace of heart he hadn't had before so that even though his past hadn't changed and the country still remained a dark place, he had hope."

Brandi bounced on the chair, her grin as wide as the open doorway. "I like that story."

"I thought you might." Leith leaned his head against the pillows. His shoulder ached, but he didn't care at the moment. "Not as good as your Daniel stories, but it's all I have."

He heard swishing skirts, and gentle hands straightened the blanket around his shoulder. A strand of hair tickled his cheek as Renna leaned over him. "I think it's a very good story. Now go back to sleep."

Even as he smiled, he had no trouble following her orders.

Night wrapped around Walden. Leith couldn't delay any longer if he wanted to return to Nalgar Castle in time for the Meeting of the Blades.

He'd found his weapons tucked under the bed and strapped them on. The left shoulder strap pressed against his wound, but he gritted his teeth.

Lord Alistair, Renna, Brandi, and Shad assembled on the front steps of Walden Manor to see him off, both Blizzard and Vane's horse saddled and waiting.

The darkness shielded them from prying eyes while the guards patrolled far enough away that they wouldn't see more than a black blob. It didn't matter if they did guess he was a Blade. If rumors got out that a Blade was working with Lord Alistair, Leith would use them to his advantage.

Leith stared at them, not sure what to do. He'd never said farewells with friends before, not friends like these anyway.

He shifted his feet a few steps closer to Blizzard. "You'll have to be careful. This area will be swarming with Blades once Respen believes the First Blade has betrayed him."

Lord Alistair's jaw tightened. "I'll make plans with the other Resistance leaders. We'll be prepared."

Leith knew better than to ask. The less he knew, the better. "And the First Blade's body will have to be well hidden."

"We buried him in the town graveyard. I doubt any of the Blades will look for him there."

"And his horse mustn't be found."

Shad held up the reins of Vane's horse. "I'm taking him away from here. Don't worry. We know what to do."

Leith glanced at Shad. The Blades wouldn't be looking for a grave, but they would be looking for Vane's horse. "You'll have to hide the tracks carefully. A number of the Blades are skilled at tracking."

Shad nodded as if Leith was telling him something he already knew. Of course Shad would be careful, but worrying about the Blades was Leith's job. They'd gotten this far without anything too major going wrong. He didn't trust that it'd stay that way.

No, that wasn't right. He should trust. Whatever happened would be God's plan.

Brandi hugged Leith so tightly his knives dug into

his ribs. "Take care of Blizzard." Her voice caught, though he couldn't be sure if the tears were for him or his horse.

Leith patted her back with his right hand. A lump formed in the back of his throat. What was he going to do at Nalgar Castle without Brandi? How long would it be before he'd have a chance to see her again? If ever? "I will. You listen to your sister. It won't be safe to wander far from Walden Manor for a while."

Brandi stepped away from him and trudged over to Blizzard to give the horse a goodbye that would probably last longer than the one she'd given Leith.

Renna gripped a knife in her hands. As she held it out to him, the faint light caught on his initials in the hilt. "Here. Thanks for letting me borrow it."

He shook his head and gently pushed it back toward her. "You keep it."

"Thank-you." She twisted her hands around it, her blue eyes flickering up at him before going back to the ground. The silence stretched on for a minute until the tension was painful.

Leith wasn't sure what he could say to her. So much had changed since the night he'd fallen into their kitchen during that blizzard. He was no longer the same Blade. Somehow, that didn't make it any easier to say goodbye.

She stepped forward and gave him a hug like Brandi had. Or, as Renna's soft hair brushed against his cheek, *not* like Brandi had. He loved Brandi like a sister, but Renna...Renna was definitely not his sister.

He swallowed, his hand hovering over her back. Perhaps he should've asked Shad for girl advice when he'd had the chance.

After a moment, she drew back. "I'll be praying for you."

"Thanks." Leith choked out the word. His brain buzzing like it'd been dropped in the moat and struck by lightning, he stumbled to his horse.

Shad held Blizzard steady while Leith placed his foot in the stirrup and swung himself into the saddle with one hand. He held his left arm close to his body, pain shooting from his shoulder.

Taking the reins, Leith gave everyone a final nod and nudged Blizzard into a lope. Leith gritted his teeth. Each drum of Blizzard's hooves jarred his shoulder.

A minute later, Shad caught up with him, riding Vane's horse. He didn't speak as they cantered their horses across the prairie. They didn't stop until they'd reached the foothills.

Shad sidled his horse next to him. "How are you holding up?"

Leith huffed a laugh, but it came out a groan. "About as well as can be expected."

He pushed the fabric of his shirt aside and touched the bandage. Only a spot in the center squished with blood. As bad as cauterizing the wound had been, it held up better than stitches.

Shad gazed into the mountains. "I guess this is where we part." At the wistful tone in Shadrach's voice, Leith guessed he was thinking about Jolene Lorraine. To preserve Leith's cover, Shad had to leave without knowing if she'd survived.

"Yep." Leith's gaze traveled along the edge of the hills and scrub brush he'd have to skirt as he headed for Nalgar Castle. Every muscle in his body screamed at him to turn and run the other way.

Why was he stepping back into Respen's clutches? A

whiff of Renna's scent, a floral something he couldn't name, drifted on the breeze. That's why.

Leith shrugged and extended a hand. "Be careful. Respen will have the Blades combing these hills looking for that horse."

"I'm a lord's son. I can handle myself." Shad shook Leith's hand. "You take care of yourself, Blade. You'll be face to face with Respen himself."

"God is with me even there." The words brought a confidence Leith hadn't fully felt before they hit the air. God would be with him, even in Respen's dark fortress.

"Godspeed." Shad wheeled Vane's horse and pointed its nose northward. It surged as it climbed its way up the twisting trail deeper into the mountains.

Leith watched until he was out of sight. When his last link to his peaceful life in Walden had vanished, he nudged Blizzard and headed west toward Nalgar Castle.

46

The gray towers of Nalgar Castle loomed over the horizon. Leith's heart thudded in time with Blizzard's hooves drumming against the cobbled ramp leading to the front gate.

To his left, the Blades' Tower rose in its five-story splendor, as if reminding everyone who entered the castle why they bowed beneath King Respen's might.

Inside the cobblestone courtyard, Leith handed Blizzard's reins to a stablehand and headed into the dark passageway below the king's apartments. Turning left, Leith strolled over the wooden bridge to the Blades' Tower. The moat reeked of stagnant scum and refuse.

As soon as he stepped inside the common room, Martyn jumped up from a bench. He wore a bandage around his head and walked with a limp. But he was alive. A lump in Leith's chest eased. He hadn't killed his friend.

Reaching Leith's side, Martyn clapped Leith on the left shoulder. Leith sucked in a breath and took a step back. "Sorry. I took a knife in that shoulder."

Martyn blew out a breath, running a hand through

his curly, blond hair. "You survived. I wondered when you didn't return last night or this morning."

Leith clenched his jaw at Martyn's admission. Martyn had worried about him. Guilt stabbed into Leith's chest. Martyn's injuries were his fault. He clapped Martyn on the shoulder as well, trying to keep his voice steady. "I'm glad you're all right."

Martyn glanced past him. "Where's the First Blade?"

"He's the one that put the knife in my shoulder." Leith winced at the words. They weren't a lie. Vane had been the one to throw the knife. But they still led Martyn to believe something other than the truth.

Martyn's eyes flared. "That scum! He sold us out? No wonder this happened!" He waved at the room, where only ten Blades gathered, not including Martyn and Leith. "Unless more straggle in, we're all that's left. Almost half of us were killed." Martyn ground his teeth. "I'm going to make Vane pay when I catch up with him."

A bitter weight sank into Leith's stomach. Martyn would be furious if he ever learned that Leith had been the one to set up the ambush.

Leith closed his eyes. He was going to lose Martyn's friendship. Deep down, he'd known he was going to have to choose—had already chosen—between Shad and the friendship of the people at Walden and Martyn and the friendship of his fellow Blades. He couldn't have both.

Martyn grasped Leith's elbow and steered him to a seat. "Sit down before you pass out."

Leith did as he was instructed and took stock of the Blades assembled in the dining room. Many of the lower Blades were missing. They wouldn't have been skilled enough to escape when ambushed. The Fifth Blade was missing, but the Fourth Blade hunched in a corner, nursing a wounded arm. The Second Blade was also missing. Hopefully the Lorraines were all right.

A chill jolted down his back. With both the First and Second Blades dead or believed to be a traitor, Leith was the new First Blade. The First Blade was Respen's right hand man. He was called in to private audiences with Respen and expected to give recommendations on the activities of all the Blades.

And Respen wouldn't be fooled for long.

Leith hunched in his seat in the meeting room.

King Respen's dark eyes sliced them. When he spoke, his deep voice rumbled like boulders tumbling down the sides of the Sheered Rock Hills. "You have failed me, my Blades. Of the eighteen Blades I sent out, only four succeeded in their goal. Eight Blades failed to return. The rest of you crawled back here licking your wounds."

Respen banged his fist on the table. Some of the Blades jumped, touching hands to bandaged heads. "You were supposed to strike fear into the hearts of my enemies. Instead, you have emboldened them! They believe they can stand up to my Blades and succeed! And right now, they would be right."

Would Respen have them all whipped to punish them for their failure? Leith steeled himself. He could take it, if that was the consequence for his decision. He'd set up this ambush. He'd have to face the results.

Many of the other Blades quaked in their seats. Even the two Blades that had stayed behind sunk low in their chairs.

Respen called the Nineteenth Blade, the lowest ranked Blade to survive. Nineteenth Blade Altin shook as he gave his report. He'd sneaked into the lord's room, only to be surrounded by fifteen guards. He'd jumped from a window, twisted his ankle, and spurred his horse into a gallop.

When Respen pronounced his failure, Altin shook harder. Leith's stomach knotted. It was Altin's third failure. Leith would be as responsible for Altin's death as he was for the deaths of the eight Blades that hadn't returned, including Vane.

King Respen slashed the third mark on Altin's left arm. "Return to your seat."

Altin, now rapidly promoted to Twelfth Blade, glanced at Respen with wide eyes. He opened his mouth, as if to ask why Respen had spared him, only to snap it shut and rush to his seat before the king changed his mind.

The other Blades sat mute, as if knowing any reaction would push Respen to keep his ultimatum that three failures meant death. Leith let out a long breath. As much as Respen ruled the Blades with an iron hand, he had to spare the twelve Blades he had left.

The rest of the Blades gave their reports. Leith gripped his chair when the four Blades reported their successes. Lord Emilin, Lord and Lady Spencer, Lady Dawson, and Lord and Lady Westin had been killed. He'd done his best, but the failure still burned.

Leith glanced around the room. They wouldn't be the last lives lost before this war was over. Respen still had twelve Blades, four more than he'd had when he'd taken over Acktar. All twelve were well-trained and deadly, though only eleven of them remained loyal.

Respen boomed Leith's name. Leith knelt, met Respen's eyes, and gave his report. "The First Blade insisted we sneak into Walden and execute our orders a day early. Inside, I discovered that Lord Alistair had been warned. The First Blade turned on me. We fought, and he threw a knife. I took it in my left shoulder."

Leith pulled back his shirt and showed Respen the bandage. At Respen's wave, Leith undid the bandage so he could see the knife wound. It still burned red, oozing blood and liquid.

Respen twisted Leith's shoulder so the light from the candles fell on the wound. Leith struggled to keep a straight face as pain shot through his body.

"You cauterized it."

"Yes." Leith's voice wiggled through his tight throat.

Respen let go of his shoulder. "So the First Blade betrayed me." He stroked the arms of his chair.

Leith held his breath. The evidence pointed to Vane. Vane had suggested they separate within Walden Manor when they'd spied on the nobles' meeting. Vane had volunteered to return to Walden to kill Renna and Brandi. It had been Vane who'd failed to kill the girls four years ago.

Respen's hard eyes narrowed. "How did you escape?"

"They let me go." It was the truth, and the only answer that could explain how Leith, wounded as he was, could've escaped a traitorous First Blade and Walden's angry guards. Reaching into his shirt, Leith pulled out the letter Lord Alistair had given him. "Lord Alistair wanted me to give you this."

Respen broke the seal and scanned the contents. Growling, he ripped the paper and tossed the shreds on the table. "He thinks he can make demands of me. I am the king. *I* control Acktar. I will destroy this religion of his and show him that his imaginary God is no match for me."

Still, Leith wasn't afraid. The God that Respen challenged was very real, and very powerful.

Respen turned back to Leith. "You have failed, my Third Blade."

The words didn't frighten Leith as they might've three months earlier. He had to work to appear contrite as he pulled up the sleeve of his left arm, the top of his shoulder unmarked.

As Respen leaned forward and sliced his arm, pressing harder and deeper than he did for a success, Leith suppressed a rush of satisfaction. In Respen's eyes, this mark represented Leith's first failure. For Leith, it marked his first success in standing up to Respen. It didn't mark a life lost but lives saved. Leith dropped his sleeve.

Respen lashed forward and gripped Leith's face. Forcing his chin up, Respen leaned closer until his breath slapped Leith's skin. Leith froze. His heart pounded in his throat as he stared into Respen's eyes.

Respen's voice deepened into a low growl, the sound a wolf made before it struck. "Listen to me, my new First Blade. You have failed me once. Do not fail me again."

As Leith met Respen's eyes, a shiver crawled down his spine. Respen knew. He didn't know exactly what Leith had done, but he knew something was not as it should be.

When he discovered the truth, Leith was going to pay in blood.

Don't Miss the Next Part of the Adventure

THE BLADES OF ACKTAR

BOOK TWO

DENY

All lies have consequences.

Promoted to the top rank among King Respen's assassins, First Blade Leith Torren hides his involvement with the Resistance. How many lies will it take to protect his secret?

Renna Faythe has done nothing but survive for the past four years, but now Leith's courage inspires her to try to be something more. If only she could figure out what that duty might be.

When the unthinkable happens, faith waivers. Friendships tear. What else will they be forced to deny?

But this time, Leith faces his greatest fear.

He can't save everyone.

THE BLADES OF ACKTAR

BOOK THREE

DEFY

Coming May 31, 2016

ACKNOWLEDGEMENTS

A debut author's list of acknowledgements is extensive. Many people have been waiting for years to see their name acknowledged in the back of a book. In case you don't wish to read through the whole thing, here's my thanks to you, my readers. I'm still awed that I *have* readers. Thank you so much for taking the time out of your busy day to read *Dare*. May it have touched you as the characters have already touched me.

Now on to all the personal thanks. This book is dedicated to all the many, many people who have helped me along the journey to publication.

To my mom Maureen for teaching me to read and write. You encouraged my dream even when I was two years old and drawing books with my crayons.

To my dad Don for listening to my idea chatter and combing my books for plot holes.

My brothers Ethan, Josh, and Andy, who helped me get the male POV and banter right and didn't laugh (too much) at my questions.

To my sister-in-law Alyssa for your enthusiasm for this book and these characters. I wouldn't have pushed through the many, many drafts of character development without you.

For my alpha readers Briana and Paula. This book wouldn't have been written without you. Literally. Your frantic texts to *Please write another chapter* made all the difference between a half-finished draft and novel.

To Ashley, both good friend and amazing cover designer. Your patience with me is almost as amazing as the cover itself.

To the rest of my friends Jill, Gabby, Megan and Susan. You put up with quite a bit to have a writer as a friend. Thank you for being my early readers.

To Marcia, Bethany, and Jeff who replied to my frantic posts on Facebook asking for names. I'm sure you'll recognize many of the names throughout the book.

For my extended family who have been waiting for years to see my name on a book and believed it would get there eventually even when I was writing nothing but junk.

To Sierra, critique partner extraordinaire. I never would've guessed a comment about corsairs would lead to such a great critique partnership and friendship.

Nadine Brandes, amazing editor and friend. Your edits not only made *Dare* a better book but also taught me to be a better writer. I wouldn't have survived this book release without you.

For Angie Brashear and Jaye L. Knight, who both helped me with my indie publishing questions.

To Kim Moss, an author friend and encourager who came along at just the right moment.

For all the rest of the authors who signed up for the blog tour, answered my questions, and welcomed me into their midst as a fellow author.

To all of my English and writing teachers and professors through the years. Every class was a baby step along this journey. You each impacted me so much, and I hope if you read this book, you can smile when you see the results of your hard work.

Most of all, to my Heavenly Father who gave me the gift of writing that I may praise Him by it. All the glory be to His name alone.

ABOUT THE AUTHOR

Tricia Mingerink is a twenty-something, book-loving, horse-riding country girl. She lives in Michigan with her family and their pack of pets. When she isn't writing, she can be found pursuing backwoods adventures across the country.

To learn more about Tricia Mingerink and get a behind the scenes peek her books, visit triciamingerink.com.

Made in the USA
Columbia, SC
23 May 2017